RACE FOR THE GOLD

RACE
FOR THE
GOLD

THORN BACON

PRESS™

Milwaukie

While based on historical events, some details have been altered for dramatic effect. Names, characters, places, and incidents featured in this publication with the exception of historical elements, either are the product of the author's imagination or are used fictitiously. Any resemblance to actual persons (living or dead), events, institutions, or locales, without satiric or historical intent, is coincidental.

M Press
10956 SE Main Street
Milwaukie, OR 97222

mpressbooks.com

Book design by Darin Fabrick
Cover by Darin Fabrick and Lia Ribacchi
Cover illustration by Thomas Yeates

Library of Congress Cataloging-in-Publication Data

Bacon, Thorn.
Race for the gold / Thorn Bacon. -- 1st M Press ed.
p. cm.
Includes bibliographical references.
ISBN-13: 978-1-59582-115-7
ISBN-10: 1-59582-115-5
I. Title.
PS3552.A285R33 2007
813'.54--dc22

2006035100

ISBN-10: 1-59582-115-5
ISBN-13: 978-1-59582-115-7

First M Press Edition: August 2007

10 9 8 7 6 5 4 3 2 1

Printed in U. S. A.

To Ursula as always

AUTHOR'S NOTE

THE DRAMA AND EXCITEMENT of men on horseback racing through the pages of history have made a deep imprint on readers. No true story of men in the West is more remarkable than that of Louis Remme who changed horses more than twenty times in a wild seven-hundred-mile race with a steamboat to rescue a fortune in gold.

Race for the Gold is based on the actual events surrounding the legendary horseback ride of Louis Remme in February 1855 from Sacramento, California to Portland, Oregon. While short versions of his story have appeared in *American Heritage Magazine* and the *Oregon Business Review*, the original account of Remme's ride was published in *The Sunday Oregonian* February 12, 1882.

The version of Remme's ride presented in this book is based on the published facts about his journey. Gaps in his personal history have been filled by careful reconstruction of events in his life which were vague, but offered a sound basis for re-creation. The author has been careful to apply his research so that it faithfully augments the description of the overland route Remme took, the people who helped him along the way, and the obstacles he had to overcome in the dead of winter to reach Portland, Oregon in six days. The excitement of his struggle to win the uneven race became a subject of vivid conversation aboard the *Pacific Mail Steamship Columbia* as new passengers who had heard about his mad dash boarded the ship at stopping points along the Oregon coast.

Wagers were made on the outcome of his wild ride and he was held up as a courageous example of the spirit of the pioneers that so entranced the national consciousness.

Justice could not have been done to Louis Remme's story without including excerpts from the history of the Indian War which took place in Oregon in 1850–1855. It was during this last year of the bloody conflict that Louis Remme faced irate, bloodthirsty Indians who were dispossessed of their traditional lands and way of life by gold miners who flooded into the Oregon Territory during this time of turmoil and called for the extermination of the native race. This climate of violence was at its apex when Louis Remme made his daring ride, escaping from vengeful Indians by his wits, fast horses, and an iron determination to win.

CHAPTER ONE

IT WAS A BRISK FEBRUARY Thursday in San Francisco when Louis Remme sat down to breakfast in his hotel dining room. A slender, wiry man of medium height, Remme was dressed for the city in a gray wool suit, red string tie, and polished black boots. He felt elegant seated at a table covered with starched white linen with a matching napkin stuffed in a polished oyster-shell ring. A tall silvered pot of coffee rested next to his cup of bone china and for his reading pleasure a copy of the *California Chronicle* thoughtfully had been placed neatly folded on the table.

Remme was amused at himself. He had never treated himself to the luxury of a grand hotel like the St. Francis, which was host to the rich and famous of San Francisco. The fancy room he had rented was priced at twenty-eight dollars a day, a lot of money for a French-Canadian cattle trader who only three days earlier had completed a long, muddy cattle drive down the Sacramento valley from the Rogue River country of Oregon. The rooms he was used to sleeping in cost a dollar per night and the papered walls breathed in and out when the wind was blowing. But he was celebrating the sale of the last of his cattle herd and had found himself with $12,500 in gold, more money than he had possessed at one time in his life. On a whim, after he deposited his gold at the Sacramento branch of Adams Express Company, he had taken the steamer to San Francisco with one thousand dollars in his pocket. He was going to enjoy himself for a few days visiting the opera, the museums, San Francisco's famous waterfront restaurants and he intended to risk a few dollars in the gambling houses which had a reputation for gaiety and entertainment.

When he checked into the St. Francis, looking prosperous in his dark wool suit, he seemed at home, unintimidated by the plush surroundings and thick Persian rugs. The lobby was a beautiful room in which several small groups of men and women were drinking tea and coffee serviced from a mobile antique cart. Their talk was animated and the subject, Remme noted, was a local bank, Page, Bacon. The name meant nothing to Remme as he signed the hotel register and accepted a key to his room from the clerk who had sized up the cattle trader as a man who was rising in the world and had given him a room with a grand brass bed and velvet drapes. He accepted gracefully.

As he finished his breakfast eggs on his first day in the hotel, and sipped his second cup of coffee, Remme thought about how San Francisco had changed in the seven years since a gold nugget had been found in Sutter's Mill, starting the Forty-Niner gold rush. He had been one of thousands who had rushed to the bonanza with the dream of gold to prod his haste.

From a sleepy town slumbering on a lovely bay, San Francisco had been transformed into a tent city by thousands of miners from every country in the world. In a few years it had grown into a bustling city with tall buildings, magnificent homes, and a population of fifty thousand people. Remme had occupied most of the years of San Francisco's gold rush growth differently than the horde of hopefuls who traveled to the Golden State. While San Francisco was prospering and changing, he had learned cattle trading the hard way. Almost penniless when he left Quebec in French-speaking Canada about a decade earlier, he had drifted south and west into Oregon territory. He had learned about cattle and horses in a dozen different jobs, working as a mule skinner's helper, a cattle drover's apprentice, a wild-horse tamer. He had driven wagons and toiled in the gold-bearing streams for a short period. Nine months he had served as an apprentice seaman on a steam-driven paddleboat until it exploded and he was thrown overboard. He had farmed for one season. He had repaired wagon wheels, learned to shape steel shoes for horses in a smithy's fire, and discovered that he liked to work leather for relaxation.

For a short period he shipped Oregon apples, cartons of eggs, and bushels of wheat to the California gold camps. The apples brought five hundred dollars for four bushels, eggs sold for a dollar a piece, and wheat demanded a price of six dollars a bushel. He had sent his produce by steamboat and the major hazard was the rough seas that tore cargo lashed to the decks free, causing expensive losses. Still, enough of his produce arrived undamaged in San Francisco for him to make a profit. With what he saved he outfitted himself for the strenuous and dangerous work of chasing wild cattle, branding and taming them.

He found his niche when he started locating "brush hoppers," domesticated cattle that strayed from herds and went wild. Rounding up wild cattle was cruel, brutal, dangerous work. Stubborn steers used to their freedom could turn on a herder suddenly and rip a man with their horns for no reason.

Little by little, Remme became known in the Oregon and the northern California frontiers as a shrewd trader, trapping and fattening wild cattle, building small herds he drove to pioneer towns where settlers needed animals for breeding at reasonable prices. He was especially appealing to lonely settlers who were starved for conversation and excitement in their lives. He was a romantic, cheerful figure when he showed up dressed in leather and wool with jingling spurs. Mounted on a lean, fast horse, he was a man who could always be counted on to carry a message to the next farm or hand-deliver a letter with a favorite recipe to a cousin in another town. He was referred to as "that crazy Frenchman" not only because he sang songs with lilting, strange words to himself, ones he had learned as a child in Quebec, but because he was admired for his free, daring life. He had a dark complexion, large brown eyes, a quick smile, and long black hair that grew to his shoulders when he was away months at a time scouring the woods for cows and building a herd.

As Remme spread butter on a hot biscuit, he realized how fortunate he was to be sitting in a fancy hotel cheerfully contemplating his future. For the first time in all the years he had been trading cattle, he had enough money in the bank to properly stock his southern Oregon cattle ranch flowing with cool water and sweet grass on which he could graze and fatten cows for market. San Francisco paid handsomely for beef and its growing population couldn't seem to get enough. It was Remme's idea to drive cattle from collection points near Mr. Shasta, far north of Sacramento, to cattle yards close to San Francisco in stages. By herding cattle slowly, the animals could graze along the way, put on weight, and arrive in the city by the bay fat and healthy. Of course, stockmen drove herds of cattle into the holding pens in the city every day. But most of the cows arrived in poor condition, thirsty, exhausted, and thinner than when they started on the trail. Remme's idea was to reverse the process. By controlling the pace of the cattle drive, the cows would be less nervous, lose less fat, and bring a much higher price when they arrived at the stockyards. He was surprised that no one else had thought of his plan. It just made sense. Buyers would pay more for plump cattle than skinny critters with trail-hardened muscles. Actually, he knew why most cattlemen in northern California didn't bother to put pounds on the cattle they raised. There was such a high demand by gold-rush miners for beef that a butcher could sell whang leather and call it steak.

But times were changing. After all, it was 1855! San Francisco was growing up and so were the tastes of its citizens. There were a dozen theaters in the city by the bay. Men and women who had endured the hardships of the gold rush years wanted more comfort and the good things of life. His own hotel, the St. Francis—the first to put sheets on the beds instead of the customary scratchy blankets which used to irritate the guests—sponsored fancy dress balls and appearances at social gatherings of famous actors and singers. Why, he had learned that the American thrush, Eliza Biscaccianti had dared to brave wild and boisterous San Francisco when other singers such as Jenny Lind and Catherine Hayes had declined. Was it any wonder that natives of San Francisco who had endured the gold rush diet of beans and bacon, wanted more comfort and better food? Tender steaks and roasts which he would soon provide from the pampered cattle he drove to town would be part of the new future. Remme was bemused for a moment with the memory of the extraordinary woman he had dined with just the night before, but was suddenly distracted by a snatch of conversation from a neighboring table. The words that caught his attention were the same he had heard spoken in the lobby of the hotel the day before.

"I'm sure we wouldn't be sitting here calmly having a cheerful breakfast if either of us had been affected by the financial ruin of Page, Bacon."

"I'm glad to hear you're okay."

"I heard Page, Bacon started paying out hundreds of thousands yesterday to depositors, but I bet the bank won't last through today."

"Of course, I heard the same news," his companion said. "At first I couldn't believe it, then I decided I couldn't take a chance that it might be true. I got to my bank late Thursday, stood in line, and saved my gold. Good thing I did, because later I saw crowds banging on the doors of Harris-Marchant which closed in the early afternoon. I thank my lucky stars I acted or I might be penniless."

Remme found the men's exchange only slightly disquieting. He was certain his own gold resting securely in the vault of Adams Express Company Bank, the fastest growing financial institution in the West, was safe. But it was unsettling to hear that one of the oldest banks in California may be shaky. The failure of the old, reliable St. Louis bank would certainly send shivers through the depositors in the San Francisco branch. The question raised was could the local bank, lacking the backing and gold reserves of the parent bank, survive the sudden rush of depositors for their money? The shrewd cattle trader knew that the fate of Page, Bacon, and Company in San Francisco would depend on how panicky its customers became. If the bank could keep paying until worried folks regained their confidence and stopped withdrawing their gold, then everything would be all right.

Concerned more than he wanted to admit, Remme decided to discover if the men at the next table had any more details to impart about the solvency of financial institutions in the city. He inclined his head to listen, pretending to read his newspaper.

"I don't know if the run on Page, Bacon and your bank has spread to the others. I did hear that Page, Bacon has a close connection to Adams Express Bank. I wonder if it's true? Adams does more business than all the others combined. It seems doubtful that they're in trouble."

The reference to Adams Express Company struck Louis Remme like a splash of cold water in his face. He dropped his napkin, rose to his feet, and stepped to the neighboring table.

"Excuse me, gentlemen," he said, his eyes resting on the larger of the two seated men. "I couldn't help but overhear your conversation and your statement, sir, that Adams Express Bank may be linked to Page, Bacon. I have money in Adams. May I ask how reliable your information is?"

Both men were gracious about Remme's intrusion and the one who had been talking last said, "I don't know how reliable it is, but the *Steamship Oregon* arrived late Wednesday bearing news that the St. Louis parent bank of our branch here went bust because of unpaid railroad loans. If Adams is interconnected to Page, Bacon that may be bad news." The man frowned, then looked sympathetically at Remme and added, "If I were you, I guess I'd try to get my money out. You can always redeposit when the panic subsides."

Remme apologized to the men for his interruption, turned to his table where he dropped a few coins next to his breakfast plate for the waiter, and walked into the hotel lobby. A dozen questions popped into his mind as he considered what his next move should be and he couldn't dismiss the sinking feeling in his stomach. Was it possible that a bank's failure half a continent away could have an echo in San Francisco? Could his personal fortune be in jeopardy? How bad was the panic? If it spread to other banks in San Francisco, the chances of it influencing his own bank in Sacramento, only ninety miles away, were probably predictable. The aspect of the bank run that worried him most was the question that had electrified him a minute ago—was Adams Express linked to the troubled Page, Bacon bank? If that was true, and if Adams Express depositors got wind of what he had heard, he knew they would start clamoring wildly for their savings. Remme had to admit to himself that his own unfounded suspicions about Adams Express were growing by leaps and bounds. A man who acted quickly when his mind was made up, Remme decided to wait no longer. He would cut his vacation short and catch the next boat upriver to Sacramento. Even as he made up his mind, he prayed to himself that he would not be too late. He realized as he paid the bill for his room and checked out of his hotel that he was acting hastily. He had absolutely no information beyond a single overheard conversation that his bank might be the target of a run simply by association with Page, Bacon, and Company. As he tipped the hotel doorman, asking him to whistle for a horse and carriage, he was determined to put a brake on his imagination. After all, the boat to Sacramento did not leave San Francisco until late afternoon. He had several hours to kill. Also a pair of boots he had ordered from a reliable boot maker on Sutter Street would not be ready before 2:00 P.M. It was only 11:00 A.M.

When Remme climbed into the carriage that responded to the call of the doorman, he told the cheerful driver to take him to the city's main square, Portsmouth Plaza. Many of San Francisco's banking institutions were located in the plaza. Remme was going to visit the offices of Adams Express Company Bank located in the plaza. He didn't know what he was going to say to the people at the bank, but he was certain he would have to be cautious and crafty if he was going to learn anything valuable about the soundness of the bank. While the certificate he owned proving he had $12,500 in gold on deposit in the Sacramento branch of Adams Express was resting in the safe at his boarding house in Sacramento, and could not be cashed unless he presented it in person to a teller or agent, Remme's idea was to gather any information which could help him to make a decision about withdrawing his gold. He doubted that the San Francisco officials of Adams Express were going to admit to him that their bank was in trouble, even if it was. But he hadn't learned over the years to trade shrewdly for cattle without discovering how to judge the motives of men, often by what they didn't say.

It had been seven years since Remme had visited Portsmouth Plaza and he didn't recognize it when he stepped down from his carriage and paid the driver. He was amazed at what he saw. Hundreds of people—men in frock coats and top hats, workmen in aprons, women in long skirts, sailors in blue jackets and brass buttons, flower sellers with baskets of asters, chrysanthemums and violets oblivious to the raw February weather, walked and mingled and exchanged greetings and comments along the wooden plank sidewalks.

The plaza was ringed with the offices of attorneys, doctors, dentists, banks, and brokerages. The old adobe city hall occupied the north edge of the square. The city's courthouse, customhouse, and surveying offices rested not far from the Parker House, Denison's Exchange, and the Empire Hotel, all of which boasted of being fireproof. Not to be missed were several saloons, a laundry, a public schoolhouse, and a grist mill.

Remme was overwhelmed by the changes. He remembered the square as a wild area of shanties and tents, cow pens and grassy mounds where animals grazed. Now, it was a bustling modern plaza with a flag to identify its public character and an atmosphere of busy commerce and enthusiasm.

As he got directions to the building in which Adams Express Company was housed, Remme realized it had been natural for companies which originally had been organized to deliver mail to thousands of California miners to merge with financial institutions that kept gold for customers. Like Adams Express Company, the smaller, but fast growing Wells Fargo had started in business just three years earlier in 1852 to transport mail. It was transformed into a banking company, spurred by the demands of miners for a safe place to deposit their gold. The flow of wealth from the incredible gold rush caused many express and banking companies to join together and they had grown tremendously prosperous. Could an established firm like Adams be in trouble?

He had to work his way through the noisy, impatient overflow crowd that was jostling for position to get into Page, Bacon located next to Adams Express to redeem their gold. Faced with a two-hour wait or longer in the long snaking line to the open doors of his own bank, Remme's resolve was strengthened by the fact that its rumored association with the floundering Page, Bacon might be the truth and Adams was staying open long enough to satisfy a few hundred worried depositors.

Once inside he saw that on the surface everything appeared normal. Several customers stood in front of tellers' cages collecting their savings. Remme saw stacks of fifty gold coins changing hands and there was the pleasant chink of gold, the rustle of currency, and the air of privacy typical of financial institutions. No one appeared hurried, or overanxious. His eyes finally came to a stop on a stern man with heavy sideburns seated at a desk behind a wooden banister. With his slight paunch, dark gray suit, and blue foulard tie, he looked like a person whose job was important.

Deciding on a story to cover the real reason for his presence in the bank, Remme removed his wide-brimmed hat, stepped up to the railing, and said, "I am a depositor in the Sacramento bank of Adams. I am in San Francisco on a holiday and I need to know about shipping some gold dust to Sonora. Can you help me?"

The sun came out on the banker's face as he smiled at Remme and invited him to push through the wooden gate in the railing and take a chair beside the desk. When Remme told the man, whose name was Harold Forbes, that he was staying at the St. Francis, the banker's attitude became respectful. It was obvious to him that Remme was a man of substance, a person whose bank patronage was valuable. After exchanging pleasantries with his visitor and discovering that Remme was a cattle trader, Forbes poised a pencil in his hand above a small white pad on his desk and said, "You spoke about shipping dust to Sonora, how much did you have in mind, Mr. Remme? You know we charge one half of one percent as our fee for transporting gold."

Remme put a frown on his forehead, pretending to be suddenly disturbed and thoughtful. He shifted in his chair and hesitated as if he were reluctant to say what was on his mind. Finally, he said, lowering his voice, "The sum I have in mind is quite large. I—"

"And you're concerned about its safety? Is that it, Mr. Remme?"

"Exactly," Remme whispered with a relieved sigh and looked worriedly into the eyes of the banker.

Smiling largely, Forbes leaned across his desk and said reassuringly, "Banish your doubts, my friend. Our shipments are carefully protected. After all, Adams Express Bank has a reputation for prudence and caution."

"Then the rumor about Adams being associated with the failure of Page, Bacon, and Company is false?"

Forbes tried to cover up the stab of panic in his eyes from Remme's surprise question, but it was too late. His sudden cautious expression gave him away. He cleared his throat and said hurriedly, "I don't know what you mean."

But Remme was already on his feet. He knew now that his whole future was in peril. He had to get to Sacramento as soon as possible and recover his gold. And he knew as he left the bank that Forbes, furious for being tricked, would never have told him whether or not Adams Express was on the verge of closing. And he was absolutely certain the banker would not have told him if fast riders had already been dispatched to the dozen or so branches of Adams Express in northern California with secret instructions to close down if the rumor grew and depositors started clamoring for their gold.

CHAPTER TWO

ON THE STEAMBOAT TO SACRAMENTO as Remme stood against the starboard railing in the cold, black windy night, the sharp chill was like a foreboding reminder of the staggering personal loss he faced if Adams Express proved to be insolvent when he took his certificate to be cashed on Monday. He had already homesteaded and bought about three thousand acres of grassland. The gold he had on deposit in the Adams Express Bank would make the purchase of more cows and improvement of his spread possible. When he deliberately shut his mind about the pending disaster, he thought of the woman who was waiting for him in Oregon. Chagrined and feeling a little guilty about his attraction to Lola Montez, when they had dined together Thursday night, he said to himself, "Fool, how could you betray Iron Bird, your French and Indian princess with a notorious flirt?" The irony was that the woman known as the "Queen of the goldrush" had asked him to help finance a wild scheme of hers that had convinced him she was mad.

He felt a little better when he compared himself to the famous European artists who had lost their heads to their fascination with the black-haired Irish beauty who could sway any man by the promise in her eyes.

The woman was none other than Lola Montez, notorious femme fatale, mistress to many famous men in Europe before she sailed to America. They included Franz Liszt, Alexander Dumas, and Victor Hugo. George Sand was an acquaintance, as was Lamartine and Balzac. Her most enduring liaison was with King Ludwig of Bavaria whom she so influenced with her feminine enchantments and radical political views that he abdicated and she sought greener pastures in America. Remme recalled vividly his first meeting with Lola six months earlier and could not forget how she had excited him with her dazzling beauty, assertive self-confidence, and the stage name she had made famous on two continents. He had learned she had been born Elizabeth Gilbert in Sligo, Ireland in 1821.

What fascinated Louis Remme was why a dark beauty of her outlandish reputation recognizable anywhere as "the belle of the California gold rush" would bother with a cattle trader like himself.

His first contact with her occurred in California when he had showed up in Grass Valley at a livestock auction to buy horses on contract for the U. S. Army stationed at Fort Humboldt. Several horses had been bid for and bought, when a beautiful gray with thoroughbred lines was presented. Remme, who was an expert judge of horseflesh, had quickly bid one hundred dollars as a starting high price. He was convinced the horse would make a fine mount for an army officer. He expected some competition, but was startled when a beautiful woman with a full cloud of dark brown hair arranged artfully in fashionable waves that hugged her face, lovely dark eyes, and a fierce challenging expression on her features, raised a short leather whip—a quirt used to smack a horse on the rump to urge a faster gait—and said in a low, intriguing voice "two hundred dollars."

Remme looked at her again, he let his eyes take in her long, sweeping dress and embroidered collar, her small waist and generous bust. In her there was a blaze of amusement and determination.

Smiling to himself, he decided to test the strength of her confidence and raised the bid to three hundred dollars—an outlandish price to pay for even a fine horse. She laughed across the room at him, then her lips flattened into a hard line of firm resolve and lifted her voice, "five hundred dollars."

Remme was astounded and a little puzzled that she, or anyone would pay such an exaggerated price for a horse.

He shrugged, walked to the auctioneer's clerk to settle in gold for the horses he had bought. He pocketed his receipt, preparing to start the trip north to Fort Humboldt on the way to Oregon, early the next day. He was halted by the woman's harsh, demanding voice, "Hey mister. Stop!"

He turned and there standing in front of him, was the famous beauty who had come to California from Europe to capture the hearts and gold of rough-and-tumble gold rush miners. They appealed to her sense of daring and she felt at home at last on the frontier.

Remme had heard wild tales about Lola Montez and the saloon in Grass Valley which she owned. It was opulently furnished, he'd heard, with fine objects of art, magnificent furniture, and rare antiques from France and Germany.

Staring at him with wicked arrogance, she said naughtily, "Don't you know that what Lola wants, Lola gets?" With an amused smile that revealed her perfect white teeth, she added, "Come with me, I'll buy you a drink at my place." She turned swiftly, climbed into an open one-horse carriage outside the auction hall, moved to the passenger's side, and handed the reins to Remme.

"You drive," she commanded.

Even at six o'clock in the afternoon Lola's saloon was crowded with miners. It was the most richly decorated cabaret Remme had ever seen. Ormolu mirrors, precious jewels given to her by King Ludwig of Bavaria, Louis XVI cabinets, a pet bear, Kanaka houseboys, a swan bed, gold leaf decorating the huge mirror behind the bar and on other graceful objects. It was plush, ornate, and its likeness could only be found in Europe in the salons patronized by the very wealthy and titled. But Lola had shrewdly appraised the wild and woolly miners. They would spend money in the atmosphere of richness, and the rude frontier of 1854 California with gold-seeking immigrants flooding into the state every day with dreams of riches beyond belief would idolize the European courtesan with her French accent and worldly ways.

For those patrons who played billiards there was a room off to one side of the main bar space and tables whose rich furnishings were grouped around a large, deep-red-top billiard table with dragons carved on its walnut legs. It was a gathering place where the governor, senators, and the newly rich could consort away from the crowd. Lola lured them in with her personality.

The single act in Lola's allure and fascination was her Spider Dance which she performed on the stage in the barroom. Famously suggestive, she whirled across the stage to the music of her choice flaunting her superb body which seemed under attack from dozens of imitation tarantulas attached to the ends of long, fine strings suspended from a thin belt around her slender waist.

She gave one performance at night and that was at eight o'clock by which time her customers were well lubricated with whisky.

Remme stayed for a meal and her performance, then she joined him briefly, pouting a little that he had to leave. She invited him to call on her at the Holbrooke Hotel in San Francisco when he ended the cattle drive which he estimated would take him to Sacramento in February of the coming year. He was driven back to his grubby hotel in Grass Valley by one of the house boys.

It was almost six months to the day at ten o'clock at night when Lola and Remme finished with their dinner and were dawdling over their wine at the Holbrooke Hotel. She told him that she kept a suite of rooms at the hotel and he wondered if this was an invitation. He found himself swimming in her dark eyes, honest with himself that it would be thrilling and dangerous to take her in his arms. He knew that she had divined his rising passion, and was an expert at love with far more experience than he. She had freely admitted and seemed pleased to take credit for several scandals with famous men. She smiled at him evocatively—a sign, he was certain, that she was willing. But a voice of caution warned Remme to go slowly. Here was a woman of such beauty, charm, and self-assurance that with a crook of her finger she could have men of wealth, power, and substance flock to her side.

What did she see in him?

Without hesitation she answered his question with a surprising reply even though he had not spoken it aloud. "I like men who are adventurous, who are not afraid to take risks, and that is what you are Louis, a man who knows what he wants and is bold enough to reach for it. Not only at the auction was I was attracted to you, for your obvious personal success, but for the excitement and deep satisfaction when a man and woman know instinctively that they belong together. I also saw in you a man who can help me make an ambitious dream come true."

When Remme asked her to describe the nature of her dream, she lifted her dark, romantic eyes to him and in them was a sudden visionary strength and brightness that was like sparks of fire struck from iron. "I make no excuses," she said, "for the woman I've become. I've learned to leave the history of my heart and moral life to a higher judge. If there were a need to defend or justify it, it should be contrasted with those of the other sex.

"I've learned how to make money at Lola's and know how important it is to make a dream come true. For me," she emphasized, "I need money to buy the influence and assistance I'll require to take California out of the union and declare its independence. And, yes, to rename it Lolaland. I will be queen and guide it to its true destiny."

Taken aback by her weird delusion spoken in such a sincere, undramatic manner, Remme made the only reply he could think of on the spur of the moment. It was the truth. "The money I've saved," he said gently, "is earmarked for the purchase of land and cattle."

Before the words were out of his mouth Lola's face had frozen; she rose quickly, disappointment and anger firming her lovely mouth. She dropped her napkin beside her plate, said she was suddenly tired, and strode away, her skirts flying.

It was 9:00 P.M. Saturday, February 24th, when Remme hurried down the gangplank of the paddlewheel steamer *Rosebud* and slogged rapidly through the trampled, clinging mud until he reached the center of Sacramento Town, his boots heavy with clumps of brown clay. He passed the City Hotel ablaze with lights, formerly John Sutter's old grist mill, which had been transformed into a fancy palace where miners could eat, drink, gamble, and sometimes sleep. At night, the hotel was a bright spot in the winter cold and noisy with music and raised voices—a smoky, raucous atmosphere too loud for Remme's taste. He trudged by, then turned up a street and paused on the steps to the wooden porch of his boarding house. A kerosene lamp hanging from a hook next to the front door cast a weak glow on a flatiron boot scraper with a sharp edge which hung from a string tied to a nail imbedded in a board next to the doorsill. As he propped first one foot then the other on a wooden stump sticking out of the ground under the nail and scraped mud in thick layers from his boots, Remme thought about how his San Francisco vacation had ended with his discovery of treachery at his bank.

After leaving Forbes behind his railing at the Express Company office, and stopping off to pay for his new boots, then hiring an open carriage to take him to the waterfront, Remme bought a late lunch and waited three hours for the steamer to start loading passengers for Sacramento. Even though the steamer would not arrive at his stop until late Saturday, he was impatient to get upstream and realized there was nothing he could do until Monday when first thing, he would take his certificate of deposit to the Sacramento offices of Adams Express Company at 46 Second Street.

His boots clean, Remme opened the door and climbed the front stairs of Miller's boarding house to the second floor. He hoped he would not encounter anybody; he was in no mood for idle talk. He unlocked the door to his room and dropped his leather suitcase and the package containing his new boots on his bed. Once in the familiar surroundings of his own room and his few valued personal possessions he felt better. On the wall there was a colorful Mexican shawl that once belonged to a Santa Fe beauty who cared for him. On a chest of drawers was a framed photo of his mother and himself. He was in a long dress and stood at her knee. He had been five years old. On the lamp stand next to his bed rested a pistol with a dark walnut handle. It had been given to him by Charles Fremont before he became California's first U.S. senator.

Remme decided to put the whole Adams Express Bank business out of his mind. There was nothing he could do until Monday and worry never accomplished anything. He fell into a restless sleep an hour after eating supper and he dreamed of swimming in a clear stream near the farm in Quebec where he grew up as a boy. He cast off his clothes in his dream and he felt the current of the river soothing and lifting his bare, lean body and he enjoyed the cool ooze of the mud between his toes. Then he heard his dog barking excitedly, her sharp voice overriding his splashing and the smooth hissing and agreeable rumble of the river. He looked up then, scanning the river bank. Through the moving curtain of spray and foam he saw his dog was circling a figure in agitation. It was a man and he was growing bigger and bigger as he drew closer to the river bank.

Remme was frightened as the man's form filled out, became taller, and wavered like a person formed out of fog, a ghost in a story, and he huddled in the stream, growing cold as he stood with his shoulders out of the water. Then he recognized the long sideburns on the man's pale cheeks, the deep scowl in his face, the slight paunch of his stomach, the dark gray suit, and the blue foulard tie. It was the banker, Forbes, who stood holding Remme's clothes and stared at him angry-eyed and frighteningly unfamiliar.

Remme felt himself pushing through the water toward the bank, unable to stop his legs from pulling him forward. He started up the slippery bank, naked and ashamed, to meet Forbes who had lifted a heavy stick in his right hand over his head and was bringing it down toward Remme's head with a whizzing, hissing sound. Remme woke up then, saving himself from the banker's blow. He breathed deeply for a few moments, then stared out of the window of his room at the bright moon hanging serenely in the blue. The rain had stopped, the clouds had disappeared, and a cluster of stars like icy brilliant diamonds pierced the sky. It was near dawn. He felt the warmth of his blankets and slipped into a light doze and then he was wandering over the wooded hills behind his old home in Quebec.

About the time Remme was dreaming about swimming in the river near his grandfather's farm in Quebec, Delos Lake, judge of the twelfth district was awakened by a loud, insistent rapping on his front door. His wife, a light sleeper, nudged him and said with a tremor in her voice, "Del, Del are you awake? Who could be at the door at this hour?"

"I have no idea," he said, glancing at the wall clock in the bedroom. He slid out of bed and straightened his long nightshirt that fell below his knees. He opened the drawer on his nightstand and found the handgun he kept handy for protection. He walked silently through the hall and living room, took a stance behind the heavy oak door, and shouted in an irate voice, "Who's there? What do you want at this hour?"

The reply came from an attorney he knew well enough, Alfred A. Cohen. "Your Honor, I have a bankruptcy petition that needs your signature tonight. I wouldn't dare bother you if it wasn't of utmost importance."

Delos Lake was well aware of the financial panic in San Francisco, but this was the first bankruptcy petition he'd been asked to sign. It had to be from one of the three largest express banks in the city that sought protection from creditors.

Grumbling, he said, "Come in," unlocked the door, and stepped into his study off the hall opposite the living room. He placed his pistol on his desk in plain sight.

Alfred Cohen stepped across the threshold carrying a battered briefcase. Shrugging off his wet coat and removing his sodden hat, his open face showed fatigue and strain in every line. Cohen's voice was ragged and unsteady when he said, "I've got men and horses waiting for Your Honor's signature to ride to every corner of California where there is an Adams Express office and order it closed to save the remaining assets. So you can see I'm in a hurry." It was obvious to Judge Lake that the tall, spare man hastily dressed, his tie slightly askew, had been roused from his own bed a few hours earlier to draft the documents that Lake's signature would make official.

As Judge Lake sat behind his desk, barely able to hide his relief from the sudden panic he'd felt as he thought about the loss of the small fortune in savings he had placed in Wells Fargo, not Adams Express, he let out his breath and sighed. Still it was a shock that Adams, the most aggressive express bank in San Francisco, was broke. As he examined the petition expertly, looking for legal flaws, he was troubled when he looked closely at the balance sheet for the company. It showed liquid assets of more than $1.5 million and one recent single unidentified withdrawal of $1.8 million bothered him. Combined debts were listed at more than two million and contingent liabilities in favor of Page, Bacon totaled another million. The officer of Adams Express who had signed the petition was I. C. Woods, the senior California partner.

Judge Lake debated briefly the idea of questioning Cohen about the seven figure withdrawal, but changed his mind. There was no question that the certified balance sheet proved Adams Express was insolvent. Cohen, whom he agreed to appoint as receiver, was anxious, as he had explained, to release his riders to thunder through the miles on early Sunday to deliver their message of misfortune to every Adams branch before they opened on Monday. More tired than when he was awakened, Judge Lake signed the petition and opened the door for Cohen. With his thanks, Cohen ran into the wall of rain that had thickened during his short visit with the judge.

It was four A.M. Sunday morning, February 25th, when an exhausted, thoroughly wet Alfred Cohen finally reached his home, shed his wet clothes, and climbed into bed.

Little did Cohen know that while he was dispatching the horsemen on their urgent errands, I. C. Woods, the resident partner of Adams Express sneaked out of his house carrying a heavy briefcase. He lived not far from the harbor in a house with a magnificent view of the Pacific Ocean. No one could remember seeing Woods keeping to the shadows of the port buildings where ships of all sizes arrived and departed at all hours. The ship Woods chose was sailing for Australia early Sunday morning.

Even though Remme arrived at the Second Street office building of Adams Express on Monday fully thirty minutes before the normal opening hour of 9:00 A.M., his heart sank. The worst of his fears had come true. At least fifty grumbling, loud-talking men were assembled in front of the wooden doors bristling with anger as they patiently waited for clerks inside the bank to raise the window shades and turn the locks. The cat was out of the bag. The San Francisco rumor describing Adams Express' involvement with the bankrupt Page, Bacon, and Company had traveled more than ninety miles almost overnight. The question was whether or not the express company was going to honor drafts or suspend payments.

Remme had obtained his certificate of deposit from the boarding house safe in his landlord's small office after breakfast and now it rested securely in his pocket. But he doubted seriously whether he was going to be able to redeem its face value. As if in answer to his question, on the dot of nine a slender, middle-aged man with thinning hair, wearing a black suit opened the front doors to the bank and pushed carefully through the crowd of men that was still growing as he stood on the steps of the bank.

"I have a notice to read," he said in a high voice. "When I have finished I will tack it to the outside of the door for anybody who wishes to examine it."

Fastening reading glasses on his nose and clearing his throat, he held the notice between his hands and read:

"The undersigned, resident partner in Sacramento of Adams Express Company of California, announces suspension of payment on this date, February 23, 1855, on all certificates of deposit, notes or acceptances, sight drafts or checks drawn upon the Adams Express Company . . ."

Howls of protest drowned the clerk's voice and several men in a rage started up the steps with the obvious intent to charge into the bank. Curiously, they stopped when the clerk raised his hand and he said calmly, "Violence will not help matters. I have a brief statement of the causes that led to this calamity."

He paused, looked gravely at the gathered men, and said, "It is well known that the demand for gold for shipment has for months far exceeded the supply of gold dust from the mines. As a result gold coin has been withdrawn from circulation at a rate of about one million dollars per month. This has left scarcely enough for the most ordinary needs of business, and has caused unusual pressure for gold. This pressure has resulted in today's announcement."

As if on cue just as the clerk completed his explanation, two burly men carrying shotguns and wearing badges on their coats stepped from behind the door of the bank and positioned themselves stiffly on each side of the clerk. It was clear they were on hand to protect the bank from anybody who decided to take matters into his own hands and force the bank to pay out what it owed.

It was Remme who stepped forward and asked the question that was on the mind of every man in the crowd, "Is the bank closed for good or is there a chance we can get our gold in a few days?"

The clerk looked down at Remme with a slight smirk on his face. "Sir," he said, "Adams Express Company is in liquidation. The receiver, Mr. Alfred Cohen, will decide on its future."

"In plain language the bank is broke? That's what you mean isn't it?" an angry man in the crown shouted.

Another man yelled, "I hear Woods has disappeared. Is it true? How much of our money did he take with him?"

The clerk stepped back cautiously and the deputies looked sharply at the men in the crowd for any sign of sudden violence.

Remme turned away bitter with disappointment. The shock of his loss was so great that for a moment he could not accept what had happened to him. He looked around and saw on the faces of the men who were drifting away a reflection of his own anger and loss. He had less than a thousand dollars in the world. He was almost broke after six years of backbreaking work chasing and corralling obstinate steers. When he tricked the banker Forbes in San Francisco on Saturday and learned Adams was in trouble, he had still hoped for the best, even though in his heart he had known his gold was probably lost. Now, everything he had worked for was gone. The ranch in Oregon would be overrun with wildlife, not stocked solid with beef. They were out of reach for a man who owned little more than a saddle, the clothes on his back, a few hundred dollars, and some personal possessions. The idea that he was back where he started six years before was unsettling for the thirty-year-old French-Canadian whose confidence in himself to face any obstacle in nature with strength and nerve had never proved to be wrong. Now, because of the dishonesty of men in banks he did not even know, his whole future was wiped out.

As Remme started back to his boarding house, he could guess what was happening when other men and women in California towns that housed branches of Adams Express Company inquired about their gold: locked doors and sheriffs' deputies protecting the closed banks. He had considered and discarded the idea of finding a horse and making a wild dash to Adams branches in Marysville or Grass Valley to cash his draft there. But he knew the news of the failure would be ahead of him everywhere he tried to get relief.

Had Remme but known it, just a few minutes earlier, the citizens of Sonora, California, learning the news of the bank collapse from a messenger who had ridden all night, had taken matters into their own hands. A mob in a hanging mood overpowered the sheriff and his deputies and broke into the Sonora office. The citizens had confiscated the gold in the vaults and forced the express company clerks at gunpoint to count it out among its rightful owners.

Lower than he had ever been in his life, Remme trudged down the muddy street unable to plan what he should do next. His mind seemed frozen with his personal disaster. Then, on an impulse which he could never later explain, he bent over and picked up a square of paper he saw lying in the mud. It probably had been discarded by one of the men in the crowd at the bank.

It was a handbill advertising the national and international banking and express delivery services of Adams Express. In one column of smaller type was a list of all the cities in the United States and Panama where the banking company had financial connections and were served by steamers. Portland, Oregon was one of them, and the *Pacific Mail* steamship *Columbia* sailed twice monthly from San Francisco to the northwest city located on the banks of the Willamette River.

Remme stared at the handbill and the small type swam in front of his eyes as he dared himself to believe there was hope for him in the printed words on the muddy sheet. Taking a deep breath and letting it out slowly, he forced himself to concentrate on the printed lines. The handbill, Remme saw, was dated February 16, 1855, about a week before he had overheard the disturbing conversation at a neighboring table while he breakfasted at his hotel. It took a moment for him to understand the importance of what he was reading, then his heart beat faster. Excited, overwhelmed by the startling idea that was forming in his mind, Remme could hardly contain himself. Then, reasserting the patience and self-discipline he had learned during a decade of working for himself, he reread the words that had excited him:

The Pacific Mail steamship* Columbia *departs San Francisco on the 14th and the 26th day of each month, barring stormy weather, and arrives in Portland, Oregon six days later. This is to certify that Dr. Steinberger is the only authorized person in Oregon to receive packages of gold to be forwarded by us from San Francisco, and to honor checks, notes or acceptances, and sight drafts, drawn upon the Adams Express Company.

With a shaky hand holding the paper that could be his salvation, Remme realized that on this very morning the *Columbia* must have already started her northern voyage and he was wasting time. He had forgotten the sailing dates of the steamship which had been important to him five years earlier when he was shipping provisions to California gold camps from Oregon. Now, he was going to risk his life on a chance, slim, preposterous, yes, even mad, but a chance that he could recover his savings.

Even as he crumpled the handbill and thrust it in his pocket, Remme's legs were carrying him in a dead run toward his boarding house. And his brain was moving just as swiftly, calculating the odds for the success of an impossible scheme: Could he beat the *Columbia* to Portland by horseback overland? He would have to ride through trackless forests, deep snow, wild rivers, and craggy mountains. If he could do it, he could turn disaster into triumph by exchanging the now worthless sight draft in his wallet for $12,500 in gold from Dr. Steinberger.

Because of Indian troubles between the Klamath and the Rogue Rivers in Oregon and also in the Pit River country, as well as lack of passable roads, there was no stagecoach service between Sacramento and Portland and no telegraph. The *Pacific Mail* steamship *Columbia* would be the first vessel to reach Portland carrying the legal papers to stop payments to all Oregon depositors and clearly, unless Remme was willing to forget the gold he had worked so hard to accumulate, he would have to ride to Portland and beat the boat.

He knew it was eight hundred miles to Portland by water; six days for the *Columbia* to plod her way up the treacherous Pacific Coast to Astoria, Oregon, then up the Columbia River and into the Willamette River which passed the city of Portland. There she would dock. The reason it took so long for the *Columbia* to reach Portland was because of the several stops the steamship had to make on her trip north. The *Columbia* picked up passengers and cargo first at Mendocino Mills, then at Humboldt Bay where Union soldiers were stationed. The next stops were at Trinidad, then Crescent City—the jumping-off point for the mining country of Northern California. The next stop for the paddlewheel steamship in Oregon Territory was at the small military post at Gardiner, then on to Astoria. Basically, the *Columbia* sailed in a straight line with a few side excursions, but the distance to Portland by horseback, as the crow flies, was just shy of seven hundred miles.

Only seven hundred miles! For that matter it may as well have been three thousand miles! For a moment the wiry French-Canadian's heart sank. Ahead of him lay some of the cruelest natural hazards in the American West. Some of the highest mountains in the continent raised their snowy heads in the Cascade Range. And they plunged into some of the deepest valleys with the fastest rivers, and the densest forests on earth. They climbed over rugged hills and pushed through valleys where the Coast Range tied to the Sierra Nevada. There were no well defined trails through the wilderness of Northern California and the Oregon Territory, only the pony forest paths of the hostile Indians and the few scattered white settlers. To make matters worse, within two hundred miles he would encounter a killing obstacle: the deep drifts and ice that locked the higher elevations in a wintry grip. He could only pray that snowfall had been light on the upland reaches.

In his room at his boarding house, after he had stopped to buy supplies at a general merchandise store, Remme was slightly giddy at the boldness of his undertaking. If he had not spent years in the California-Oregon wilderness, he might not have been so aware of the dangers ahead of him. Dozens of brash, foolish men—prospectors, trappers, hunters—disappeared every year because they challenged the wilderness without experience or respect for its harshness. They were smashed to death in a dozen violent ways. Not only was Remme going to pit himself against the mountains and the raw elements in the dead of winter when the hazards were multiplied, but he was going to have to push himself far beyond ordinary human endurance to have a chance to win his solitary race. The fact that he would have to ride at a breakneck pace also meant increasing the risk of accidents or the single mistake that could take his life.

Among the purchases Remme had made at the store and packed into a set of sturdy saddlebags was a one pound sack of coffee beans. On long night vigils in the past he had chewed on the bitter beans, strong with caffeine, to keep awake. Since he had to travel light, but knew body warmth was vital, he packed a spare pair of longjohns, the red woolen underwear that would keep much of his body heat from escaping. There were three pounds of beef jerkey to chew on in his saddlebags, a spare shirt, another pair of warm deerskin pants, two dozen hard biscuits, six cans of beans, three jars of peaches, four candles, two dozen wooden clothespins, matches in a Prince Albert can and a new flint with punk, two boxes of bullets for his rifle, three pairs of heavy long woolen stockings, earmuffs, wooden snowshoes, and a long heavy woolen scarf. An eighteen foot tightly woven and oiled pigskin whip which he often used to pop over the heads of stubborn steers or mules with a sharp snap was coiled and stuffed in his bags. Used as a weapon, it was deadly.

With his saddlebags, his sheepskin coat, a heavy wool blanket tied in a roll, and two canteens to add to his own body weight of 155 pounds, Remme would be asking the horses he rode to carry more than two hundred pounds. The load was still lighter than the average strong horse was used to bearing, but every pound Remme gained in reduced load meant extra miles for mounts that would carry him.

Into a thin leather pouch, Remme carefully placed his certificate of deposit. Then he inserted the leather pouch into an oilskin envelope which he tied securely with string, and thrust the envelope into a space between his shirt and undershirt.

CHAPTER THREE

IT WAS NOON MONDAY, FEBRUARY 26—three days after the financial disaster that many Californians later were to call Black Friday—that Remme caught a small paddlewheel steamer north from Sacramento to Knight's Landing. As he stood at the rail watching waves curl under the bow of the little steamer, Remme learned from a passenger returning from San Francisco that the *Columbia* had weighed anchor early in the morning even while Remme thought up his impossible idea. There was no time to lose. He dared not even stop to think his cause was hopeless, and that even supposing he could find the horses to make the grueling trip ahead of him—and he would need at least two dozen hardy ponies capable of bearing him long distances at a steady run—how was he going to hold up to almost a week of continuous days and nights in the saddle without sleep? He didn't know the answer, but he refused to be daunted by the question.

It was while Remme leaned on the railing close to the bow of the steamer that he thought he recognized a man a few feet away brooding into the water. The bitter expression on the man's face led Remme to say, "You're one of the men I saw yesterday in the crowd trying to recover gold from Adams Express."

Turning his deep-gray angry eyes on the cattle trader, the disillusioned man said, "I recognize you. You're the sucker who asked that little nobody if there was a chance of getting your money back." The contempt in the man's voice was so thick that it made Remme bristle. He turned to walk away, but the stranger said, "Forgive me if I seemed hostile to you. You're just one of the uninformed who lost your life savings in that corrupt bank. The irony is when the *Columbia* sailed from long wharf at seven this morning she had in her safe at least $1.8 million belonging to depositors like you and me. When she reaches Portland all that money will become bankrupt assets of Adams Express. And who do you think is earmarked to receive preferential treatment in the distribution of assets? Not small depositors with less than $15,000 to lose. It's the big concerns like Page, Bacon, Burogne and Company, the North Pacific Trading Company. I've been told that just prior to Judge Lake's signing of the writ of attachment, Page, Bacon got a whopping $378,000. Of course, Page, Bacon is going under too, but the bankruptcy laws allow payment to big depositors when the decision to file for relief is made.

"How do I know all this?" the man asked. "I'm Jedediah Franklin, a partner in a New York law firm. I was sent to protect the assets a few of our clients had in Adams. But I arrived too late to do any good. We knew Page, Bacon was in trouble because of unpaid loans extended to the Ohio and Missouri Railroad, and it was financially linked to Adams, but we acted too late."

Remme was shocked and furious with the knowledge. He'd been cheated. The information imparted by Franklin's admission was like a punch in his stomach, it took his breath away. Preferential treatment was unfair and unjust and his anger brimmed over.

"I don't believe what you've just told me is true. Why, it's legalized thievery."

"No my friend, not criminal," Franklin said with a bitter smile. "It's simply an example of the present state of federal bankruptcy laws that the politicians in Washington were bribed to allow when they wrote the bill for Congress."

Remme's frustration had no enemy upon which to discharge his disillusionment. Washington politics had made such favoritism a specialty.

Sensing Remme's state of mind, Franklin, in a more friendly and reasonable voice, said, "My friend your anger is justified. One of our clients is Westervelt and Mackay of New York who built the *Columbia*, and another is Novelty Iron Works who installed the engine they built for Pacific Mail Steamship Company for a total cost of $169,044. That bill was paid. But other ships Pacific ordered will never be completed. The *Columbia* which weighed anchor this morning and is carrying depositors' money, is a wooden side-wheeled steamer, with three decks, three masts, round stern. She weighs seven hundred seventy tons and is one hundred ninety three feet long. Like most of Pacific's fleet of thirteen steamers, she can accommodate at least one hundred fifty passengers. The irony is that Adams Express was the banker of the boat's owner, Pacific Mail Ship Company. It owes Pacific a lot of money it will never see."

Remme thanked Franklin for his information and walked away to get his gear. Knight's Landing was in view and if he had been determined to save his gold before Franklin's explanation, his mind was now cast in iron with one objective: at all costs, he would beat the *Columbia* to Portland. When he scooped his gold into his saddle-bags, he would not hesitate to describe the deceptive and deceitful character of Adams Express to its Portland agent.

When Remme carried his saddle, saddlebags packed with his provisions, and his bedroll off of the steamer, *Lydia*, at Knight's Landing, he looked almost like a different man. Gone was his dark suit, string tie, and the shiny black boots. Instead, he wore the new rough cowhide boots he bought in San Francisco. They covered his legs up to his knees. His buckskin pants, wrapped tightly around his legs, were thrust into the top of his boots. His long sheepskin coat worn open now, reached almost to his knees. Around his waist, he wore a wide belt to which was attached a sheath for a long sharp knife with an elkhorn handle. Another belt, riding lower on his hips, supported a dark brown leather holster with a row of cartridges. The belt held the black pistol given to Remme by John Charles Fremont. It was loaded and ready to fire.

With his saddle thrown over his shoulder, his heavy, gray, flat-brimmed felt hat pulled snugly down over his forehead, Remme could never be taken for the smiling dandy who had sipped coffee in the dining room of the St. Francis Hotel. Even his expression was changed. His piercing brown eyes in his lean face looked fierce beneath his heavy black brows and his jaw was set in a determined thrust as he strode down the gangplank of the *Lydia* and walked briskly toward the livery stable where he purchased a solid roan horse, a mare, for eighty dollars and threw his saddle and bedroll on her back. He checked to make certain his range rifle was resting securely in its leather scabbard, mounted his new horse, and clattered out onto the trail north.

Remme soon discovered the roan needed little urging to stretch her legs in ground-covering strides and he let the animal have her head until she began to falter and show signs of fatigue as they neared Grand Isle several hours later.

Remme had carefully planned ahead of time how to exchange winded horses with friends without disturbing them. He didn't want to have to take the time to explain his mission to men with whom he traded horses until he absolutely had to. To begin with they might think he was crazy to be racing overland against a steamship. Then, when they decided he was actually trying to restore his life savings in an impossible race, they would probably want to know more about the bank failures and he would have to waste precious minutes to explain. Also, when some of them learned that he was going to push the horses he borrowed, or bought, to the limits of their endurance, they might try to pawn off second-rate animals on him, fearing he would ruin good ponies by riding them too hard.

Remme knew that as long as he rode within two hundred miles of Sacramento, his name would be known and trusted by anyone he was likely to borrow a horse from. He hit upon the idea of leaving a handwritten note pinned to the mane of each horse he had to leave behind. The wooden clothespins he packed in his belongings were for this purpose.

The first note he wrote was addressed to an old friend of his, Judge Diefendorf at Grand Isle. It read:

"Judge: I borrowed your sorrel. In awful hurry chasing a horse thief. Leaving the roan. She's sound and you've got the best of the bargain. See you in about a month. Louis Remme."

Remme had to chuckle to himself as he tightened the cinch of his saddle on the big sorrel and leaped into the familiar leather seat. His idea of blaming a nonexistent horse thief for his hurry was a good touch. There was no crime in the West considered to be worse than stealing a horse. Murderers got lighter sentences in a miner's court than a horse thief who often was hanged on the spot. Remme's friends would understand in an instant the urgency of a chase after a horse thief. When they found a strange horse with his note, they would wish him luck and Godspeed. Of course the note acknowledging the exchange of horses was very important. That's why it had to be secured to the horse in a fashion that guaranteed it would be found and not flicked off. The clothespins would do the trick, Remme decided, even if rain wetted the paper. He smiled as he looked at the note paper pinned high on the roan's mane where it grew between her ears. It was a safe place. The horse couldn't reach it to dislodge it, and it looked pretty, almost like a decorative bow.

The next stretch took Remme about thirty miles west of Marysville and into a small valley he knew about. He pulled Judge Diefendorf's winded sorrel pony to a halt in a pasture where several mares were grazing. The animal he was riding was tired and breathing heavily as he walked it slowly toward the clustered horses whose ears started twitching as they raised their heads and stared at the intruder. Remme's eyes were on a gray, a sleek, long-legged mare with a blaze on her forehead. Carefully he shook out his lariat and let the loop dangle harmlessly next to his right boot.

When he kneed the sorrel as close to the mares as he dared to without spooking them, Remme suddenly swung his lariat in a large flowing circle that dropped over the head of the gray fifteen feet away, even as the other mares bolted and ran. Quickly, Remme wrapped the free end of his rope around the pommel of his saddle to keep it from being jerked out of his hand as the gray lunged against the loop. Dropping to the ground, he ran to the gray and pulled her head down. She quieted as he murmured to her and smoothed her neck with one hand.

Ten minutes later, Remme, aboard the tall, slender gray, clattered swiftly out of the pasture, headed north. He smiled to himself as he thought about the owner and what she would say to herself about Remme when she found the strange sorrel horse with the note clothespinned to her mane.

Remme knew the gray's owner, Lola Montez, loved the companionship of animals. When she came to stay in a plain small cottage not far from the valley of the horses to be away from her saloon, she occupied herself with a brown bear on a chain, dogs, parrots, cats, and a goat. After their parting a few nights ago she would be furious when she learned that he had borrowed her favorite horse.

Remme laughed to himself as he pictured Lola's wrath. She was a beautiful woman with a famous temper and he was grateful she had disillusioned him with her strange fantasy of making herself Queen of California.

Pounding north on the gray through the flat land on the wagon trail to Red Bluff, Remme knew the easy part of his ride was behind him. The last of the day's light gradually disappeared and the horse beneath him lost its sharp outline. Shadows made the trail ahead obscure, but he refused to allow the gray to slacken her pace, fully aware how dangerous it was to be running at full gallop as the twilight deepened. An unseen small animal or bird seeking a nesting place for the night could cross the trail, collide with the gray, startle her, and cause injury to the horse.

With the light gone, the chances of the gray stepping into a gopher hole were a hundred times greater. Still, Remme could not let up. In his imagination he could see the *Columbia* plowing through the ocean unimpeded by nightfall. Every minute of speed was precious to him if he was going to beat the *Columbia* to Portland.

There would be dozens of times on the trail ahead when natural obstacles would reduce his progress to a walk. But the boat wouldn't stop; it would beat northward relentlessly mile after mile, not dependent on horsepower and fighting spirit.

Remme refused to worry about the hazards he could not see. He had strong faith that luck was riding with him and a belief that if he let the horse have her head, her own sense of the contours of the earth beneath her feet, coupled with her night vision, would prevent a spill. On he rode, his body bent forward in the saddle, his mind and sinews urging his mount forward.

Aware that chewing coffee beans to keep awake during the long hours in the saddle would not be enough to keep his eyes from closing, Remme focused on his short four-month experience five years earlier in 1850 when he took on the rewarding job as a one-man express agent who collected letters from isolated miners for a fee, then delivered them to ships docked in San Francisco. He delivered the mail then bought up used copies of the *New York Herald Tribune* from passengers for one dollar a copy and resold them ashore for eight dollars each. Next, he hired himself out as an apprentice seaman on the steamer *New World.* Remme's duties kept him running—cleaning tables and washing the dishes of the passengers, swabbing the decks, relieving the fireman loading the boiler with hard wood chunks, keeping the captain's coffee cup full, making certain the sails wrapped around each of the two masts were tied securely by ropes preventing them from flapping in the wind. He oiled machinery and performed a dozen other menial chores.

June 3, 1851 was the day he never forgot because he came closest to losing his life from a catastrophic event that had never been equalled before or since in his life. Even though it seemed that every minute of his waking day at sea was devoted to some mundane chore, he did have time to speculate on the competition between Adams Express and Wells Fargo. The two banking companies encouraged a reckless rivalry by its messengers who raced by horseback, by stage, and by paddleboat to be the first to deliver mail, collecting deposits from miners and carrying the news of the world from New York and from widely separated California towns where each company had branch offices. The struggles of the two express companies for supremacy and to enhance their reputations for speedy delivery was the subject of pride and admiration often described in dramatic fashion in California's newspapers. Editors knew their readers loved to consume details about racing steamboats and took a particular pleasure in those who were favorites and on which heavy betting was an exciting pastime. The spirit of the madcap competition between Adams Express and Wells Fargo was dramatic and dangerous. Newspapers noted that the age of steam had sharpened the competition between the two rivals.

Remme saw firsthand among the passengers of the *New World* their enthusiasm as praise for steamboat racing and their loyalty to a particular paddleboat by betting heavily on it being first in a race to dock at a river port. But Remme couldn't convince himself the engineer was not flirting with disaster when he observed the man's practice of tying an oar across the lever of the safety valve, allowing the steam pressure to rise dangerously near the point of explosion.

It was just this sort of folly responsible for the *New World*—charging ahead of the *Henry Clay* and *Wilson G. Hunt* plunging down the Sacramento River into the waters of lower San Francisco Bay—to blow the cap off her steam chest, killed the fireman and one passenger, and flung three others overboard. Charles Youmans, the clerk of the boat, was badly scalded while checking his sacks of bullion. Remme was at the stern of the boat coiling rope when the eruption blasted the forward structure of the paddleboat, reducing it to kindling. The force of the explosion dipped the stern and Remme was thrown into the bay. Shocked but uninjured, he saw one of the passengers struggling in the water and swam to him, grabbed him by the collar of his coat, and swam to shore with his burden.

When Remme was satisfied the man was breathing normally, he walked away, convinced he would never again work on a steamboat. In view of the boiler explosions during the next four years, Remme accused himself of poor judgment in selecting Adams Express as his banking institution. Now he was paying the price riding through the frozen night with his woolen scarf pulled up over his nose to protect him from an icy wind.

There seemed to be no end to rushing competition that ended in tragedy. Just a year earlier the toll of human lives from over-stressing defective iron used to build boilers and the reckless spirit of competition between Adams Express and Wells Fargo were directly responsible for the deaths of more than four hundred passengers who risked their lives aboard the imperfect steamboats. They seemed to be made to be fancy and dangerous, in an era when relentless rain made winter stagecoaching virtually a form of navigation.

It was near midnight, having covered more than forty miles on the tireless gray, when the animal began to stumble and weave. She was dangerously winded and Remme, stiff and numb from hours in the saddle, stepped down to the ground and almost fell on his face. His feet were like blocks of wood, void of feeling. Gradually as he walked around the horse and stamped his boots and swung his arms, circulation returned. When Remme could feel his toes again, he led the gray toward a campfire a hundred yards or so west of the trail.

A light drizzle was falling and a three-quarter moon sailed high in the murky sky between night clouds. Drawing closer to the fire, Remme shouted in a loud voice, "Hello the camp. Anybody home?"

The answer that came from a man Remme could not see froze his blood:

"Show yourself against the firelight. Slow and easy now, unless you hanker for a lead bellyache!"

Holding the reins of his horse with one hand and with the other clearly in view, Remme stepped into the cheerful circle of light thrown by the fire, pulling the gray behind him. He turned his head as he heard a step and a tall man clad in buckskin with a white beard and flowing hair stationed himself in the half shadows just beyond the fire's glow. In his hands rested a rile. The barrel was pointed straight at Remme's heart.

"Now, what do you want this time of night?"

"I'm chasing a horse thief," Remme said, thinking quickly that the idea he had struck on earlier would be a good explanation to strangers whose help he needed.

The bearded man lowered his rifle and glided into the firelight. Remme breathed easier and got a better look at the remarkable figure he had disturbed. Obviously a trapper, the man had the appearance of a person who spent most of his life outdoors and slept in his clothes. His buckskins were dirty brown, but neatly patched with lighter, newer squares of hide. He wore a red kerchief around his neck and moccasin boots that reached to below his knees. His face was hawkish with a wide mouth, hooked nose, and fierce gray eyes. He looked sharply at Remme for a moment, then dropped to his knees, stirred the fire with a stick, and poured coffee from a blackened pot into an empty clay cup. He held it out to Remme. "Here, drink this."

As Remme thanked the trapper and sipped the strong brew he saw the man sizing up the gray which was trembling with fatigue, her head lowered.

"That's a fine horse you're riding. I'll swap you mine and get the best of the bargain."

"It's a borrowed horse," Remme said, "I'll have to swap back with you after I catch the man I'm after."

The trapper nodded. "I'll throw your saddle on my bay while you finish your coffee. How far ahead is the thief?"

Remme thought about the *Columbia's* ocean passage and shook his head, "Could be only a few hours if I'm lucky," he said.

The trapper grunted and patted the gray's neck then swiftly unstrapped Remme's saddle and carried it over his shoulder into the darkness beyond the fire. When he returned a few minutes later, he was leading an ugly, square-headed bay, a big, lumpy horse with knobby knees, a slight sway back, and high shoulders with bones that seemed to poke through the skin.

"He ain't much to look at, but he just keeps going. Feels like you're sitting in a rocking chair on his back. I call him Shorty 'cause he's so tall."

As Remme swallowed the last bitter taste of the trapper's coffee, he swung up to the saddle and took the reins from the trapper.

"Listen," the man said, "keep your eyes peeled for Injuns and watch your hair. They say the Klamaths and the Modocs have been ranging south of the Oregon border. And the Modocs are the worst of the lot." With that sparse advice, the trapper slapped Shorty on the rump and the big bay jumped into the night.

True to his word, the trapper's Shorty was a dream horse to ride. A powerful animal with a wide back and strong legs, he lunged north eagerly carrying his rider in a comfortable see-saw motion. Guided by Remme's light touch on the reins, Shorty fell into a long, loping rhythm that ate up the ground beneath his hooves.

Grateful though he was for the pleasant rocking of his horse, Remme had been in the saddle since noon—almost thirteen hours. He was not tired so much as he was sleepy. The boost from the coffee he had drunk at the trapper's fire was fading and he reached into his pocket and found a handful of roasted coffee beans he had placed there. The bitter flavor of the beans bit into his tongue as he chewed them, but he swallowed the juice and soon felt more alert. Hungry, he broke a stick of dried beef jerky he took from a bundle in his saddlebags. The jerky was as hard as nails and in order for him to eat it he sucked on it until it softened in his mouth. A few minutes after he crunched the coffee beans and swallowed the jerky, Remme was refreshed. He felt more in tune with the thundering hooves of the pole horse.

As he broke through the night on Shorty with a cold wind rising from the west buffeting his body with sudden puffs of force, a new sound arched above the wind. Even though he had heard it many times in different places, it always reminded him of his own solitary life. He respected and was wary of the watchers in the wilderness who traveled together with yellow eyes gleaming and called to one another in their high, sobbing voices. Shorty had veered slightly in his forward stride when the wolf howled, proving the big horse also felt threatened by the gray hunters.

Remme frowned, thinking the near presence of the wolves in the valley below the mountains might be a sign of something that did not bode well for him. If the critters were hunting in the low hills and valleys, it might be because the snow was too thick and too deep higher up for them to find game. If that was the case in a hundred miles or so he could be facing winter passes blocked with snow. He wished now for a glimpse of the gray travelers. One look at the fur a wolf was wearing would tell him a tale of the weather. If the hairs were as long as his little finger, gray and thick as a rain cloud, he could probably count on bitter cold and heavy snow the higher he went.

It was near Towerhouse, five miles northwest of Whiskey Town an hour after dawn of the second day in the saddle, that Remme got his answer to the mountain weather. For seven hours he had ridden the willing Shorty hell-for-leather through the night. The big horse had seemed tireless as he carried Remme mile after mile through the darkness. All night the moon played hide and seek, darting behind clouds and hiding the wagon path Remme was following. Shorty had thundered on faithfully, flying through the patches of light and dark without hesitation. If Remme had admired the gray for her beauty and grace, he was impressed by the strength and endurance of the big white. He promised himself to barter with the trapper for the horse when he came back from Oregon—if he won his race.

Thoughts of bartering for Shorty flew out of Remme's head a moment later when he heard the unmistakable sounds of hard breathing and the pad of many feet following Shorty's swift legs pounding the earth. Twisting in the saddle for a quick look behind him, a chilling stab of fear ran through Remme and his mind froze for a moment. Not ten feet from his thundering horse was a pack of hungry gray wolves—their sharp teeth showing white in their open mouths. From the instant he glimpsed them, he was certain of their strategy. Five of them were drawing closer, their long legs narrowing the gap between man and horse, their lonely prey. But two were running wide of the pack, loping parallel to Shorty. Their intention was clear—charge ahead of the big horse and at the right moment hurl themselves at his head and neck, sinking their teeth in his nose. Just as Remme twisted his body again with his handgun drawn,

Shorty's scream and sudden lunge to the right almost unseated Remme. He grabbed for the pommel of his saddle, missed, and he was jolted precariously to the left.

Unbalanced, his right boot pulling free of his stirrup, Remme felt himself slipping down the left leathery side of his horse. If he fell the hooves of the hysterical horse could trample him to death. He had no choice but to claw for Shorty's rough mane. He buried his left hand desperately in Shorty's long flowing hair, knotting his fist in the mane and pulling himself upright. With his right hand, still gripping the pistol, he turned his body and fired once. He heard the high yelp, felt a sudden spurt of satisfaction, then yanked on the reins with all his strength, to pull himself into the saddle. The bit dug into Shorty's tongue, but the horse ignored the pain and charged ahead. The sleek, fast wolf on the right to the rear of Shorty launched herself onto Shorty's buttocks, sinking her teeth in his thick hide, with her long claws trying to dig furrows into Shorty's skin. At the same moment Shorty squealed in pain, Remme twisted his body and pointed the handgun at the wolf's skull. The explosion tore the scalp away from the skull in a spurt of blood and the creature dropped to the ground beneath Shorty's feet.

Just after Remme killed the rear-running wolf, Shorty shrieked, and lunged to the left to avoid the attack of the lead wolf. His sudden veering almost unseated Remme again. Still gripping his gun in his right hand, he grabbed for the pommel of his saddle. He missed, jolted further to the left by Shorty's sudden sliding to a jarring momentary stop and turning in a desperate half-circle to face the wolf with his hooves raised above his body. Down he trod, crushing the wolf's head. At the same moment Shorty turned, Remme, losing his balance, had kicked himself free of the saddle and lunged off Shorty's back. He struck the ground, rolling, still holding his pistol firmly in his right hand. When he stopped turning over, he raised himself on his elbows, pointing his pistol at the mouth of a big wolf whose teeth had pierced Remme's sheepskin jacket. Tearing his teeth away from the cloth, the animal sprang forward on his haunches, airborne, covering the four feet to Remme with his fangs bared. Then his mouth exploded in a spray of blood when Remme fired twice. The force of the two slugs tumbled the wild beast in an awkward backward flip and he landed heavily in the dark wet grass, the life gone out of him.

With no time to discover if any of the other predators were still alive, Remme quickly rose on one knee and took in the scene. Shorty was no place to be seen. The wolves were gone except for three bodies. One attacker was whining. It was trying to limp away; his right leg was shattered from the first bullet Remme fired. The bullet had made a long bloody streak which had stripped away the thick fur on his right side, exposing a bleeding horizontal furrow. Remme's first shot had broken a front leg and denuded the hair from the wolf's skin, leaving a bleeding swath a half-inch wide.

Taking the wolf's life would save it from its own kind who would attack, kill it, then tear it to pieces and consume it. Remme took careful aim at the wolf's head and fired. It was dead before it collapsed.

Dark though it was and suddenly still, the wagon road was faintly illuminated by an intermittent moon, hiding, then revealing its pale face between hurrying clouds that obscured its brightness as they sailed past. Remme was certain that Shorty could not be far, probably standing still shivering with fear, afraid to reveal himself, still trembling from the attack by the wolves, uncertain they would not reappear and that his rider was lost, leaving him alone without direction or the welcome companionship of the man he had come to trust. When Remme made out the horse's unmoving form in the dark, the greeting from Shorty when he smelled Remme as he headed for him in the dark was a grateful nickering. Relieved, Remme stroked Shorty's neck affectionately until the big animal stopped shaking. Quickly, Remme climbed into his saddle and turned the eager horse north.

Now, Shorty was winded. Streaks and bubbles of lather painted his neck and shoulders like a film of soap. He stood with his head lowered behind the hitching rail in front of the livery stable in Clear Creek. He was gulping air and wheezing. Remme was proud of the hammer-headed, speckled white and when he told the owner of the stable how the big, knobby horse had carried him almost sixty miles in seven hours, the hostler smoothed his hand over Shorty's back, clucked his tongue, and said, "That's some horse. Wish he was yours to sell. I'll loan you a good mount and rest and feed this one. It'll cost you three dollars. I'll saddle Becky for you while you get breakfast."

Remme agreed, paid the man, and trudged across the street to the towerhouse.

As he walked he reflected that the stablemaster had not been surprised when he rode up and told his story about chasing a horse thief. He had accepted the lie as true and commented that the thief and stolen horse had not stopped at his stable. Remme was the only stranger he had seen in two days. Remme began to realize that the men to whom he told his tale swallowed his story because to them his pursuit of the thief was an example of frontier justice, and by helping Remme along the way with horses they were participating in the small drama of his chase.

CHAPTER FOUR

TOWERHOUSE WAS ONLY THREE years old when Remme sat down in the dining room for a quick breakfast. The hotel was doing a brisk business mostly with miners who searched for gold in Clear Creek and the surrounding Trinity Mountain area. The hotel was known as the best roadhouse in California and Remme had taken meals in the dining hall many times. While he waited for his eggs and ham, he asked a man seated across from him at the long oak table what the weather was like in the mountains a few miles north.

It was plain to Remme that the man was a miner and his clothes were a dead giveaway that he was an Oregon Trail immigrant who had probably started west from St. Louis, arrived in Oregon, then decided to try his luck in the California gold camps. There was no mystery in Remme's deduction. The miner's clothes revealed his origin. Because of Oregon's isolation many settlers were outfitted in styles that outsiders considered peculiar. They all wore broad-brimmed black, soft hats. Their long hair was combed back behind their ears, protecting their necks from the cold, just like the man sitting across from Remme. Also typical was the canvas material from which his clothes were made. It came from the tents and wagon covers that had sheltered emigrant families from Missouri to the Columbia River. Raincoats and outer garments were reinforced with remnants of old woolen garments. Broad collars and cuffs were faced with beaver or otter fur. These hardy homespun garments were practical and inexpensive.

The miner admitted he was digging for gold and his hands gave him away. They were red and chapped from washing gravel in a rocker at Clear Creek. His boots and heavy coat wore tell-tale streaks of dried mud. Between bites of hot biscuit and sausage, the miner, whose name was Pearson, said, "It's been a bad one in the mountains to the north, I hear. If you're headin' that way, you'd better veer west as far as you can and keep to the valleys unless you want to get blown off your horse. The winds have been sweeping down the chute like a blast from the North Pole. Even down here, I've been chipping ice in the mornings all winter."

Remme thanked the miner for his information and tackled his eggs when they were delivered. He realized as he hurried through his breakfast that it was probably the last hot meal he would eat for several days. A few miles north of Clear Creek, the wagon road ended and the tall mountains of pointed firs and pines rolled away to the north in a labyrinth of interlocking ranges, plunging canyons, and craggy, broken summits. There were forest trails known to men like himself, but as yet only a few wagons had creased the valley floors beyond the mining camps. The country ahead of him was wild, lonely, and dangerous, with a thousand tricks to snare and trap an unwary horseman. It was no domain for breakneck riding, for whisking through the cloud-broken night hugging the neck of a fast horse. His progress would be much slower because it would be necessary for him to make time-consuming detours.

Sometimes the only way to overcome the mountains was to skirt them. Climbing them was impossible. At this time of year, some of the slopes were buried in twenty or thirty feet of snow, clinging to the hidden earth so precariously that a martin's cry would be enough to start a landslide. Remme knew how destructive the moving side of a mountain could be. It was awesome. But skirting the mountains often meant swinging wide east or west through canyons that eventually would lead him to paths north. In some cases to gain a mile, he would have to ride five. But Remme had not underestimated the obstacles facing him when he started on his mad race.

Even though his passage through the wilderness would be hampered by dozens of setbacks, his estimate of the sailing time from stop to stop of the *Columbia* was more than guesswork. Four years earlier when the *Columbia* first reached Portland from San Francisco, he had been one of her first customers to send freight to San Francisco—eggs, apples, and wheat for the gold camps of California. She was the first true steamboat in Oregon waters. But aside from that distinction, the *Columbia* had little to brag about. A three-masted sidewheeler, only ninety feet long, doubled-ended, and resembling a ferryboat, the sturdy wooden vessel of about 770 tons lacked both style and comfort. Her speed seldom exceeded four to five miles an hour. A year after her maiden voyage the Columbia made two runs a month to Portland. For passage, travelers paid twenty-five dollars each way and had to furnish their own blankets and food.

The steamer's slow speed was the factor that gave Remme hope he could keep ahead of her overland, despite the obstacles. By water, it was about 710 miles on a straight course from San Francisco to the mouth of the Columbia River where the vessel had to cross the most treacherous and destructive bar in the world. After the hazardous crossing, the ship plowed up the Columbia about ninety miles into the Willamette River to dock in Portland, which had settled mostly on the west bank.

Remme's calculations of the steamer's speed were not based on dividing nautical miles by hourly speed. He factored into the equation the extra time consumed by the paddleboat to make five coastal stops on the way to Portland. Loading and unloading passengers and cargo, maneuvering in and out of small bays and docking and undocking safely added significantly to her running time. That was why six days enroute was the sensible estimate before she could drop anchor in the Willamette River.

If he could stick in the saddle six days and nights, sleeping as he rode, eating when he could catch a meal, avoiding natural hazards, angry Indians, and violent weather, with luck on his side, he was convinced he could beat the steamship to Portland. He knew it was going to be close, closer and tougher than any challenge he'd ever faced. And he knew deep inside him that he would win if he refused to doubt the outcome. He would use every trick he'd ever learned to outwit the wilderness, to encourage and infuse the mounts he rode with the faith in himself he would transmit to them. With the courage and passion to run like the wind, he would urge them on. Into their ears he would whisper, "Match your hoofbeats to my heartbeat and we'll win. Oats for you and steak for me!"

Setting his jaw, Remme took the last sip of his coffee, paid for his breakfast, and hurried across the street to the livery stable. He climbed on a medium black horse which the stablemaster claimed had a strong heart and clattered over the wooden bridge that spanned Clear Creek.

There were two routes roughly parallel that Remme could take north. Each one was hazardous; both of them had been made by miners exploring creeks and rivers in the Trinity Creek wilderness. Remme decided on the western route because it was further removed by a few miles from the influence of Mount Shasta whose snowy peaks reared fourteen thousand feet into the sky. Also on the western trail there were more gold camps where he could trade horses with the hardy miners who braved the winter working their claims.

By late afternoon Remme put Weaverville behind him and was picking his way round snowcapped boulders and thick trees wearing a coat of white. He had discovered that Becky was a determined horse plodding patiently through snow drifts that were often chest high. As the afternoon wore on, Remme realized that the color of the sky was changing and the temperature was dropping rapidly. The air was becoming heavier and a leaden pall was spreading over everything. All the signs convinced him that a bad storm was brewing and he and Becky had no choice but to face it. He had to keep going because to wait for the storm to subside after it struck might mean a delay of a day or so while it blew itself out. Riding through a storm was not a safe decision, but every minute counted. The steamship *Columbia* had no serious obstacles to overcome, unless of course she encountered a storm at sea and had to run for shelter. He couldn't plan on such luck.

Even as he made his decision to push Becky forward, the wind suddenly picked up and drove at him with a sudden gust that held a sharp, freezing edge. Quickly, Remme reached into his saddlebags and pulled out the heavy woolen scarf he had packed. He folded the scarf lengthwise so that it resembled a long thick bandage and looped it over the crown of his hat and tied the ends tightly under his chin. He pulled the collar of his coat up to protect the back of his neck and fastened the top button in front. Now, with his hat pulled down close to his ears which were covered by the scarf and with his collar raised, the Frenchman looked like an old woman peeking from her shawl. Only his eyes, shaded by the lowered brim of his hat, peered out brightly taking in the slanting snow as it whipped at him and his horse.

Within minutes, Remme knew he was facing one of the most vicious storms of his life. He could only pray that he could push Becky through the worst of it. While he urged the game little horse to keep a constant trot, he let her have her head choosing the path forward. He had no choice. The snow was drilling him with thousands of needle pricks. It was blown by a wind that hugged the ground and screamed like an angry wildcat. It carried icy blasts that filled the air with biting particles fine as dust. It swooped in a horizontal stream peppering everything in its path with tiny pellets of frozen white fire. Soon, Remme could not see Becky's ears, so thick was the snow. With his head bowed, the main force of the wind struck the top of his hat and wobbled it on his head, trying to lift it from his scalp. Remme tightened the scarf under his chin feeling the crust of snow building up on the wool. In less than five minutes a layer of snow three inches deep covered the front of his coat. When he lifted his eyes to look ahead, the wind flung snow under the brim of his hat and with swift cold fingers searched cleverly for openings to his skin around the collar of his coat.

Becky swayed and stumbled and ran blindly, terrified by the thick howling snow that clogged her ears and filled the hollows of her eyes. She kept going, urged by the pressure of Remme's knees and her own growing panic to escape the blizzard.

It was when Becky started heaving and shaking her head wildly that Remme pulled on the reins and dragged himself out of the saddle. Holding tightly to the reins, he pushed himself against the wind to reach Becky's head. The snow was like a thick cloud surrounding, drowning, covering everything that had a surface with layers of crystals and ice. Trees carried such a burden of snow that their shapes were lost; they were shaggy white mysteries, like miniature mountains sprouting from the ground. A sudden, brief let-up in the snow allowed Remme to see Becky's head in the white glare. What he glimpsed in that instant scared him and he reached for the knife in his belt. The worst of his fears had come true. Becky was suffocating, barely breathing through a mask of ice that covered her head from her muzzle to her ears. Her own hot breath condensing as moisture and blown back into her face by the icy wind had frozen to her hairy skin. Remme knew about killing ice. He had found cattle dead on the range, smothered in treacherous weather when their own warm breaths created the moisture that formed frozen hoods encasing their heads in glistening white sacs. Finally the ice closed off their nostrils and they suffocated.

Quickly, Remme cut breathing holes in the ice blocking Becky's nostrils and she snorted wildly, took several ragged breaths, shook herself, and stamped her feet. Remme pulled her around so that her tail faced into the blowing wind, then, with extreme care he cut into the ice that had glazed over her eyes. When she could blink and moisture started running from the corners of her eyes, Remme opened his saddle bags and pulled out a spare cloth shirt. With the wind making puffs and billows in the fabric he succeeded, after two attempts, tying the arms of the shirt around Becky's neck. Then he pulled the body of the shirt over her eyes and nose. With a piece of rawhide string, he tied the shirttails closed beneath the horse's muzzle. When he finished, his shirt flapped and pulled around Becky's head, but it was secure protecting her face from the freezing wind. Eventually, the moisture from her lungs and breath would saturate the cloth and the shirt would freeze hard as a board. But Remme was betting that the cloth would not stick to the horse's skin. She could breathe through the shirt even though her vision was blocked.

He wasn't concerned about Becky's hampered sight. She was a trail horse and answered to directions from the reins and the pressure of his knees in her ribs. He wiped the snow from his saddle and pulled himself on Becky's back, thankful that her actions had given him a warning of what was happening to her. He told himself he should have expected the wind to freeze the horse's breath. He should have examined her before she started having trouble.

Remme had no choice but to drive Becky once more into the cutting wind and snow. To stop meant death. Within minutes without shelter horse and rider would be blanketed with snow; body temperatures would drop and the end would be inevitable. He had a vague idea that they were still traveling north, but could not have sworn to it. He plowed ahead on the black horse, brushing snow out of her mane, urging her on, rubbing his own nose and cheeks to keep the blood moving in his face. He listened to the voice of the crying wind for any change of tone or pitch that meant the storm was letting up. He knew it was not unusual for snow storms like this one to last for days. If it didn't let up soon he'd have to find shelter for Becky and himself—if he could find it. That would mean the end of his race and the loss of everything he'd worked for.

It was an hour later when the storm died and the snow stopped. It was suddenly so quiet that Remme could hear Becky's soft breathing as she stood up to her chest in a snowdrift. Vapor and sweat converted to steam rose smoking from her hide.

As Remme cut his shirt off of Becky's head, he whispered a prayer of thanks. The frozen cloth hood covering Becky's face was imbedded with particles of ice and horse hair. She nickered when he removed the frozen tail of his shirt from her eyes, then blinked and swung her head up and down as if to express her relief that she could see again. When he climbed back on his horse, one look at the snow scene that surrounded him told him how lucky he had been to survive the storm. If Becky had bolted when he had removed the ice mask from her head, as many horses would have done, he could have been lost in the storm. And, careful as he had been with his knife, he saw that he had cut the skin on the inside of the horse's left nostril when he freed her air passages of ice. The wound had bled and frozen.

Remme patted Becky's neck affectionately and looked around him. As far as he could see snow blanketed the ground to a depth of three or four feet, high enough to come just under Becky's belly. Mountain shrubs like rabbit brush, and ocean spray—the sturdy plant that the Indians used as stock for their arrows—looked like huge footstools slip-covered with snow. Then, suddenly the white world around him blazed as the sun broke free of the clouds and poured golden light on the carpet of snow. The glare was so fierce that for a moment Remme was blinded by the reflection. He threw up his arm to protect his eyes and Becky started back nervously. When Remme opened his eyes again there appeared, as if it had just been made, Mount Shasta, reaching into the sky like a white dream. There it stood, probably eighty miles away, forever distant, aloof, a shining pinnacle whose reaches no man had climbed. It commanded the four directions of the wind and beneath its covering of snow a volcanic heart of fire reached deep into the earth.

Remme had seen the mountain many times, but never had it appeared so grand and remote. Even as it blazed fiercely white against the blue of the sky, the sun went behind a cloud and the mountain receded into the horizon. It was still to be seen, but its outline was faint and dim.

A man who had spent most of his life in the wilderness, Remme was convinced that the sudden appearance of Mount Shasta was an omen of good fortune. He had witnessed some strange tricks of the weather in the wilderness but he did not judge an event as mysterious or odd, or as an act of God. Why something happened wasn't important. He couldn't control the sun or move the stars, but he could be grateful when nature favored him with a stroke of luck. Not only had Shasta cheered him after a grim night of shrieking snow and ice, but it stood in a vast field of featureless snow as his directional beacon. He knew the mountain was northeast of the trail to Trinity Creek. He couldn't be more than five miles from Cox's Store. There he could swap Becky for a fresh horse, catch a few hours of sleep, and ride on. Despite his sense of urgency, he knew he had to sleep. He had to restore his strength. He had been awake almost forty-eight hours, and in the saddle for most of that time. His vision was playing tricks on him—spots that didn't exist swam in his eyes, the hairs on Becky's ears seemed much larger than they were, the horizon shifted when he tried to focus his eyes. He was jittery, nodding in the saddle, and his body, tough as it was, was aching with fatigue.

When Remme dismounted from his horse at Cox's Store, he staggered when he put his feet on the ground. Major Isaac Cox, a bearded man who operated the store on the south bank of the Trinity River, took one look at Remme, whom he knew—red eyed, with a two-day beard on his face—and guided him into the storeroom. There among canned goods, leather harnesses, shovels, gold pans, and sacks of cornmeal and flour, Remme sprawled and was asleep almost before his head touched the floor.

It was five hours later when Remme felt Cox's hand on his arm. True to his word, Cox awakened the Frenchman at 2:00 P.M. Groggy, but refreshed, Remme grunted his thanks to Cox, clumped through the two-room store, and outside scooped up a double handful of snow and pushed his face into it. When his skin began to tingle, Remme dropped the melting snow, shook water from his fingers, and put his hat back on. He accepted a cup of coffee from Cox who told Remme he had fed Becky and transferred the saddle to a motley gray-white horse Cox had taken in trade from a miner for provisions.

"I've ridden him, Louis," he said. "And he's sturdy. A gelding. Wants his own head. Stubborn. Reminds me of you. Now, what's this story you told me about chasing a horse thief?"

Remme had repeated his tale of chasing a horse thief to Cox before he fell asleep. He had had to tell the store owner something to cover his strange request to be awakened in five hours with a fresh horse waiting for him.

Spooning peaches into his mouth from a jar he purchased from Cox, he enlarged his story, between bites, of the imaginary horse thief.

Taking in Remme's dusty appearance, the horse-lather stains on his coat and pants, the circles under his eyes, Cox said, "That must be some horse to chase a man as far as you've come. I hope you catch him."

Remme thanked Cox for his good wishes, then asked the question that had been burning in his mind, "What about the Indians?"

"Well, that's a different story," Cox said. "The Modocs have been raiding all along the frontier—along the Oregon border. I hear they've attacked villages and taken slaves from the Shastas, the Pit Rivers, and the Paiutes. 'Course they've been doing that for a hundred years. If the man you're chasing is heading up into Oregon, I hope for your sake he's steering clear of Tule Lake. There's been no wagon trains with settlers since early fall. But, heck, you probably know that the Modocs and some of the Klamaths have been killing whites near Bloody Point. And all winter, I hear, they've been stealing horses anywhere they can find them. Somebody's got to get a posse together and go after the devils like Ben Wright did back in 'fifty-two."

Remme nodded his head. He remembered three years earlier hearing about the sole survivor of an Indian massacre who rode into Yreka with a grizzly tale. The Modocs had attacked a wagon train near a place that became famous as Bloody Point. The man who escaped with his life told of the slaughter of sixty-four men, women, and children. All of the bodies had been horribly mutilated and scalped. An armed posse of men had stormed out of the town headed by Ben Wright, an Indian fighter who wore his hair as long as any brave. By flaunting his shoulder-length curls, he was making his scalp valuable to the Indians as a battle trophy and he was proving his own courage and daring. Remme, who wore his own hair long, thought Wright was a reckless fool. He knew the man had become an Indian agent for the tribes that lived near the mouth of the Rogue River in Oregon. He thought Wright's determination to make a target of himself for renegade Indians was the kind of arrogance that endangered the lives of the men who rode with him. One day he'd pay for his bravado with his own scalp.

Remme knew that the hunting party from Yreka headed by Wright tracked and killed several Modocs, but the Indians continued to prey on settlers headed to Oregon and the Applegate Cutoff into the Willamette Valley. The French-Canadian was fully aware that a lone horseman like himself was a favorite target of roving bands of braves. One of the games they loved to play was for one brave with two horses to chase a solitary horseman. If the man alone was mounted on a swift pony, the sport was more fun because the brave had to switch horses on the run, finally overtaking the rider on the fresher exchange horse. The horseman was rarely left alive when the whole party of braves caught up with him and his Indian pursuer.

"What Ben Wright did was for his own warped sense of glory," Remme said. "Wright's bloodletting probably did more in Southern Oregon than any man to incite the Modocs, who were sure guilty of killing. The truth of the matter is, his men buried the bodies of the immigrants and by October, most of Wright's volunteers returned to Yreka. A few men stayed behind in case of more trouble from the Modocs. The part that made me sick when I heard it was that the volunteers invited the Indians to a feast in November. Only a few Modocs came. The Indians were scared off by rumors of poison. Later in the month Wright and his men attacked a village whose people were preparing for winter. Only five of the forty-six Indians survived, including women and children. Then the heroes mutilated the bodies of their victims and paraded into Yreka with the scalps they'd taken. Then the miners staged a seven-day drunk. Did that make them any better than the Modocs?"

Cox nodded grimly.

"Well, hell, I'll watch my hair, times a' wasting."

As Remme climbed on his horse, Cox said, "Fellow stopped by about a week ago and told me that your Oregon exterminators killed a bunch of Rogues they tricked into believing they were peaceful on Christmas Day."

"I heard about that," Remme said, and waved his hand as he touched his heels to his fresh horse.

Remme dropped his empty peach jar into a wooden refuse barrel. "I'll watch my hair, Isaac," he said to the storekeeper, and thanked Cox for his information about the Modocs.

As Remme turned the gelding north from Cox's store, he knew he was moving into hostile country. In the next one hundred and fifty miles the danger to himself from attack would increase tenfold. One of the reasons for that was that he was in mountain country, a rising land of volcanic peaks surrounded by white bark pines and red fir forests. A perfectly rounded cone, called Black Butte, composed of millions of small, black lava rocks thrust its domed peak more than a mile into the sky just southeast of his path. But due north of him was a wide stretch of open, treeless, gently rolling sagebrush country, dotted with volcanic debris that had been scattered for miles when Shasta stirred to life in the past erupting with smoke and thunder and sending thousands of tons of red-hot rocks into the valley below it. Putting two and two together, he had decided when he first saw the prairie-like land north and west of Mount Shasta years before, that the mountain's fiery lava had burned the area clear of trees. It was a land of cold cinders and sagebrush. For a solitary traveler like himself, the miles of open space, where a horse and rider silhouetted against the sky stuck out like a sore thumb, were dangerous. There was no place to hide. A chase would be won by the rider with the fastest horse. And Remme knew when he reached Calahan's ranch less than fifty miles from where he was that he had to decide how to get across the wide stretch ending near the Oregon border. Dozens of unknown men had been run down by Indians who hunted the area for antelope and deer. They disappeared with only their bones to mark the places where they fell.

As Remme pushed the gelding north along a track where the snow was thinner on the ground, he thought about the heavy price the pioneers who came west paid for the land they were eager to settle. He had been a green young man when he saw his first covered wagon pull out of Saint Louis for the Oregon Trail. That had been ten years earlier. Since then waves of settlers had pointed their wagons west into country previously populated only by the free-ranging natives. The lives of the pioneers taken by the Indians to defend their land were negligible compared to the ones sacrificed to the hardships of the trail. Every mile west elongated the prairie graveyard for hundreds of men, women, and children who did not survive the trek.

Better than most frontiersmen, Remme understood the anger of the various Indian tribes that attacked covered wagons with pioneer families and lone riders whose horses would give braves who stole them new mobility and tribal recognition. Chief among the reasons for the wrath of the Modocs and the Klamaths was the fact that wagon trails ran through summer hunting grounds, scaring the game away. Another bitter complaint was the diseases brought by the immigrants that killed hundreds of Indians. Whole villages were wiped out. But all of the Indians' bitterness could be summed up in one sentence: Their way of life was being threatened and the whites were responsible.

The Christmas Eve slaughter of a band of the Rogues Cox had mentioned earlier to Remme had been described to the Frenchman about two months earlier by a lone rider who had stopped for coffee and to exchange gossip with the cattle trader in Red Bluff, California. That was in early January. Remme and three hired drovers had been resting his large herd of cows on pasture grass he'd leased, before pushing the cattle on to Sacramento. He had planned on selling the remainder of his herd there.

According to the rider, two companies of volunteers assured the Indians of their peace and friendship but that was a dirty-faced lie. The exterminators had scouted the camp of the Butte Creek Rogues the previous day, then on the afternoon of Christmas, the next day, they attacked the unsuspecting Rogues—killing nineteen men—burned the band's supplies, and left the women and children to die in the snow from exposure. The next week when the expedition was crossing through the hills behind Jacksonville, another band of Rogues fired into the line of march. Martin Angel, one of the agitators who had screamed for the hanging of a seven-year-old native boy two years earlier, was blown out of his saddle. The exterminators continued on to the river but a mule carrying ammunition for the howitzer slipped over a cliff and into the bottom of a deep pool in the stream. This was but one incident in the undeclared war between the whites and Rogues that Oregon miners and settlers favored.

In the uplands beyond Cox's store, Remme had left the craggy columns, the rosy quartz, and flaky granite of Old Baldy, with its foundation embedded in dense carpets of cedar and pine. Across the creek, climbing for the sun, loomed tall bare mountains which, as he well knew, rolled away to the north in a labyrinth of interlocking ranges, deep gorges, and jagged broken summits. But the trail was a familiar one to the cattle drover. All that day he rode, climbing and swinging back around bold headlands, as he drove the gelding further north, leaving springtime far below. Snow shrieked and moaned in the higher canyons and a fierce wind howled on Trinity Mountain, shaking tall firs and bending tamaracks in creaking protest. It was under black forests at night that he reached Trinity Creek. Here none of his gold pieces would buy a horse, but one good-natured miner listened to Remme's story—told more than a dozen times by now—cursed, and said, "I've got a spare horse and he's fast. When you catch the horse thief fetch him back on my horse and I'll help you hang him."

Remme was grateful for the miner's generosity. Was it only seven years earlier that he had done backbreaking work for himself on a small tributary of the Trinity panning for gold? He had worked in the icy waters bending his back over a gold pan until he thought he could not lift another pan of sand with a hint of the glitter that drove men crazy. Yes, he acknowledged to himself that he had been one of the adventurers that Lindsay Applegate had organized in '48 to take the Applegate trail in reverse and locate a place on California's gold-bearing streams out of which the Oregonians could reap a fortune if they were lucky. But Remme had never forgotten the travail he had suffered, the disappointments, the loss of his body weight, the aches and pains that seemed never to end, and the tremors that made him shake from wading in icy streams. Every night he propped himself in front of a wood fire that gradually returned warmth and circulation to his feet and legs.

When Remme thought about what he'd been through his only consolation was the gold he had taken out of the creeks that allowed him to buy the Big Strawberry Patch ranch when he returned to Oregon and started his cattle business.

CHAPTER FIVE

AT A SPOT NEAR A large boulder jutting out into a small ice-fringed stream, Remme pulled back on the reins of the horse he had borrowed from the miner and came to a halt. For less than a minute he studied the creek and how it flowed around the big granite rock. He took in the leafless poplar trees standing like slender naked sentinels near the water's edge and the shaggy evergreens that huddled close by. Even with the light coating of snow on the ground he recognized the location where he had labored to glean gold from the sands of the creek. It had been seven years since he'd sweated, strained, and endured chills and crippling leg cramps to eke out the yellow stuff from the cold mountain stream that yielded its riches to the stubborn and lucky or denied them to the unfortunate and feckless.

As he touched his heels to the sides of his horse and rode north, he recalled that it wasn't until August of '48 that the news of the gold rush in California raced over mountains through valleys and over hills, exciting Oregonians of every stripe to head for the golden state.

It was Lindsay Applegate, who had convinced Remme to join the advance party of the Oregon expedition.

Remme learned from Lindsay about the man who had started the gold bonanza. A former Oregon carpenter considered moody, untalkative, self-possessed, and hard working, was chosen by happenstance, or by gods of fortune to be responsible for a discovery that changed California overnight and drained Oregon of most of its able-bodied men when the one-word exclamation "Gold!" traveled from Sacramento around the world. James Marshall, working at Sutter's millrace, was the first to be curious about a peculiar little lump of rock shaped like a small pea. At first glance, hardly impressive, resembling—as someone said later—"a piece of spruce gum just out of a schoolgirl's mouth, but slightly more yellow in color." Marshall didn't know what it was, except that it glimmered in the water. He found it soft when he bit it, tasteless and metallic. Soon he'd gathered several of the pea-size curiosities—and learned how valuable they were.

Marshall was bending over Sutter's little California stream on a crisp, clear morning in January of 1848. Friends of his in Oregon didn't learn about the bonanza until August.

So many Oregonians were drawn to California's rivers and creekbeds by the lure of Marshall's discovery in 1848 that it was estimated two thirds of all the men in the territory left their farms and women behind with promises they would return with their saddlebags heavy with gold nuggets as easy to pick from shallow streams as ripe cherries from a tree.

Lindsay Applegate, trailblazer Jesse's brother, lost no time organizing the California expedition. By keeping its initial numbers small, the advance party could move faster than the main group of hopefuls numbering about one hundred and fifty who would follow. The high optimism of the large contingent led by James Marshall was comprised of no ordinary crowd. Oregon merchants, physicians, lawyers, schoolmasters, and clergymen bumped shoulders with schemers, ne'er do-wells, and just plain loafers who were always willing to try anything that required small effort for big returns.

Lindsay and a small group of men who led the majority decided the Applegate trail was to be the route to the gold fields south. That decision, as they later discovered, was a mistake. Lindsay blamed himself for choosing the Applegate trail as the path to follow. He was chagrined to realize that he and Jesse had scouted the route north for emigrants coming into Oregon, *not leaving it.*

The heavier rigs, which were pulled by three teams of oxen, with provisions and tools, were of necessity drawn by the plodding beasts over the rough inclines in the Umpqua country. Abandoning these wagons was unthinkable. The stubborn drivers struggled on, lurching up the precipitous eastern spur of the Siskiyous, and rattling down and across the grueling basin and range terrain of the Klamath region.

"By the time we passed through the rugged, arid plateaus skirting the marshlands, a few men considered doing harm to me," Lindsay commented to Remme. But fortunately as Lindsay related to Remme later, "What calmed them down, was that the scouts and I discovered a far less difficult trail into the Pitt River Valley. This was where the gold-bearing country began."

The gold-seekers congratulated themselves as well. How fortunate the Oregon webfoots were to find themselves already on the Pacific Coast before the rest of the country—or the rest of the world—got excited about what winked in the streams of California. Except for the local settlers, their Indian helpers, a crowd of Mexicans, and a few Mormons, the Oregonians had found the rainbow first.

Though Remme struck out for California on his horse with Lindsay and the advance group, he changed his direction. With a mule in tow loaded with his "necessaries," he headed for the Trinity River about which he'd heard a treasure trove of gold had been mined. The Trinity was fed by several smaller streams and it made sense to him to pan for the yellow metal in one of those. It was late August of '48 when he set up camp on a tributary of the Trinity west of Scott Valley.

As soon as Remme started wading streams to sample for the presence of gold, he learned that prospecting—shifting sand in a heavy pan with a circular motion, or working a rocker, was brutally hard work. It was not long before he started to experience the symptoms of strenuous labor in near freezing water up to his knees. His head ached and he was taken with dizzy spells. Since his whole purpose was to glean gold from the streams, he worked from daylight to dark. After a hasty supper, he was too exhausted to light a kerosene lamp and read from one of the three books he always carried with him. His favorite was the Holy Bible—not because it was the history of what became the foundation of Christianity, for he was not devoted to any faith, but because it was great literature and in it he found wisdom. The other was the *Adventures of Marco Polo* and the third was the *Plays of Euripides*.

But much as he loved to study the thoughts of men of the mind and soul, his body ached with terrible fatigue and he was unable to keep his eyes open after cooking his meals which were as mediocre as their lack of variety.

During the day his body fought an exhausting war against hot and cold. Chilblains, terrible leg cramps, and loss of feeling in his feet drove him out of the water a dozen times a day to stamp his feet to return blood circulation, as he dug and explored the streams for the golden muck. His battered felt hat, worn against the sun's merciless radiation, magnified the heat until sweat poured down into his eyes from his wet scalp and he was forced to dunk his head in the snow-fed waters for relief. After a few weeks his sunburned face was covered with a matted beard behind which nervous tics were hidden. Worst of all was his poor steady diet of fried pork, beans, and biscuits, invariably burned on the bottom. Canned fruit he'd packed with him, kept his diarrhea in check.

But slowly, Remme was collecting gold dust at a high personal price. A wiry, toughened man, he soon discovered a weakness in his knees and legs from constant exposure to the melting snow of Mt. Shasta in the east. His bowels betrayed him at times with a sudden loosening.

It was about three weeks after Remme started prospecting the streams flowing into the Trinity that he found a vigorous creek that showed no trampling of footprints. Remme sampled the sands in several places with poor results. Determined to explore around a granite boulder before moving on, Remme saw that a big rock jutting out from the shade of a streamside tree formed a natural catch-flow for minerals. Out of that pocket in three weeks or so he extracted about fifteen hundred dollars in tiny nuggets and gold dust.

Three months later, Remme decided he had enough of a stake—almost seven thousand dollars—to buy the land which had never left his mind and which he called Big Strawberry Patch. During the period of his hard labor panning for gold more than one suspicious character stopped by and asked how his luck was. While most of the miners were straight shooters, California had attracted its share of dishonest, shifty, and murderous men and women and it was best not to put your trust in any strangers.

Several men, card sharks, confidence men, thieves, had stopped by Remme's camp, but they moved on when they judged there were victims less wary than Remme.

One shifty-eyed, friendly faced man in his forties with a scar running six inches along his right jaw, said he thought he'd step off his horse and join Remme for coffee resting on an iron pot holder over the coals of a fire. Before the lanky stranger in checkered plaid pants and a corduroy jacket could lift his right leg over his saddle, a metallic click froze him in position. He eased back into his saddle and faced Remme with his hand gun pointing straight at his heart.

"It's customary to be invited for coffee, mister, and I don't need your company," Remme said in a cold voice.

"Didn't mean no offense, mister," the man apologized. "I'll just ease along."

That evening while it was still light, Remme decided to change where he slept. Next to a tall pine lay a boulder about the size of a big black bear. There, with his back against a tree, he laid out his bedroll.

He lay awake late that night imagining the man in the checkered pants might be lying in wait for him to go to sleep. He wasn't the first stranger to keep Remme awake, until exhaustion closed his eyes.

But now as he listened to the noises of the night; the wind brushing leaves together, the nearby murmuring voice of the stream that spoke louder when a log moved where it had been trapped or small boulders were unsettled by a change in the current, they seemed more threatening. During the three months he'd camped by the stream, sleep had been restless for he knew that because of bad luck or bad habits men who were untrustworthy resorted to thievery and murder. If the victim was awakened, a swift knife across his throat silenced him forever.

That night in his bedroll with his fingers wrapped loosely around his handgun, Remme decided he'd had enough. His beard was a nest for "no see 'ums," his bedroll stank of his sour body, and his longjohns itched from their constant wear. It was time to leave. He fell asleep at last that night with one hand protecting his leather money belt; and his hand gun close by. Despite his precautions, no inkling or forewarning had ever made Remme hesitate about his decision to prospect for gold, or how it would result a few years later in dangerous threats to his life and set him on the epic journey that would require a feat of strength, courage, endurance, and determination few men had ever forced themselves to perform.

Remme was no more than six miles from his Trinity River site, an early fall chill in the air and the leaves on some birches had turned yellow as the elusive gold in the streams, when he heard his name called. Apprehensive, turning quickly in his saddle, he spotted the familiar face of Lindsay Applegate. Like Remme, he was packed to travel with two mules burdened with mining supplies, a tarp, sieves, collapsible stove, gold pans, and other paraphernalia.

As Lindsey drew near, he said, "You're the last one I expected to see out here. You look like you're heading for home."

"I am and you look like you could use some of Betty's cooking. You're twenty pounds light."

"Gold mining ain't no picnic, I'll tell you that, and I've never worked so hard in my life. You've slimmed down more than a little yourself. To tell the truth, both of us look thinner and a lot smarter about slaving for gold."

A sudden surprised thought flashed on Lindsay's face. "Two bits to a dollar, you were going to take the trail Jessie and I blazed home?"

Remme nodded, puzzled by the question. "Do you know a better way?"

"Sure, join up with us five, all from Oregon. We're meeting at the Tower House. There's a man who runs a hostelry there who'll give us a fair price for our mules and equipment. Then we'll ride to Red Bluff and catch a coach to Knight's Landing. There we'll take a steamer for San Francisco. We're going to sail home in style."

The appeal of an ocean voyage over six hundred miles on horseback in time to beat the winter rains of Oregon was overwhelming to Remme. "You bet I'll join you and pay my share of the fare," he smiled.

A day later Lindsay and Remme had a good meal at the Tower House, got reacquainted with the five men who had accompanied Lindsey to California and, after a stiff drink, mounted their horses and headed for Red Bluff. Three days later the men from Oregon clattered aboard a small ship they chartered on San Francisco's infamous Barbary Coast and paid in gold for their passage north.

The seven men who met in San Francisco not far from the wharf where the small steamer *Sierra Bell* was tied up converged on the *Red Slipper* by three o'clock to meet the skipper. It was a Wednesday and the boilers of the steamer that would take the Oregonians home were building pressure for a five o'clock departure.

Remme and the other six had slept in at a small hotel—three dollars a night for a tiny room—hardly big enough to turn around in and lucky to get from what they'd been told. Sightseeing and purchases of presents for families waiting in Oregon occupied most of the day until their appointment with Captain Charles Morgan.

Remme was astonished by the activity in San Francisco. Everybody seemed to be in the grip of intense excitement and optimism. Gold was the spirit, adventure, lure, and fortune-making on the minds of men and women from dishwashers to room maids, merchants, miners and dance hall girls, seamen and carpenters.

Morgan was a large, florid man—full of himself was Remme's opinion—and the grandiose way he talked gave the impression that he was personally responsible for the world's greatest treasure rush since the days when the conquistadors sacked Mexico.

After the Oregonians paid out the aggregate sum of twelve hundred dollars for their passage to Portland, Morgan insisted on buying several rounds of drinks and while they were being consumed, the captain explained that in just seven months since Marshall's discovery, ships of every nature and every port were crowding the docks.

"Why, before gold was found half a dozen ships would have been a rarity on our waterfront. At least two hundred thousand so far have transported passengers to our port and they keep coming!"

He explained that the previous July the number of houses in the city were no more than two hundred. "They've grown to two thousand, to four thousand. Our population has expanded from four hundred and sixty, including Indians, to six thousand, fifteen, thirty. Yes sir, we're the busiest port on earth!"

Jangling dance halls and whooping saloons, gold erupting from the ground. It all seemed to be true. But Remme didn't trust Charlie Morgan and he limited himself to two drinks of whiskey before they boarded the steamer.

It was Remme, unused to sleeping in a soft bed, who awakened about four in the morning with a feeling of disorientation. During his short stint as an apprentice seaman on the *New World* before she exploded, he had learned about the currents and wave directions in San Francisco Bay and beyond, and something felt wrong. Dressing quickly and pulling on his boots, he creeped quietly down the carpeted corridor between the staterooms, opened the door to the main deck quietly, and stepped outside. It took but a minute for Remme to realize the ship was sailing south not north. Even the greenest youth would know the position of the North Star in the dark blue sky was misplaced. The ship was chugging south, not north, which was its destination.

Quietly, Remme slipped back into the corridor of the ship and tried the doorknob to Lindsay's room. To his surprise, the door opened, Remme slipped inside and in a whispered voice said, "Lindsay, wake up. We're in trouble." He shook the Oregonian until he rolled over. "It's Remme, wake up!" he said again, deliberately careful not to frighten Lindsay. He was certain the trailblazer would have cultivated the habit of sleeping with a Colt under his pillow. A sudden surprise and the gun would emerge while the sleeper was reacting to the danger of an unfamiliar touch.

When Lindsay blinked awake after he heard Remme speak his name a second time, he pushed himself up in bed quickly, his hand under the pillow.

"Lindsay, it's me, Remme! Wake up, we're in trouble."

It only required a moment for Lindsay to get his bearings, swing his feet over his bed, and ask, "What's so important this time of night?"

"Only that we're sailing in the wrong direction." Then, Remme explained his strange awakening and his trip to the deck. There was no doubt about it. They were sailing south. Remme believed that the captain was in league with some bushwhackers who could be expected to board the ship when it was far enough out to sea to make the shoreline indistinguishable. Even a seaman with experience would have trouble identifying the ship's direction if no landmarks were visible.

"This man is after our gold and our lives in the bargain. If we don't act quickly we're going to lose them both."

"By God, you must be right, man. Let's get the rest of the men with their arms and prod the son of a bitch awake."

In less than five minutes the seven miners from Oregon—some dressed, others wearing nightclothes—were standing quietly in front of the captain's cabin. One of the men, Jake Hardy, weighed 250 pounds, stood six feet five and carried a twelve gauge shotgun. It was decided that he would burst through the door, tearing it off its hinges. Hardy hated cheats and it was a pleasure to make them pay their due. With his broad right shoulder and a smile of cheerful malice on his face Hardy stepped back a foot or two and rushed forward, his huge body snapping the cabin door to the floor with a shattering crash. Captain Charles Morgan woke up in his bed with a startled fright on his face which turned white when he saw the arms of the miners aimed at his body. He started to sputter what were they thinking, but Lindsay told him to shut his mouth if he wanted to live and said, "Louis Remme will explain. He's the one who discovered what a crook you are. While he does that my men will round up your crew who are part of your dirty scheme to rob us of our gold and kill us."

Four of the miners quickly left the room and Remme ordered the captain out of his bed. "Your first duty is to turn this piece of junk north. If you hesitate, we will throw you overboard just like you've done to others you've gotten drunk and murdered in their sleep. Now get out of that bed and turn this boat on a heading for Astoria."

Remme's threat was genuine and the captain, barefooted, hurried to the pilot's room where the seaman at the wheel, taking in the situation at a glance reached for a handgun on the chart table. He was far too slow, for Remme smashed his knuckles with a swift blow of his heavy Colt. The man screamed in pain, and without a thought Remme cracked the seaman's head with another blow from his gun and the man slumped to the floor.

In a voice as deadly as the grave, Remme directed the captain to his seat and spelled out the conditions under which Captain Morgan would sail his ship to Astoria. He would be under constant surveillance, his clothes would consist of his nightgown and a slicker to ward off the weather and rubber boots. He would be subject to chilling drafts and windy sprays from the sea. He would also be allowed, under guard to relieve himself when it was necessary; his meals, since there was no kitchen on the Sierra Bell, would have to come from prepared food he'd brought on board and would be served in the pilot house, and he would be required to stand twelve-hour shifts without relief. There would be no refueling stops and average time, without stops, of ten miles an hour would be expected to sight Astoria in eighty hours. The slightest deviation from the routine Remme spelled out would result in his punishment. A rope looped around the captain's chest would drag him through icy water.

It was explained by Remme that the engineer would suffer from similar discipline and water dunking for disobedience. The two able seamen were to be shackled and would perform their duties without complaint if they expected to live. The other able seaman whose knuckles Remme broke was locked in a small room that served as a brig.

Remme left the small steamer at the mouth of the Umpqua—after demanding a refund of his fare and advised Lindsay Applegate to turn the man and his crew over to the law when they reached Portland. By leaving the steamer south of Astoria, he would shorten his journey cross-country to the small village of Roseburg. The captain, within sight of the Columbia River, refused to take his ship across the bar. It was too dangerous.

As for Remme when he heard later about Captain Morgan's reluctance to pass over the bar, he was disappointed in Lindsay. All seven of the Oregonians could have lost their lives, and instead Lindsay acted in a conciliatory fashion to all the pirates in the conspiracy. After the steamer breasted the violent waters where the Columbia met the Pacific, everybody on board celebrated with champagne and the crooks were forgiven.

Remme soon forgot about Lindsay's reconciliation with the pirate. A day's ride took him to the donation claims offices in Roseburg. There he filed the papers that made him legal owner of 640 homestead acres in Big Strawberry Patch and he was given the name of a land broker with whom he could deal for more acreage.

Soon after his land was secure, Remme paid for his passage back to San Francisco. He had an idea how to make money collecting letters from miners who were writing home. He would charge a fee for each letter he carried to steamships sailing east.

CHAPTER SIX

TWELVE HOURS AFTER REMME had left Cox's store behind, he was almost too groggy to stand. When he tumbled off his horse in Scott Valley he curled up in his blankets and slept till noon. When he woke his eyes took in the soaring dome of Shasta looming like a big white beacon to the southeast. Far out at sea the folk on the plodding *Columbia* were probably also gazing at that lofty peak. Thoughts of the *Columbia* thrashing its slow way northward spurred Remme on. The steamer carried two companies of soldiers on board, one to land at Fort Humboldt on the bay and tame the Indians, the other to garrison the fort at the mouth of the Rogue River. Though he did not know of it, these and other stops by the paddlewheeler would delay the *Columbia*.

His recollections of the San Francisco where seven years ago he'd met the scoundrel Charles Morgan was no comparison to the amazing city where a few days earlier he had learned of his personal disaster.

Combined with his rancorous memory of the pirate Charles Morgan, his contempt for the thieves of Adams Express, his determination to beat the *Columbia*, put them all in the same class of detestable crooks. He swore to himself never to let the *Columbia* outpace him. He was betting his life that he'd win.

Trouble came for Remme not where he expected it, but shortly after he crossed the Oregon border. He had exchanged horses three more times, once at Calahan's ranch, again with a miner in Scott

Valley, and in Yreka on the morning of his third day. There he borrowed a pony from Horsley and Brothers Mountain Express where he repeated his story of chasing a horse thief. Impressed by his determination and nerve, the man who operated the delivery service loaned him their fastest horse, a piebald, brown and gray with one white foot. Before he mounted the piebald, Tom Horsley detained Remme with a warning. "I know you aren't nobody's fool when it comes to watching your back, but I'd be extra cautious was I you. The Modocs are real soreheaded because an idiot miner pulled a stunt about thirty miles west of here where they made a small gold strike. Nothing big and it'll play out in a month or less is my bet.

"Anyway, four white men camped near Little Bear Creek for the night and headed out to find wood to build a fire. Three of them gathered scarce driftwood from the creek bank. When their fire was going, two Modocs showed up and kicked it out. One of the miners, the way we heard it, ran for the rifle on his saddle, but the other three stopped him before he could shed any blood. They asked the Indians what the trouble was.

" 'This is our country,' they said, 'and you white men pass through it. You take our grass and water, and burn our wood. For that we do not care; but this man came to our burying ground and cut down the monuments on the graves of our fathers.'

"That trigger-happy fool had made firewood from the scaffolds those Modocs built for their dead. They went away but they weren't happy."

With Horsley's warning still fresh in his mind, four hours later after crossing the open stretch of sagebrush land he dreaded without a challenge, Remme, cold and weary urged his mount up the long snowy slope eleven miles north of where he forded the Klamath River. It was in the Siskiyou Mountains when he slid out of his saddle in front of a huge pile of smooth stones which was heaped in a triangular shape around a small oak tree. The tree's lower boughs had been cut away with an ax and part of the trunk that projected above the stones bore the curious mark of United States Surveyors.

The tree and the stones around it marked the boundary line between California and Oregon territory.

Remme studied the surveyor's symbol cut deeply into the bark for a moment and sighed, "Thank God for Oregon." Then he kneeled in the snow on the bank of Hungry Creek nearby and cracked ice with the handle of his knife. He drank deeply and splashed the freezing water in his face. As he turned, refreshed, to mount his horse he saw them. Three Indian braves sat on their horses not two hundred yards away. They were staring directly at him. Were they Modocs bent on revenge for the miner's act of stupidity?

Remme had confronted Indians in the wilderness before. Sometimes they meant no harm, finding satisfaction in studying the habits of white men from a distance. They were like children curious about new neighbors. Often they were fascinated by items of clothing—belt buckles, suspenders, felt hats, women's bonnets—or even the skin texture on the face of white strangers. But something about these three spelled menace to Remme. Carefully, he mounted the piebald, swinging his right leg over the saddle in a quick, effortless motion, never taking his eyes off of the trio. He was not surprised when they did not move, but continued to sit on their horses, motionless, like figures carved out of wood, and stared at him. Staring a man down was an old trick of some Indians Remme had learned about years before. Often it was harmless, but equally often it was a deadly game whose rules were known only to the Indians. For them, it was a duel of wits to see who would make the first move. A frightened man who decided to run for it might be pursued by nothing more dangerous than laughter from the Indians, tickled that they had outwitted a white man. On the other hand, swift arrows might be launched at the back of the rider who bolted.

Remme wasn't sure which tribe the three Indians came from. Two of them wore buckskin shirts and pants, rawhide leggings, and blankets over their shoulders. They were bareheaded with their black hair divided in braids that fell on either side of their faces. The third brave was dressed in the same fashion except his buckskin shirt fell down to his thighs which were bare. His heavy leggings covered his skin up to his knees. Also, like the others, over his right shoulder hung a tightly strung bow and quiver with arrows. The horses on which the braves were mounted were small and shaggy, but looked fresh and spirited. As far as Remme could make out none of the three was armed with a rifle, although around their waists each of them wore a belt with a long knife attached. These men were a small hunting party. The question was was it wild game they were after, or the scalp of a solitary rider after they rode him down and took his horse and weapons?

Remme's decision to turn his horse and move slowly was based on his hunch that the longer he stayed the more determined the Indians would become to win the staring contest. Also the longer nothing happened, the longer the braves would have to work up their courage and decide that three against one, even if the one was armed with a rifle and pistol, were good odds. He was certain the braves were smart enough to figure out the way to attack a man armed with guns was to separate and come at him from three different directions. One of them was bound to get through.

As Remme clucked to the piebald and turned his head north, he was aware that the Indians probably had a big advantage over him. The piebald was not fresh. He had carried Remme forty miles and was almost played out. Maybe the dappled horse had another five miles in him, but he wasn't up to a lengthy chase.

For an hour Remme guided the piebald north, deeper and deeper and gradually higher up a mountain slope through crusty, day-old snow that reached at times up to the chest of the pony. The Indians followed, never decreasing the distance between them and Remme, but never allowing the gap to widen. All the while he moved forward with the Indians trailing behind, the back of Remme's neck tingled with the threat they represented. It took all of his self-control to force himself not to turn anxiously in his saddle to see if the braves were creeping up on him—getting within arrow range of his back. Remme knew the situation had to change. Sooner or later the braves would lose patience and suddenly whoop with blood-curdling yells and plunge after him. The piebald was making it easier for the Indians to catch up by breaking trail for them. It was after two hours of playing a deadly cat and mouse game near the summit of a small mountain pass that the Indians broke loose. With shrill cries, they whipped their horses and tore up the snow in a wild charge.

Remme drove the piebald over the crest of the pass and down the other side of the mountain in a flurry of snow. Tired as he was, the horse headed down in a series of jumps that surprised Remme. Almost rabbit-like, the piebald sprang forward in leaps, pushing with the powerful muscles of his hind legs. The ride for Remme was like staying on a bucking horse. As the piebald's feet struck the ground, spraying snow in small explosions, his hind feet were in the air and Remme was suspended momentarily above his saddle until the piebald's rear feet came to earth with a jarring thump. The French-Canadian cattle trader managed to cast a glance backward only once during his wild descent and then he saw something that gave his heart a lift and chilled his blood at the same time. The brave wearing the long buckskin blouse and leggings had forged ahead of his companions who had stopped at the top of the hill. He was pushing his horse, like the piebald, in lunging jumps that covered about six feet at a time, seesawing down the slope in a cloud of snow. The fact that two of the Indians were holding back meant only one thing to Remme. The one brave who came after him had decided the white man was a worthy challenge to his manhood. He would earn praise from his tribe by capturing the man's horse and guns and taking his scalp unaided by his friends. The prize was even worthier because the brave was not armed like his opponent and would have to catch the white man by wit and cunning.

As Remme drove the piebald foot after foot up the next mountain through the snow, sensing the fatigue in the horse's legs, hearing his heavy breathing, the faltering strength in his stride, he noticed something in the air that disturbed him. It was nothing he could name—a feeling, a tension, a shimmering pressure that warned him of danger far greater than the lone warrior who was coming after him. When he understood what it was, he brought the piebald to a halt and turned him so Remme could see the top of the mountain far above hidden in a cloud, and the deep bottom in the white valley below. If he could have described the threatening quality of the mountain that frightened him it was like a quivering in the air before thunder strikes—as if everything around him, the ice-smooth rock faces, the snow-covered cedar trees, the short, ragged pines, the deep snow blanket clinging to the mountain, were suspended and waiting. Remme thought about drawing his rifle and shooting at the brave to discourage him from coming up. But the loud cracking sound of the rifle would hasten what he knew was going to happen.

He started to yell to the Indian to turn around when he realized it was too late. At the last instant before the danger struck, the brave's eyes popped open wide with fright when he felt the ground stir and shake. One moment, the Indian was mounted on his horse not two hundred feet away from Remme and the next, still clinging to his pony with his legs, he and the animal, facing forward, started moving down hill rapidly, powered by a force that stripped snow from the side of the mountain like a sharp knife. The snow slide started just six feet below where Remme and the piebald stood. A huge wedge of snow five hundred feet wide and five or six feet deep separated from the snow pack where Remme and his horse waited. It thundered and rumbled down the mountain like the tide rushing out, leaving a ragged gap that widened swiftly. Neither Remme nor the piebald dared to move. They were stunned by the avalanche and Remme was amazed to see the brave throw himself off of his horse as it sank. Face down, he landed, turned himself, and flung his arms outward in a swimming motion, trying to keep above the snow pouring in waves down the mountain. With a wild scream his pony fell on his back and was quickly drowned as the rushing snow piled over him, creating a mound in the surface that disappeared in the flow. The avalanche swept the struggling Indian—paddling in the same downward direction—hundreds of yards down the slope before

Remme rode down the mountain. As he drew the piebald abreast of the Indian he saw the man was not deeply buried and he was not dead.

He had been stripped as naked as a skinned potato. Not a shred of his clothes remained and cuts and bruises covered his body. A cap of snow crowned his matted and snarled hair. He pulled himself to his feet standing up to his waist in snow and stared bitterly at Remme as if the avalanche was his fault. Remme rode away from the naked man awed that only six feet had separated him and his horse from the edge of the snow slide.

The tired piebald needed little encouragement from Remme to stumble ahead slowly. Both horse and rider had been going on nerve during the last two hours of the chase by the Indians. Remme decided the redskins had been from a band of Klamaths that roamed between the Klamath and Rogue rivers. They attacked settlers and horsemen riding alone, but they weren't as bad as the deadly and murderous bunch that roamed the Grave Creek hills further north. They were known to attack without warning from ambush. He had been lucky evading the three braves who had chased him, and his life seemed charmed to have been saved by a few feet from the avalanche that stripped the single Klamath bare and killed his horse. But Remme dared not trust his fate to a tired mount when he entered the Grave Creek region. As it was, he and the piebald were so exhausted that neither was alert to danger. Luckily, Jacksonville, Oregon was just a few miles away. There he would find oats for the horse and a place to sleep for himself. He had to sleep for an hour or two. His body craved rest.

Remme looked even worse than he felt. His sheepskin coat was spattered with mud, melted snow, and horse-lather stains. The warm white collar of his coat was bedraggled and gray. His shirt, pants, and boots were speckled with grass, pine needles, and streaks of dirt thrown up by the hooves of the horses he had ridden. His hat looked as if it had been thrown in the mud, then stamped on. He could never remember being so tired in all of his life. He had been in the saddle for three and one half days with only seven hours of sleep. All of that time his tough body had been hammered mile after mile by the jarring hoofbeats of the horses he rode. His muscles ached from the beating they had received. During the eighty hours since he had left Sacramento he had munched coffee beans, chewed on dried jerky and hard biscuits, and had eaten only two hot meals, one at Clear Creek and one at Yreka. The pursuit of the Klamaths had tired him more than he was willing to admit. As the piebald jogged along wearily, Remme's eyes kept falling shut. Unconsciously, his body slumped and his head fell forward on his chest. Twice in an hour he woke with a start, shaken that the piebald was not moving. The horse halted when he felt the reins go slack and the man in saddle released control.

Each time this happened, Remme awoke, shook himself like a wet dog shedding water, looked around to get his bearings, then urged the piebald into a trot. He finally managed to force his eyes open by thinking about the steamship *Columbia*. Where was she now? he wondered, and with a sinking feeling estimated that she must be plowing ahead of him on a direct line paralleling the rugged Oregon coast.

More important than the rest his body desperately demanded, the Bobtail Range came into view capped with snow and ice. It stood between him and Jacksonville where he would exchange horses, get a meal, and sleep for a couple of hours. He had to make a decision despite the despairing fatigue of his aching muscles and his dulled mind. Even at this distance the stirring of the wind off the mountain ran chills through his body and set the piebald to shivering.

Remme's escape from the Indian who had lost his clothes in the snowslide had convinced him that he had to face the worst winter could throw at him and there was no way to avoid it. He estimated that within a mile or two he would reach the eastern side of the Rogue Valley.

Along the eastern side of the valley rose the ancient Siskiyous. These mountains, Remme knew from experience, were eroded and tree covered. On their slopes were outcroppings and boulders, freeze-shattered from extreme cold into gravel. Traces of nickel and tailings from mine shafts drifted with the spring freshets down among the azaleas and rhododendrons growing on the hills. In the upper part of the valley the Siskiyous melted winter snow with spring warmth and it spilled into Bear Creek. Down river the Applegate River and Galice Creek emptied into the Rogue. Farther west the Illinois River was supplied by drainage from the limestone hills near the Oregon Caves and the swampy bottom lands in the prairies of the Josephine Valley. The Illinois wandered among the Siskiyous until it entered the Rogue about forty miles from the Pacific coast. He had to cross each one of these rivers which were iced at the edges and most of them overflowing.

The northern edge of the Rogue Valley was formed by a series of tumbled hills referred to as the Umpqua Mountains, well known by the Applegates and their emigrant followers. Although not high and seldom covered with snow, the Umpqua range was rugged enough to make the pioneers dread its slopes and canyons. These hills sent Jump Off Joe Creek, Grave Creek, and Wolf Creek into the Rogue. Cow Creek wandered through them, then suddenly swung away and flowed into the South Umpqua.

The rains in the region on the west side of the the Siskiyous facing the sea often were torrential in nature. On the east side, the velocity of the downpours, approaching eighty miles an hour, whistled over the crests with a fury of snow and rain so strong that trees and rocks were uprooted. The wind screamed like a wildcat and was cold enough to paralyze any human or beast. It painted a curtain of frost as opaque as thin wool blinding a man or horse for a distance of more than three feet. The name the mountaineers tacked to the killing stream of air—the White Death—was appropriate because the number of frozen corpses turned into blocks of ice by its frozen breath were too many to count.

Remme had heard stories of emigrants who toiled down the treacherous Siskiyous too late to avoid the arctic freeze. They paid for their folly with their lives. But he had no choice. To reverse his course and take the southern route would cost two days of delays and would mean the loss of his race. He couldn't tolerate that thought.

Quickly, with no more hesitation, he unwrapped his bedroll and looped it over and around his horse's head. He fed her a handful of oats, tore the scarf off his neck, and wrapped it over his eyes and nose. He fastened his battered hat tightly under his chin. He slipped over his leather riding gloves a pair of woolen mittens and he clucked encouragement to the piebald and led the horse onto a tumbling path that gradually descended to the bottom of the mountain. Three times Remme was injured. He was swept off his feet by the fierce, numbing wind that buffeted his body with such ferocity that he was pounded against solid rock, leaving freezing bloodstains of the harm he suffered. The piebald shrieked, fearing she'd lost contact with her rider when he was battered against the mountain.

By the time horse and rider stumbled to the bottom, neither could feel blood in their feet or their legs. Remme feared frostbite. Worst of all was the freezing of their eyelashes. Blasted by the wind, Remme awkwardly wiped the frozen moisture from the eyes of the piebald and his own. He repeated the process at least a dozen times, preventing the ice from building barriers of blindness in their bleeding eyes.

Stiff, bruised, numbed, even when Remme and the piebald reached the bottom Remme forced himself and his horse—though it was close to freezing—to stumble on, until blessed sight, he saw not far away, a ramshackle, poorly made log cabin, a deserted relic long abandoned. Man and animal stumbled on bloodless legs, forward. If they were to survive from the dread chill that had driven the blood deep beneath their skin, they had to find warmth or die.

As he looked at the shack Remme wondered if he had the strength to break open the door. He pushed with all his might against the stubborn door swollen shut by rain, then sealed by ice. But it wouldn't budge. In desperation, he backed away a few feet and threw himself against the wooden slab that closed the opening. The blow from his body cracked the ice. Recovering, Remme forced the door open. There were patches of snow inside and unbelievably a stack of wood leaned against a broken chimney. Pulling the piebald behind him, Remme removed his gloves and chafed his frozen skin until he could feel movement in his fingers.

Then he reached into his snow-covered saddlebags on the suffering piebald and found a Prince Albert can. He pounded the can against the uneven floor until the seal of ice was broken. Then clumsily, he fished out a wooden match, hoping it was not too damp to light.

From a small leather bag he untied the top and sprinkled tinder on kindling he scraped from the wood pile. He was exhausted.

Carefully, asking for God's blessing, Remme struck the match and held it to the tinder on the floor. The match blossomed and, cupping its flame carefully in his stiffened hands around the small pile of wood sticks, he watched it grow.

Half an hour later, a hot fire blazed in the cabin, smoke filling the space so that he had to open the door slightly to make a draft.

It was late morning when Remme and the piebald stepped out into cold sunshine. Drained of snow and ice, legs and joints aching but free of numbness, Remme mounted his horse and she started off eagerly, prancing with her enthusiasm for the feeling of blood coursing through her muscles and veins again. The deserted cabin was ablaze with the fire he had built. Isolated, not close to trees or shrubs that could catch and blaze, he was certain the pile of wood would burn to cinders.

CHAPTER SEVEN

AS REMME AND THE PIEBALD came within shouting distance of Jacksonville on the late afternoon of his third day in the saddle, his memories of the mining town two years earlier were bitter with the antagonism of the whites against the various Indian tribes. It was inevitable to Remme that the community had become a gold mining camp that seemed to sprout tents out of the rich Oregon soil like some strange human variety of the camas lily. But if Jacksonville had exploded from a sprawling collection of temporary shelters to ones built of wood frames, it also became the center of anti-Indian activity in Southern Oregon in 1852. Many miners called for the extermination of the whole native race. This hatred had grown more poisonous as miners from California moved into the territory. An event had occurred to Remme four years after he returned from his single gold-mining venture in the streams of California's Trinity River. Ultimately it led him to Jacksonville as a sympathizer of the Rogues.

With the stake he brought back to Oregon, he had spent long hours every day building a cabin, holding pens for cattle, a barn, and long days roaming the whole of the Rogue River Valley south almost into California. He was looking for cattle to buy cheap or to capture wild cows—brush hoppers—if the opportunity arose. It also was an opportunity for him to explore the three thousand acres that made up his spread. He had never thoroughly investigated all the meadows, creeks, trees, and pastures that were part of the Big Strawberry Patch ranch.

He was a gallant figure on a horse, sturdy, tough, and intriguing to settlers with his French accent and the strange tunes he sang to himself in his native tongue.

After he made a livable cabin on Big Strawberry Patch, he was friendly to the Rogue Indians, often giving away a cow as a sign of friendship. Since he was no threat to the Indians they left him alone and welcomed the gift of beef he gave away.

His generosity and reputation for fairness and respect for the land made him welcome wherever he went.

It was late July of 1852 after he completed the basic improvements on his land that he started herd building in earnest. His roving took him all over Southern Oregon on a horse which he named Diablo. The horse was a beautiful, high-stepping Andalusian with a dark coat, almost black with a sheen of brown. He was a proud animal with huge, wide, deep eyes that Remme imagined looked like the purple of deep night, with glints of gold. Sturdy, long legged, Diablo loved to run.

Remme had bought the horse from a farmer who described him as "too spirited" for plowing and pulling a wagon. But the Frenchman saw pride and endurance in the horse.

When Remme brought Diablo to the Strawberry Patch, his response had been almost identical to the strong fascination of Tony Jo, the horse Remme sold before setting out on his gold-mining venture. He had never forgotten that it was early in 1848 when his exploration for the right piece of land had taken him occasionally from his job as a horseshoe maker for a blacksmith near Roseburg. On one trip, he roamed southwest for about two days until he allowed his horse to wander into a forested area and sniffed the air eagerly. That was when an aging, scrawny, toothless Indian appeared and indicated Remme should stop. Chewing tobacco was what he wanted and the Frenchman always carried small squares because they were favorites with the Indians. The toothless old man laughed at the Frenchman, sharing the obvious fact that he had nothing in his mouth to chew with.

Then pocketing the tobacco, he made it clear to Remme that he had seen the white man before and it was plain he was looking for grass land. He beckoned Remme to follow him and started in a direction that led far down a dim footpath that was so faint it often disappeared. But the old Indian kept jogging tirelessly on a southwesterly heading until he came to a stop. Then with his thin arm pointing, he insisted Remme drive his horse through a barricade of tall, lacy fern entwined with thick-stemmed grass and wild growth. Staring ahead at the wild tangle of thick leaves, Remme was puzzled. What did the old man want him to do? He frowned, turned for some sign of explanation but the old man was gone

Remme could not fathom how he had disappeared. The thin copper-skinned ancient had vanished, as if plucked by the wind and carried off in a twinkling.

Long ago, Remme had learned to respect the strange ways of the Indians in Oregon. The insistence of the old man pointing stubbornly at the bushy barrier was like a secret sign Remme was supposed to penetrate. A strange feeling of mystery urged him to push his horse through the thick wall of brush.

On the other side the lay of the land changed. The air seemed warmer here and there was no biting wind to chafe his face and lips or to sneak into his clothes with icy fingers. The foothills were much closer and higher. June, in that gentle country he traversed, seemed to have advanced. It was while they were passing through the first little valley that Diablo, like Tony Jo before him, bent his ears forward and twitched his nose. He seemed eager to plunge ahead and Remme couldn't help but notice his horse was livelier and he kept his nose into the gentle breeze as if it carried a secret message that excited him. Soon Diablo picked up his pace and was running as if something in the distance was compelling him to get to it. Remme had learned to let a horse have his head if it was set on reaching an objective.

Diablo galloped under him following a winding stream, which was wider than any Remme had seen that afternoon. After a half an hour of hard riding, Remme though it might be a good idea to bring his horse to a halt, but changed his mind since Diablo appeared not to want to let up and showed no sign of wearying. The cattleman's curiosity was aroused.

The sun dropped lower on the horizon and Diablo kept plunging on a straight line. Soon they were passing through the lush wild pasture Remme had first seen in 1848. The grass was so high it stroked the sides of Remme's horse. Then he dismounted and stood in the thick of it and it was no wonder that his horse was acting like he had galloped into heaven. Later, Remme tried to remember how to describe the sweet fragrance in the air and the best he could do was to compare it with the rich aroma of his mother's spice drawer when she opened it.

That night when Remme curled up in his blankets, he slept soundly and rose at daylight full of vigor from the best sleep he'd had in years. His dreams had been filled with a sort of pink haze, a pleasant lethargy. That day Remme rediscovered not just one valley, but many of them, one leading into the next. The long scented grass was everywhere and covered the bottom lands in a thick high carpet. The rolling hills gave way to it, and they were almost free of timber and scratchy underbrush. When he first made camp, four years ago in the same spot, he had been much taken by the spectacle of those soft hills. Their smooth curved slopes were like gentle mounds of velvet.

Remme's find that first day settled a question in his mind which he thought was the result of some trick of the sun painting the grass with a reddish tinge. Then, walking into the tall grass, often rising to his shoulders, he found wild strawberries—the size of his thumb—so sweet, thick, and luscious to swallow that they seemed to swell in the sun, reflecting a ripe redness for acres and acres. He had found a paradise with water in lakes and in streams everywhere. Several creeks appeared large enough to provide power for gristing wood.

Remme was not certain of his location, except that it was many miles south of the Willamette Valley, probably close to the

Rogue River country where the firs grew tall and granite outcroppings were plentiful. One thing he knew for certain. He had found the place he would homestead. There were no signs of other men or encroaching civilization. Long dead campfires were evidence of other explorers. But it was unused land and it was perfect for cattle. It would be his. Cattle would thrive on the tall grass. It was his sworn oath on that day never to reveal the remarkable location until he could buy it. Tony Jo had been able to lead him to the tall grass country because he could smell it miles before it came into sight. Still, on his way back to Roseburg, Remme on that first trip marked his trail with signs only he could understand.

He swore then that he would find enough gold in California to buy the land that would ever be his.

And of course, he did.

It had taken Remme almost four years after his return to Oregon to homestead his ranch and erect the buildings he would need to shelter himself and the cattle he planned to acquire. It was then that he went roaming with his horse and money belt to find cattle, or work to increase his stash.

Back at his ranch was an old Mexican vaquero who had tended cattle in Texas. How he arrived in Oregon Territory was a story he refused to tell, except that he'd been drawn to gold. He felt comfortable with Remme, was probably in his seventies, still hard and lean, satisfied to have a roof over his head, a few dollars for whiskey, and the freedom and the responsibility to watch over the ranch and the few cattle Remme had collected.

On one trip Remme had allowed Diablo to drift and. after a lazy day. realized he could smell the ocean not far away. Diablo's ears picked up and his nostrils flared as a fresh sea breeze flowed through a densely thick forested area. Remme was riding through heavily timbered country. As he jinked along on Diablo's back, it was bottom land through which they were passing. Among the huge aromatic trees were myrtles, big-leaf maples, alder, and tangles of wild cucumber vines. Remme had learned to recognize and avoid the hillsides abundantly blanketed with poison oak.

Crossing one ridge in the lower part of a small mountain, Remme came to a fork of a finger-like stream. One of the fingers was stronger and was moving faster and Remme recognized the seaward flow of a tidal current.

As he guided his horse beneath the branches a few feet from the stream, it was the time of day when light faded fast. He dismounted, let the horse drink long from the stream, while he stood hearing a frog sing and the murmurous rustle and bustle of animals and birds making ready for the night.

In the cool, he felt his face still hot from the long glare of the day. He got on his belly and drank.

From his saddlebags he pulled a tin cup and a canvas bag of parched ground corn sweetened with sugar. It was a staple of long riders on the Northeastern frontier where he'd been raised and in other parts of the country. In the Southwest, too hot and dusty for Remme, it was called *pinole*—a Spanish word. When he scooped up water in the cup, he poured some of the pale meal into it, and stirred with his finger. Sitting in the grass against a tree he ate his gruel from the cup, while his horse was pulling strongly on the damp grass with deep roots, munching comfortably, moving faintly in the lengthening shadows of the lost day.

The bright north star, whose sparkle in the sky never failed to mystify and make Remme feel welcome, stood high above the giant trees when he put the reins over the black neck and swung into the saddle. He cut across the shallow stream up the slope at an easy walk in the starlight, through thick grass, low shrubs, and ferns wet with moisture. He caught the offshore breeze which had strengthened and with it the faint roaring sound of the ocean.

"Not far to the big water, black one," he said conversationally to his horse. "I'll bet you've never heard the voice of the Pacific. It's like a mother to all of us, old black horse. We'll camp nearby and let the waves lull us to sleep."

Awake early the next morning, Remme was aware that the constant roar of the ocean made Diablo skittish. When the big horse snorted and lunged to the right it was already too late for Remme to control the sudden fright of Diablo when he saw one squawking red-headed woodpecker chasing another down the beach, both shrieking like shrews. Dipping and rising in fury above the white sand to escape his pursuer, the one in front dived suddenly under the belly of Diablo with a swish of feathers, then climbed for the sky. There was no time. The woodpecker had brushed the right foreleg, skimmed under the belly and was gone. As Diablo jumped to one side, rearing on his hind legs, Remme's clutch on the reins pulled the horse backward and higher. Too high, pawing the air. The wild-tangled black mane covered Remme's face. He threw himself to the left, knowing the big black head and outstretched neck was descending on him. He fell with a white flash in his head and a stabbing pain in his pinned leg. In his clenched right hand the reins jerked as the horse scrambled to his feet, towering and shivering.

Remme opened his eyes, blurred from shock and pain. Diablo's head and neck had driven his left leg into the soft sand. It hurt horribly. He tried to flex the muscles of his calf and wiggle his toes. If his leg was broken he could not have moved as he had without excruciating pain. But the leg was injured. Nobody had to tell him he couldn't stand on it. It was then that he saw Indians, men, women, and children, scurrying up to him and looking down at him curiously. They were from the Rogue culture, called Takelman, and dwelled on the coast. Remme knew that much about them and that they traded with other tribes such as the Rogues in the mountains and the Shastas who were hill people. The men wore shirts, buckskin leggings, moccasins, and often blankets of deerskin. All of the men wore hats of bear or deer scalps, some with the ears still attached. The women wore buckskin dresses, fringed with tassels of white grass, reaching to their knees. Those who wore hats had fashioned them from twined grass shaped like round baskets. Both men and women wore long hair tied in a roll and twisted around their heads, with a piece of skin or ragged cloth.

One of the men crouched next to Remme and tried to convey with signs that a chief was coming to help him. He looked down the beach, pointing to a medium-size Indian who was approaching. He was hatless, his long hair in braids with a single eagle feather tied to a lock of hair, which Remme took as a sign of authority. The Indians surrounding Remme made an opening in their circle and the smallish man bent over and touched his hand to Remme's leg and squeezed gently. Sweat broke out on the Frenchman's forehead and he clenched his teeth against the sudden pain.

Squatting beside the recumbent cattle trader, the chief said in jargon that was a mixture of his native language and English, "Me cut off boot. Leg hurt no bro . . . ken." Without another word, he reached for the knife encased in leather on Remme's hip. Remme started to object, but the man pointed a finger at his chest. "Me Taylor, no hurt." Then slipping the long sharp blade into the top of Remme's boot he ran it down the leather, cutting a lengthwise seam to the ankle. The sudden release of pressure made Remme shudder with relief as Taylor pulled the two flaps apart. Next, giving Remme an encouraging signal, Taylor grasped the heel of the boot firmly and pulled it away from Remme's foot. Holding back the urge to scream at the cold touch of the knife on his skin, the Frenchman took a deep breath and wiped his drenched, sandy face with his shirt sleeve. There was no question about his injury. His leg was swollen from below the ankle to mid-calf. The skin was bluish around the ankle surrounded by an angry bloated redness.

Taylor slipped Remme's knife in his waistband, turned to four men, and in their language instructed them to lift Remme and take him to their village. As he was lifted, two men holding his legs and two supporting his shoulders, Taylor walked beside. It was obvious he was thinking how to say something complicated to the white man. Finally he said haltingly, "You big, nice to my brothers, nobody hurt you. Leg need rest."

Remme was taken to a brush hut, his saddle, saddlebags, and bedroll laid out so he could reach anything he desired. The women, very shy, did not know what to do about Diablo, who stood outside the hut with his reins trailing. With effort, Remme made them understand that the leather reins should be removed from the black horse. There was tall grass aplenty nearby and he would drink from the fresh stream flowing into the sea.

Taylor instructed the women to prop Remme's foot up on a basket so it would heal faster.

"No broke," were the only words Taylor had mastered that would explain Remme's condition.

Not only did the women furnish a basket to elevate his foot, but they conceived a rudimentary splint. The Rogue women were excellent weavers. They decorated their baskets with individual designs. Out of bull grass and the stipe of the maidenhair fern, their nimble fingers fashioned cradleboards for their infants, large storage baskets for acorns and dried salmon, and tightly woven containers for hot stones to boil water for seafood.

On the second day Remme, a prisoner of a bad sprain, welcomed two women who cautiously cut away the lower part of the one pants leg destroyed when Taylor sliced the leather and cloth to release his leg. Then, they carefully fit an infant's cradleboard to his leg and bound it tightly enough with woven basket threads to keep it stationary.

The taller of the two women had features resembling the women of the Plains Indians. She stood three inches higher than the Rogue women, more reserved, and was lighter skinned. Her face was sharper, more well defined with a fierce aspect, like a hawk. With her sloping brown eyes, full black hair, and teeth like white pearls she made a strong, handsome presence. She wasn't shy like the coast women chattering happily and laughing merrily at the tribal gossip that made innocent fun of a particular man or woman.

When the two had finished with the cradleboard, the tall one pointed a thumb at her chest and said, "Zinjcala Maza." That didn't sound like the Rogue dialect to Remme. She was looking at him intensely as if she were expecting a question from him. On a hunch he asked "Do you speak English?"

Before she answered she said something rapidly to the Rogue woman who giggled, nodded her head, and ran out of the hut.

Haltingly Zinjcala Maza said she had fled for her life when the Cayuse Indians massacred Marcus Whitman at his Walla Walla mission in '47. She was afraid for her life from the Oregon volunteers who came to punish the Cayuse. She had been unofficially adopted by the missionary when she made her way into the northwest after the death of her father in New Mexico. She had a half sister who lived in Walla Walla and since it was too painful for her to stay with the Navajos where memories of her father were too overwhelming to bear, she traveled north. There was sadness in her eyes and she apologized for the uncertain way she spoke with clicking sounds in her throat. Then she said when she heard there was an injured white man in the camp she asked Chief Taylor if she might talk to him.

Remme learned that her name Zinjcala Maza meant Iron Bird in the Sioux language. Her father, born a Dakota Sioux, had left the tribe when the part Indian woman he wanted to marry lived in the New Mexico desert near Window Rock. He left the Sioux, was adopted as a Navajo, but kept his Sioux name George Blue Horse. Iron Bird's mother spoke English and insisted her daughter also learned to speak it. When she was twelve, her mother, mostly of French extraction, ran off with a white man.

Iron Bird bowed her head for a moment and when she looked up again at Remme, her eyes were moist with tears.

"People tell me that she was beautiful and that I look like her. But it was my father who taught me how much the people he lived with loved their children. He was an adopted Navajo, and he loved me and I worshiped him."

Iron Bird's eyes suddenly filled. She wiped away her tears, looked sharply at Remme as if she dared him to comfort her, then said in a low voice. "He knew he was dying, but had hidden it from me. He sent me away. And I never saw him again. His Dakota Sioux name which he kept even after he was an adopted Navaho, was Tasunke-

Hinto, which means Blue Horse. The last thing he did for me was to sing a Hozhonji song."

Fascinated Remme asked, "What is it for?"

"They are holy songs of the Navajo to protect people from all evil. A man or a woman will often sing a Hozhonji song before starting on a long journey. Blue Horse and I sang one for me the night before he put me on a horse and sent me off to live with my half sister."

Iron Bird lifted her eyes and looked directly into Remme's. "I like to speak English but with the way things are now it's hard to know who to trust."

Iron Bird paused for a moment and sipped water from a hollowed gourd. Then, she offered the gourd to Remme and when she leaned forward to hand it to him her breasts pressed appealingly against her bleached deerskin shirt which was open at the throat enough to reveal the smooth ivory skin of her neck descending attractively into the deepening cleft that divided the swelling firmness of her chest.

Her hands fluttered like startled birds when she realized the view she had presented and quickly pulled the collars of her shirt together. There was confusion in her eyes as if she had been deliberately immodest, and Remme found the blush on her face attractive. She was a head turner with her hair let down instead of bound tightly in a bun at the back of her neck as most of the Rogue women wore their hair.

Iron Bird stood up quickly. "Thank you for talking to me. I will go now and find a tree from which I can cut a crutch for you."

Before Remme could say a word she was gone. He felt her absence sharply and realized with wonder that he was entranced with her. She was beautiful and his pulse beat faster when she was near to him. How could deep feelings happen so fast? Were they shared by her?

Iron Bird found a madrona tree with a limb that branched in two directions. She stripped the bark and padded the crotch with moss and bound it in place, so that a week after his accident, Remme could manage with help to walk with the crutch, leg suspended by a sling from his belt. Remme was not unaware of

Iron Bird's signs of caring for him, and he was certain that he was not the only one in the village who had noticed. The gossip ran from mouth to mouth and Iron Bird pretended not to hear the excited whispers and giggles from the women.

Remme had always loved seafood and was amazed how the female weavers could construct baskets that were nearly watertight. A coat of hot pitch sealed the fibers together. By tossing in heated rocks, the Indian women brewed fish heads and tails, clams, crayfish, and mussels.

Because they did not have horses, but were often visited by horsemen, the Rogues were fascinated by Diablo. During the last week of his confinement, Remme introduced the women to his horse, encouraged them to run their hands over his hide. When they were confident the big black horse wouldn't eat children, they placed the little ones on his back and watched Iron Bird take them for rides.

Gradually, Remme reached the point in his recovery when he could place the whole weight of his body on both of his feet. He still limped, but could climb up on Diablo's back and absorb the thud of his hooves without too much discomfort.

Remme was bedeviled by a worrisome question. What made the white settlers, miners, and farmers, hate the Indians so? These people had been kind and good to him, asking nothing in return. They were industrious, courteous to one another, and lived with nature the way it was intended—as old Morey Whitetail taught him all those years ago when he was a boy.

He was restless with his questions and stepped outside one night to look at the July moon, long risen and sickly between black clouds. The yellow moonfire brought an edge to the night shapes, making wan patches along deep blurs of shadow, and giving definition to a wisp of mist low on the retreating tide. When Iron Bird, silent as a ghost, came to his side and slipped her hand in his, it felt as natural as breathing. Both of them stood together as the wind from the sea came rushing into the timber, rousing at the stillness, making a rumbling voice to the night, blowing clouds across the moon. They thickened above the trees and a harsh invisible rain came striking in the wind, cutting at their faces. There were no answers but one. He and Iron Bird came together and, in each other's arms, found peace and excitement and knew a longing that would unify them for as long as each of them lived.

He had taken his spill from Diablo's back near one of the Rogues' temporary camps along the beaches where the smelt spawned during the summer months. With scoop nets made of woven iris fibers and pounded roots, the Rogues gathered thousands of fish which enriched the air as they dried in the sun. Indian women, searching the rocky shore, filled their tightly woven baskets with mussels, clams, barnacles, and chitons. Iron Bird was an expert at finding clams.

As his leg improved he followed Iron Bird and the young Rogues to their favorite fishing rocks in the rivers. To these traditional places, sometimes shared by several villages, the men brought their lift nets. Vine maple frames covered with woven mesh easily captured a silvery flood of chinook or steelhead. When the run of fish was slight, the men fished the deeper pools with bone and horn hooks. Often, almost every inhabitant of a village stationed himself at the weirs in the rivers or their tributary streams. The fish were so plentiful that men, women, and children shouting and thrashing gleefully in the water, clubbed and speared the fish that would feed them for a year. Wet and happy, her deerskin dress warped to the shape of her body, Iron Bird grinned at Remme, unashamed of how her dress revealed her womanly gifts. In all their splashing, the Rogues ignored the pebbles of gold in the streams. They lived free and uncaring as they had for hundreds of years.

Remme came to like the Rogues and admired how they entertained themselves and taught their children about life, death, nature, and God by reciting myths. Many of their stories were centered on Coyote the trickster, the cleverest of all warriors who could assume any physical appearance. Iron Bird was popular as the storyteller of the mythical Coyote who was recognizable in the culture and stories of tribes living on the Oregon Coast, in the Columbia River valley far to the north, and as the shrewd coyote hero in tales spread among the tribes of the plains indians.

The day Remme left the village, he walked Diablo to the hut where Chief Taylor was visiting relatives. The old man saw him coming and when Remme stopped, he raised his hand in the peaceful friendship sign. Taylor smiled, then solemnly reached into his waistband, pulled out Remme's knife he had used to cut his boot free, and, reversing the blade so that it pointed at his own body, passed it to the Frenchman.

Remme accepted the knife, appreciated the significance of the ceremony, then reversing the blade as Taylor had done, gave it back to him. Taylor nodded his head. No words were needed to express the trust between the two. He waved at the Rogue chief and headed inland, wearing knee-high moccasin boots the Rogue women had made for him.

Leading his horse, Remme walked out of the village with Iron Bird quiet at his side. He had told her he had work to do, but would come and find her. He would take her to the Strawberry Patch and make their home. She nodded, took him in her arms, and said she would be patient with the waiting. Leaving her was one of the hardest things he had ever done.

When Remme arrived in Jacksonville three days later, he found a frontier town of hostile miners, and though he was hired as a teamster to haul supplies as far north as Eugene, he couldn't escape the conviction that the whole area of southwest Oregon was bristling with hate and resentment for the Indians. He soon learned that the Rogue tribes in the Siskiyous and in the Grave Creek area had begun a murderous campaign of revenge against the white man for too many bitter memories, too many past wrongs and injustices, too many deaths from sickness and starvation. Too many attempts at their extermination had deliberately been encouraged for them ever to trust any white man again. The earlier actions of James Lupton, "the Indian exterminator" at a town meeting in Jacksonville to stir up the tempers of miners to become part of a volunteer force of Indian killers was evidence enough of the deadly intentions of the white men. But the Rogues struck first. Pushing down river toward the wilderness in the coast mountains their raiding party set fire to the Jacob B. Wagner ranch. They killed Mrs. Wagner and her daughter. In the smoking ruins was the charred body of Miss Sarah Rellete, a temperance lecturer on her way to Jacksonville.

Had the settlers been warned of a poisonous Jacksonville meeting, perhaps those along the Rogue River who lived at Gold Hill and Vahnoy's Ferry could have saved the lives of the three women. Remme learned of the bloodletting in early October while he was delivering supplies to the general store in Grants Pass. It wasn't a day later when a terrified woman and her bedraggled daughter and son, having hidden near their burned out home in the dark hostile night—rain water dripping through the shaggy firs to add to their misery—at dawn stumbled down a farm path and were met by military troops looking for survivors the next morning.

The story she told was hair raising:

Her husband, George W. Harris was splitting shingles in the yard while his wife was washing clothes behind the house. Harris looked up to see Indians pouring out of the woods and running toward him. He seized his rifle and ran with the family for the cabin but was shot as he attempted to close the door. He fired his gun twice then staggered across the room and fainted. Sophie, his eleven-year-old daughter, ran to the door to let down the horizontal bar to keep the intruders out, but was shot through the arm before she could drop the bar. Harris's wife, when her husband revived, loaded his pistols, but, to her anguish and despair, he grabbed his chest and he died of a heart attack in her arms. Alone with a wounded daughter, the Indians yelling and burning the outbuildings on the farm, and fearful for her son hiding out in the fields, she defended the cabin for more than five hours. When the Indians left, the woman hid with her son and wounded daughter in the forest until the next morning.

In the short period Remme had been driving a team of mules out of Jacksonville, he had come to detest James Lupton, whose purpose was to stir up miners against the Rogues whom he hated. He came to Jacksonville with the self-given title of major—a former member of a mounted rifle regiment out of Yreka—and proved to be an effective agitator. He also liked to brag about his exploits killing Indians.

It was in a Jacksonville saloon that Remme, over-tired from a long haul, stopped for a drink before heading for his hotel room. He was standing at the end of the bar near the saloon door when a young boy about fourteen burst in, swallowing and breathing hard. "I came to report," he said to Lupton, "that at the first light, when I was at the lookout, the one in the rocks that looks out on the southern mountains, I heard it. Then I saw. I thought it was Indians, but it was the Grayson boy from his dad's farm. His horse foundered, that blue-nosed gray. He couldn't speak, the boy. He fell in a fit when he saw me. Then he told me. The ranch was burning. The people, screaming! His family, his mother, God keep us! His father—his farm."

"They all dead?" Lupton asked.

"I don't know sir. Some Rogues got killed."

"That make you sad? It shouldn't. Vermin. Just like you'd squash a spider with the heel of your boot, the more dead Indians the better. Have to be exterminated. We'll get organized right away and go after the bastards. Have a drink on me boy. Calm your nerves."

Sick with sudden deep anger, cold eyed and deadly calm, Remme regarded Lupton with deep disgust. "You encourage killing do you? You like it? You're the one they call the Exterminator. Who gave you permission to raise hate against the Rogues? Don't you know that fools like you are responsible for the deaths of settlers?"

A hush, like breathing stopped, silenced the room. Not one of the thirty or so miners in the bar dared to open their mouths, waiting on Lupton's reply to Remme's insult. Except for the pistol in its holster worn in a cartridge belt around Remme's waist, not one, not a single man staring at Louis Remme, was armed.

Lupton, aware of the dozens of eyes fixed on him to take in his response, seemed unable to speak; his mouth was open and his reddening face expressed his unuttered bluster.

"Listen man," Remme goaded him, "Don't just stand there with your mouth as wide open as a church door on Sunday, give me an answer."

Lupton seemed to shrink. "I've got to go," he croaked faintly. "Work to be done . . ." he trailed off, then brushed by the man who had humiliated him and rushed out of the door. Remme finished his drink in an atmosphere turned sullen, threw some silver on the bar, and left the saloon. He knew he had made an enemy, probably more than one. But he didn't care. He should have kept his mouth shut. No criticism of his was going to stop the killing.

Serious hostilities had reached the boiling point in Jacksonville. The animosities of a few settlers, the hatred and self-importance of men like Lupton, the fears of many others, and the cruelty of men without principles or respect for themselves, had heated the tensions that gripped the inhabitants of southern Oregon. An all-out war against the Indians was the only solution the white miners advocated heatedly. The unsympathetic attitude of miners who resented the native people was ready to explode. The sense of excitement, of being on the edge of war with the savages, brought dozens of spectators and idlers into the settlement. Their grievances became boasts; and, fatefully for the Indians, the end of a way of life.

As Remme sank into his bed that night he reached the conclusion that no miner, settler, volunteer, pioneer, militiaman, or ordinary citizen of Oregon Territory would ever be punished for killing one or a hundred Indians.

On that thought, he fell asleep with the decision to leave his job as a teamster as soon as the man who employed him could find a replacement.

It was late in December and Remme's pack train boss had deliberately, Remme suspected, not sought a replacement. He faced the man and gave him an ultimatum. "You've got one week to find somebody else to drive for you. I'll collect what you owe me then and leave." Remme could not be swayed to reconsider. On his last trip nature played a hand in delaying his return to Jacksonville with a load of supplies. A heavy storm hit the valley; in the last month of 1852, then a silver thaw—freezing rain and arctic wind—paralyzed the region for eighteen days. Pack trains like the one Remme was driving were unable to bring in supplies. When he finally crawled into Jacksonville with his string of mules, Remme learned that flour had become so scarce that it sold for between one dollar and a dollar and a half a pound. Salt was not available anywhere. The hotel at Jacksonville sold meals for $1.50 to $2 each and kept a doorkeeper at the dining room to collect in advance as miners and other citizens entered to eat. Those who had no money were clubbed away from the door.

The incident that helplessly enraged Remme occurred in the mountains where miners were exploring the gravel bars for gold. While Remme had been delayed, in late December a number of miners were working near the mouth of Galice Creek deep in the coast range where the Rogue River cut a gorge through the hills toward the ocean. For many days nothing was heard from them; then a few bodies were found. The miners in the valley believed that the Indians of Chief Taylor's band on Grave Creek had killed the prospectors. When questioned about the missing men, the Indians said they were certain the men had drowned—for it was a well known fact that the Rogue could rise rapidly during sudden December rains.

A little later in December, Chief Taylor and his men became suspect again by miners who lived near the mouth of the Applegate River. Gold dust was showing up from the Grave Creek Indians who seldom had money to spend. They decided that Taylor's band had killed the seven men missing on Galice Creek. Taking matters into their own hands, the miners grabbed Chief Taylor and several of his warriors. Quickly hoisting Chief Taylor on a white horse, they gave him a pipe to smoke, and dropped a noose around his neck. Before the old man could draw in a lungful of smoke, one of the men smacked the horse's rump with a board and Taylor swung in the air.

The miners bound the hands of the other men behind their backs and told them to run. Helpless, the Indians, hampered by their imprisoned arms, stumbled across the meadow. The white men opened fire. Each of the Rogues fell mortally wounded. Nobody volunteered to bury the warriors or cut down their dead chief.

Remme was sick at heart when he learned about Taylor's death. He was certain the man had been accused and killed wrongly. It was the tipping point for Remme. He quickly packed his clothing and stuffed them in his saddlebags and with his handgun and cartridge belt buckled around his waist, walked directly to the stable where Diablo would be waiting.

There were dozens of minor fatal skirmishes between the whites and the Indians in 1853, but the outcome of the spreading war was inevitable. Mounted on Diablo, he left Jacksonville behind and with it Jacksonville's treacherous history of the elimination of hundreds of native people.

He was soured and depressed when he headed to his own ranch, Strawberry Patch, for which he'd paid a total of three thousand from the proceeds of his California mining and other adventures. Now, with another seven hundred in his money belt his total capital was $6,700, less a few dollars for eating money, and he was prepared to waste no time and build a sizable herd for the hungry California beef market.

Remme thought about going back to the coast, to bring Iron Bird to the Strawberry Patch, but his herd-building plans meant that he would be absent from her for weeks at a time. He couldn't risk leaving her with his Mexican caretaker. The fact that her skin was almost white and she carried herself with pride and a certain aloofness would not change the stigma that she was Indian and fair game for the exterminators. They had demonstrated that women and children would not escape their wrath. He couldn't bear the thought that he might lose her. She was safer in the isolated coastal village where few white men ever ventured.

CHAPTER EIGHT

AS REMME NEARED JACKSONVILLE two years after he had left it behind, he vowed he would stop long enough for a meal, an exchange of horses, and perhaps an hour's nap. He could never remember being so tired in all of his life. As he topped a rise and spotted Jacksonville, only three years old, he swore to himself he would not let his anxiety about the progress of the *Columbia* defeat him. It took six days for the boat to sail between San Francisco and Portland. The captain of the ship didn't know a crazy Frenchman was racing his craft to Portland. He had no urgent reason to pour on the steam or break any records. If the *Columbia* was on schedule, Remme guessed the position of the boat was slightly in advance of him, probably ten miles out on a line with the mouth of the Rogue River. If that was the case, he still had a chance. The worst of the snow country was behind him, although there were still fifty miles of mountainous terrain he had to cross before he reached the south end of the Willamette Valley.

When Remme stepped off the piebald in Jacksonville, he handed the reins to the hostler at the livery stable and said, "I'm bushed. Been chasing a horse thief and I'm all in. Give my horse oats, brush him down, and let him rest. He deserves it. I've got to sleep. Do you have a stall with clean hay?"

"We got a hotel here. Just around the corner," the hostler said.

"Too tired to walk that far," Remme said. "Here's five dollars to care for the horse. Will you wake me in an hour and find me a fresh horse? A fast one?"

"Sure," the man said, pocketing the money. "Take the fifth stall. It's clean."

Remme untied the blanket roll on his saddle, trudged to the empty stall, and spread his blanket on the hay. He curled up and was asleep in seconds. He didn't hear the stablemaster grumble to himself, "Never heard of a man who'd sleep on hay when he could rent a hotel bed."

True to his promise the hostler had wakened Remme after an hour and, barely able to keep his eyes open, the cattle trader dunked his head in the horse trough and stumbled across the street to the hotel and plunked himself at the bar. It was the same bar where he had confronted James Lupton, the Indian killer. Was it only two years ago?

"Coffee and plenty of it," he said to the bar man. "And a double shot of brandy. Then I'll have breakfast, please," he added.

A man dressed in a heavy coat, jeans, and scuffed boots seated himself at a stool a few feet away from Remme, ordered whiskey, sipped, then turned to say, "Man, you look like you've been chased up a tree, bear-hugged, and tossed out as not worth eatin'."

Braced by his coffee and brandy, Remme eyed his neighbor, and decided the man's description was a friendly gesture.

"I've been in the saddle day and night for almost three days chasing a horse thief."

"Nothin' worse than a horse thief," the man said, then extended his hand. "Hale's my name. Run the country store here. Which way's your man headed?"

"Portland, if he keeps true to the path he's taken."

"Portland, huh! Won't get far unless he can swim. I heard it straight from the captain of a small steamer that the Rogue is way past flood stage. Told me he was headed upriver from the coast to deliver cargo to merchants near Winchester he does business with.

"Darnedest thing he said. He was still some miles off shore, and was amazed to see a spread of muddy water, like a brown stain two, three miles wide gushing from the river. He took it for a flood, for he's seen floods before, but never one of such magnitude. Floating in that fresh, dirty water were barns, sheds, and even a two-story log cabin. Riding the crest were a milk bucket, an outhouse, a single blue Chinese vase, and a chamber pot. Then, there were bobbing chicken coops with chickens still roosting in them, uprooted fences and posts, a rocking chair with the seat missing. Even haystacks passed by. Then came the dead animals, drowned sheep and cattle, not to mention pigs, their troughs, and every other convenience important to farm life.

"When he finally got upriver, he found that save for one or two houses built on much higher ground, most of the cabins people he knew lived in were gone. Just empty spaces where they once stood. I think a lot of people were swept away."

Remme thanked the country store proprietor for his warning, got up from the bar, and went to a corner table where his breakfast had been laid.

The news conveyed to him by Hale made Remme both jubilant and concerned. If the flooding in the Rogue was as bad as Hale had heard, it meant the *Columbia* which stopped near Gold Beach where the river joined the sea would have a hard time unloading or taking on new cargo and passengers. That news could not have been better, for the *Columbia's* delay was an advantage to Remme. On the other hand, he had to cross the Rogue himself in a few miles. If it was beyond flood stage, swift, violent, and destructive, it might create an impossible barrier.

After brandy and coffee, steak and potatoes, biscuits, beans, and a piece of apple pie, Remme was ready for the next stage of his journey. With an hour of sleep and a solid meal under his belt he felt like a new man as he had paid for his meal and asked the cook, a jolly plump woman, what was the news about the Indians.

She smiled at Remme, wiping her hands on her apron and said, "Plenty of them." Then she threw back her head and laughed with a funny screeching sound.

A few minutes later when the stablemaster asked Remme if Crazy Annie had fed him well, Remme asked, "Why do they call her that?"

"Lost her whole family to Indians up around the Dardanelles," the man said. "Hasn't been right in the head since then, but she can sure cook."

Remme rode southeast for almost two hours before he reached the banks of the Rogue River. The horse he rode, furnished by the stablemaster in Jacksonville, was an eager black filly only four years old. Her name was Idaho and she was the smallest of the horses Remme had bought or borrowed. The stablemaster claimed she loved to run and could outdistance many bigger horses.

With Remme on her back, Idaho started out quickly and proved she liked to run. She also demonstrated that she was steady and didn't startle easy when Remme was guiding her down a seldom used trail near Elk Mountain. It was early afternoon, a break in the tumbling sky making the day sunny and glistening on the spikes of new Indian grass just beginning to bloom. The sight of the pale yellow pompoms in a meadow cheered Remme. He was riding into spring, even though there were patches of snow on the ground and higher up snow and ice still lay frozen on the peaks. As he steered Idaho past a thicket of stunted hemlock, there was a thrashing in the lower branches and the horse sidestepped smartly and froze. A blue grouse, plump as a setting hen, hopped out from beneath the tree and strutted in a circle eyeing Remme and Idaho, then boldly fluttered back into hiding.

Remme patted Idaho's neck and laughed at the hen. For some reason she reminded him of the laughing cook in Jacksonville who had lost touch with reality after her family had been massacred. While he knew Iron Bird was alert to every danger, it had been too long since he'd held her in his arms and he vowed he would go to her as soon as he cashed his certificate in Portland.

His mind turned to the weather, for Oregon was well known for its rainfall and if the weeping skies flooded the land as thoroughly as they had in '47 he'd be in deep trouble.

Even though he had been new to the Oregon territory then, he had been astonished as the volume of rain made continuous lakes of the land. String together six or seven autumns and you'd get a fair measure of the daily downpour that fell from the wounded heavens in that one season.

When the rain stopped for a day, it was only long enough for settlers to wonder why they'd ever left Missouri. If the rain quit coming for a short period, it was replaced by sleet and snow. By November of that year rain had fallen all over Oregon, all over the valleys, hills, and flatlands. The land was engorged with thick moisture half frozen under a membrane of muck and ice that slicked over rocks, roads, bridges, and whole towns—some of which never recovered. It seemed like punishment for sins of the past or those not yet committed.

The whole of the Willamette Valley looked like an inland sea, said travelers who were forced to turn back. The hilltops appeared like islands poking up from the placid water like islands, or "the forested breasts of nature," one prosy native was quoted as saying. Creeks, streams, and rivers sought to unify all across the valley floors and drown or sweep away any structure erected by man.

Farther south, in the hundred valleys of the Rogue drainage, the river and all its forks and tributaries surged across the lowlands and climbed the foothills with creeping fingers.

Little waters became big waters that November, wider, deeper, and more threatening than any settler had ever seen. As the rains fell, and the snows froze and then thawed in what seemed an unending sequence, the common winter ailment of "cabin fever" put many of the discouraged into bed with emotional sickness. Even little Elk Creek thundered and reached across the land.

What most concerned Remme was that if the huge runoff of the Rogue was an indication that its overflow merging with other rivers and streams would have closed roads north and south as well as to the coastal settlements. Anyone desperate to travel had to stick to the older trails used by Indians and pioneer freight packers that followed the hilltops and ridges. These back ways took twice as long and there was no alternative to Nature's "long way around."

Many settlers became bedridden, nursing one ailment or another. Terrible outbreaks of boils, pleurisy, colds, and stomach miseries were commonplace. Even those who remained relatively healthy but trapped by the weather pined away, for there were whole families, men, women, and children, Remme knew, who did not get off their home places for months during the rainy season. As a consequence they developed homespun ailments quaintly known as "cabin fever." The miserable weather required strong personal fortitude to overcome the miseries.

The weather in Oregon was always a chancy affair, but the signs didn't seem right to Remme for a repetition of the floods of '47, still, it was going to be tricky for Remme to stay in the saddle crossing the Rogue River on Idaho. Swift and cold, lapping both banks with the massive, moody overflow from melting mountain snow, the river was wild, swift, and noisy, and certainly dangerous. It was strong enough to tear a man off his horse and tumble animal and rider like stones along its sandy bottom. The voice of the Rogue was a steady roar as Remme searched upstream for a shallow break in the current. There was no sign of the Pioneer Ferry, washed away he was certain by the flood. He had to cross the river, yet he couldn't afford to spend the time to scout up and down to find the safest place to make his entry. But he could shed his clothes and pack them in his rubber case to keep them dry. It meant he was going into the river naked, exposing himself to an icy embrace that would take his breath away.

The best place he's seen to ford was a flat bar in the middle that divided the river with an island. Thickets of willows grew on the island and a tall gray crane was standing on one leg. Into the main channel, he would jump Idaho, counting on her to swim against the current and scramble onto the island as the river swept her close to the bar.

Quickly, standing under a tree, Remme removed his rubber case from his saddlebags on Idaho's back, opened the flexible cover, and took off every stitch he wore. As for his hat, it was already wet, but it still retained its shape and he stuck it on his head.

Into his rubber case went his clothes, including his money belt, the bandanna around his neck, and three pair of socks. Last to go in the expanded rubber container were his boots, cartridge belt, handgun, and the sealskin envelope containing his certificate of deposit. Then buckling the bulky rubber bag, he tied it securely to the pommel of his saddle

Idaho seemed to know exactly what was expected of her as Remme turned her to face the river with a head start of about two hundred feet. When he flicked the reins and nudged her with his heels, she sailed off the bank, brushing through tall grass, and splashed into the water with a huge, shocking spray about fifteen feet out from the bank. Despite his preparation, cold shock took Remme's breath away and unseated him as Idaho sank, then came blowing to the surface swimming furiously to buck the strong flow of the Rogue. Though he was floating free of his horse, naked as the day he was born and chilled to the bone, Remme did not relinquish his grip on the pommel of his saddle. His hat flooded with water, still hung around his neck from its rawhide drawstring; he jammed it on his head. Head above the water, he watched the powerful little horse churn the water with her legs, going against the downstream drag of the mighty current. As Idaho's front hooves touched the island, she pulled herself out of the clinging water with a sudden lurch and heave and stood shaking herself, spraying the air with a shower of drops. The gray crane, startled, hopped twice, flapped his long wings, and took to the air, disgruntled that he had been disturbed.

Holding Idaho's reins and giving her an encouraging pat, he walked to the far side of the island with the horse. The distance to the bank was about three hundred yards. The water ran in streams and steam rose from Idaho's hide in the cold air as he climbed into the saddle and barely touched the reins before she was in the water swimming. The current less vicious on the lee side of the island, deposited horse and rider about an eighth of a mile downstream.

After Idaho shook herself again from her Rogue bath, Remme, standing in a weak patch of sunshine, squeezed as much water from his coat as he could. Once again he checked the slim leather case inside the sealskin pouch in which he carried his certificate of deposit from Adams Express. It was still dry when he opened the flap.

Redressing, he shivered, his teeth chattering, as he pulled his clothes on. He was grateful for the foresight he'd been given years earlier by a Chinese merchant in St. Louis who had sold him the thin rubber container which, when it was empty, rolled into the shape of a thick sausage.

Five hours after Remme crossed the Rogue River on Idaho, he was plodding carefully through a mountain pass with fog lying in high patches of ground-hugging gray clouds. They towered above the firs, blocking portions of his trail, decorating the trees with long, wispy beards. He and Idaho drifted through the thick, clinging mist like ghosts appearing and disappearing. It was when they emerged from a long, dense layer of fog, clammy with moisture which goose-pimpled Remme's skin, that the shots came. He felt the whipping breeze of bullets whizzing past his head at the same moment he heard the crack of rifles.

Remme kicked Idaho in the ribs, threw a hasty glance over his shoulder, and leaned against the horse's neck as the eager pony jumped into a racing run. As Idaho headed down between natural breaks in the trees, Remme heard the thunder of horses following and Indian voices raised in excitement. Unmistakable was the bloodthirsty ring in the chilling yells of the pursuers. They were no casual hunting party that had discovered a lone rider by chance and decided to play a game of chase with him. These were riders of vengeance whose murderous intent was to overtake Remme quickly, kill him, take his scalp as a trophy, and leave his body for the turkey buzzards. Remme had eluded Indians more than once during his years on the frontier, but something told him this encounter was the most dangerous of all. He was determined not to panic as he lay close to Idaho's neck with her flying mane brushing his right cheek. By molding his body as close to his running horse as possible, he was reducing the target area his back presented to the Indians' bullets. As if to emphasize his thought rifles cracked again and Remme felt something pluck at his coat sleeve and hat. Another bullet made a hole in the hide of his sheepskin, barely missing his skin. He hunched lower on Idaho's back, urging her to run faster as she flew down the mountain.

No sooner did Remme discover how close the single bullet had come to reaching its mark than several more shots sounded closer behind him. Like angry bees, lead whizzed by him picking at his clothes and cutting hairs from Idaho's flying mane. He cast a look to his rear and saw the Indians pressing closer. He swallowed hard as he glimpsed the grim faces, painted with bars and stripes. The heat of the chase was reflected in the narrowed eyes of the warriors and they glittered with hostility.

Gazing ahead of his horse, reading the terrain for deadly obstacles that could prove as fatal as any bullet if Idaho were to misjudge her footing, Remme thought of something his grandfather had once said to him. "Never forget, some Remmes are more dangerous when they are almost dead."

He didn't understand what his grandfather meant until the old man told him about his narrow escapes while fighting against the British alongside the treacherous Hurons who tried to kill him. Once, they left him for dead with a terrible scalp wound. Found at last by French soldiers, he heard one of them say, "This one's too far gone to bother with."

"Like hell I am," Paul Remme said. He lived to fight again and raise a family. There had been Remmes fighting Indians and working the land since 1740.

Now, like his grandfather, Remme was not going to let the angry Indians chasing him frighten him into making a mistake. He cast another glance over his shoulder and made out five men on horses.

All of them were armed with rifles and they were gaining. He had to think of something quickly to give himself an edge. Idaho was running straight out, but she couldn't keep the pace going very long. Strong-hearted as she was, no horse her size had the stamina for a drawn-out chase, and the Indians were pushing hard. That was when Remme spotted the rocky area ahead and to the east of the path Idaho was taking. The decision he made took only a moment, yet it was filled with the clear knowledge of the risk he was taking with his own life, and the damage he was exposing his horse to. It was a gamble that could win the race for him, or it could be the last mistake he ever made.

What he had seen ahead of him was the disguised result of what nature had done thousands of years earlier. The whole Cascade range—nine hundred miles of it—a mountain wall stretching from Canada to northern California—was the result of volcanos erupting, lifting, and forming a long ridge of peaks. Though Remme was unaware of the geological history of the mountains, he knew there were scattered areas where lava rocks had boiled out of the mountains long ago to cool and form beds of stone like dragon's teeth rising from the earth. There were some areas to the east of him where vast fields of lava spread for miles over mountains and prairies. Eventually, in some areas the forests roasted by the hot lava fires grew back, taking root in chinks in the lava. As time went by more soil formed and spread over the lava rocks. Plants and bushes grew, and in some places they concealed the protruding teeth. But the jagged stones were still there, potent and deadly, more vicious because they lay in wait to shred the feet or hooves of any animal unwise enough to trod the ground that barely covered them.

The area where Remme directed Idaho was grassed over and there were brave splashes of Indian paintbrush, clumps of rabbit brush, and dust-colored sagebrush growing in the shade of cedar and fir trees. Patches of snow lay thinly on the ground. Remme winced as he urged Idaho into the hidden lava teeth and heard her squeal with pain. Brave horse, she clattered on, stumbling, dodging, dancing, and swerving to avoid the cruel cutting edges of the rocks. She penetrated almost half a mile into the lava rock region before Remme brought her to a halt.

Howls of rage and disappointment from the Indians was accompanied by furious rifle fire from them as their horses encountered the rocks. Unable to reach Remme by horseback without maiming the feet of their unshod ponies, three of the warriors dismounted and started to cautiously follow Remme on foot. Remme was waiting for them. Pulling Idaho behind a tree for partial protection, he threw himself off his horse, yanking his rifle from its sling as his feet touched the ground. He fired rapidly at the three in the distance, levering a fresh shell into the firing chamber of his rifle as fast as he jacked a smoking one out. He saw one of the Indians fall back and grab his leg. His companions lifted him quickly and retreated. Remme continued to fire until finally, the small band of Indians withdrew. He remained crouched beside the tree for half an hour, scanning every possible approach to his position before he placed his rifle in its sling and bent to examine Idaho's hooves.

What he saw drew a deep breath of regret from him and he shook his head sadly. Idaho was standing on three feet, holding her left front foot off of the ground. When Remme examined it carefully, he saw the long deep tear in the skin with blood running down her leg from above the fetlock into the top of the hoof. A rock had sliced her leg as wickedly as a knife, cutting through the tendon. She had no control over her hoof. The tough sinew connecting it to the muscle was severed.

The brave little pony had saved Remme's life at the expense of her own. She was helpless; she could only move by hobbling. And without the use of her wounded leg, she would be easy prey for the wolves. Remme knew what he had to do as he unstrapped his saddle and his saddle blanket from Idaho's back. He ran his hand affectionately over her soft muzzle and when she nickered, he felt miserable and couldn't force himself to look into her trusting brown eyes. He drew his pistol quickly, pointed the barrel beneath her left ear, and pulled the trigger. Her legs crumpled and she fell in a motionless heap even as the flat bark of the pistol died away. Leaving the saddle and blanket where they lay, Remme slung his saddlebags and bedroll over his shoulder, tucked his rifle beneath his arm, and stepped away from the fallen horse, knowing that he would remember her sacrifice whenever he thought of the bravest ponies he had ever ridden.

As he trudged ahead over the submerged lava carefully picking his way to avoid the sharp stone teeth, he thought about the wooden hobby horse his father made for him when he was five years old. It was remarkable, he thought, as he visualized the shiny horse balancing on its rockers, how he could actually smell the last coat of varnish his father had brushed on the smooth wood. The sharp, tangy odor was a memory he always associated with Christmas, and oranges, hot minced pie, turkey and cider, the green tree, fragrant and decorated with precious ornaments his grandmother had brought to the new world from France.

Clever with his hands, his father had carved the pony out of a solid piece of walnut. Lovingly, he fashioned a flying mane on the horse, arched his neck, and stretched his legs so that the spirited wooden animal appeared to be running at full stride. With his red painted saddle, eyes of brown glass, stirrups, and reins of real leather, Remme felt grown up when he mounted his steed and rode away in his imagination to explore the forest and hills surrounding his grandfather's farm. Remme's pride and attachment to his hobby horse was transferred later to the favorite horses he encountered after he left home and learned to become an expert horse handler. He realized with surprise a feeling of sadness as he broke free of the lava-toothed region. Idaho had reminded him of his first horse, his swift hobby horse, which was probably gathering dust now in the woodshed of his grandfather's farm in Quebec.

It had begun to snow as Remme started down a long sloping incline to a broad valley. He had walked about two miles and thought he was somewhere near the Dardanelles. As the snow quickened, he felt a sense of panic. He had no idea how many hours of trudging he had to do before he found another horse. His sense of time passing, leaving him behind the steamship *Columbia* sailing far ahead of him, plunged him into a black feeling of loss. Had not his whole venture been a foolish escapade? What had made him think that he could do what few men would have dared to try? Piercing the unforgiving winter wilderness of the Cascades was madness! Even the great mountain men, Levi Scott, Joe Meek, the Applegate brothers, who blazed the Southern Immigrant Trail, would have shunned the idea of winning an overland race against a steamship whose only hindrance was the time it took to sail from San Francisco to Portland, Oregon. He had been extravagant with the strength of the horses he rode, finally killing one, all because of an impossible task. All because of his pride, his arrogance—his belief that he could do what other men would have described as crazy.

As the snow fell more quickly, thickening, sticking to his sheepskin coat, piling a crust on the brim of his hat, saddlebags, and bedroll, Remme reached the lowest point of his life. He was dead tired, every muscle in his body throbbed; his head pounded like a drum, swelling and beating inside his ears. His legs were leaden and unsteady as his feet slipped on the new snow, his boots scuffing up small waves of the white. When he lost his footing, slipped, and fell, his chin skidding like a small plow in the snow, he lay still. The skin on his hands burned with the cold; his clothes, moldy and damp and clinging were clammy and smelled rankly of horse sweat and mildew and his own unwashed body.

He was far behind the schedule he had imposed on himself to beat the *Columbia*. As he lay wondering bleakly about his future, and how unfair life was, he suddenly heard his grandfather's stormy voice in his mind. "Get up from there! Get on your feet! Shame on you for thinking about quitting. Remmes don't give in!"

If he hadn't known better, Remme could have sworn his grandfather was standing over him shouting in his ear. He pushed himself up on his knees, looked around him, and saw nothing but the dark shape of trees and falling snow. He shouldered his saddlebags and bedroll and started walking again. His grandfather's disappointment had been so sharp, his commands so clear, that his words still echoed in Remme's mind: "Remmes don't give in."

As he trudged through the slanting waves of snow, Remme could not shake off the strong sensation that the old man's voice from the past had reached him, not from his mind, but from beyond Paul Remme's grave. It was a strange, haunting, and comforting feeling. He felt ashamed that even for a few minutes he had given in to the idea of defeat. He had to go on. He had to make up the time he'd lost as a result of the Indian ambush that had cost Idaho's life and had stolen precious time from him. He had come almost four hundred miles. He couldn't give up now. He had to play out the hand he had dealt to himself to the bitter end.

For a moment Remme let his thoughts return to the Rogues who had chased him and caused Idaho's death. They were defending what had been theirs for so long. To them he was one of the hated white enemy, but even as they clung to their past and fought for their survival, he knew the end had come for the Rogues of the valley. Those who had tried to take his life were fighting a battle already lost.

In the mountains to the west of him along the canyon of the Rogue River, which Idaho had dared so willingly, were the confused and hostile survivors of the white men in the valley. These broken families had not had time to collect acorns or preserve enough salmon from the fall runs. Scattered behind them were their tools and intricate baskets, their woodpecker scalps and deerskins, and their strings of long white dentalium shells harvested from the sea. These primitive people were from the same clan as those on the coast that had treated him with such simple kindness when he fell under Diablo. Now, their relatives, valley and mountain inhabitants, were lost. In the snowbound hills they huddled around fires or shared crowded plank houses with small bands whose villages were sure to be destroyed.

God, he prayed, let nothing happen to Iron Bird, for she represented the meaning in his life.

The snow was mixed with rain as the bedraggled cattle trader topped a rise on a hill several miles later and saw dimly in a valley ahead a farmhouse with smoke rising from a chimney. There was a barn and animals in the barnyard surrounded by wooden fences. He heaved a sigh of relief and headed down into the valley. It was late in the afternoon, the snow transformed into a wavering line of insistent, icy rain that chilled him to the bone when he stopped a few yards from the front porch of the farmhouse and shouted "Hello!"

The sight he presented to anyone observing him was that of a dirty, bowed figure whose pale, drawn face was surrounded by a scruffy, four-day growth of hair bristling with drops of rain. His eyes were bloodshot and had a wild look; his arms trembled from the chilblains—a result of exposure to cold and damp for hours on end. And he swayed slightly from the dizziness that overcame him from time to time. His trousers and boots were muddy and shapeless. His sheepskin looked like it had been dragged in the snow and mud behind a wagon for several miles. Unknown to Remme were three long bullet tears from Indian rifles in the greasy collar of his coat and other holes in his hat.

What Remme could not know as he waited for the door of the farmhouse to open was the slowed state of the *Columbia*'s progress. It would have cheered him beyond words. Because of Indian troubles, the steamship had been carrying two companies of soldiers from San Francisco, as well as supplies to reinforce the army post on Humboldt Bay in Northern California and the army fort at Gardiner located at the mouth of the Umpqua River in Oregon. The boat had dropped off troops at Humboldt Bay and had been delayed again for several hours to unload men and horses at her last stop. About the time Remme was buying a strong horse from a stout Irish farmer named Kavanaugh who welcomed the cattle trader into his house when he heard him call, the *Columbia's* Captain Dall was aiming his steamship out to sea again. He had disembarked the last of the soldiers in Oregon. Remme was ahead of the steamship—but only by a few miles!

Kavanaugh was a big, cheerful man who promised Remme that the horse he was willing to sell for $80 was an even-tempered plodder. He was certainly no bolt of lightning like the horse Remme lost to the Rogue Indians. "Shasties is what they was," Kavanaugh insisted, using the frontier slang word for the tribe which had been named after the great mountain in California. The horse Remme bought from the cheerful farmer was a big, whitish animal with a Roman nose and huge feet from a Percheron ancestor. Whitey stood sixteen hands high, was broad in the shoulders, and had been trained to the plow.

"Ain't nothin' fancy about him," Kavanaugh said, "but he'll getcha where you're goin'. You may have to pester him some to make him stretch his legs but he's steady."

The shrewd farmer agreed to part with a dusty saddle covered with cobwebs that hung in the barn. It had seen better days but with a blanket thrown into the bargain it suited Remme and he agreed to pay ten dollars for it. Before Mrs. Kavanaugh would allow Remme to depart, she insisted that he eat a thick meatloaf sandwich. He consumed it gratefully, standing next to a potbellied iron stove that drove evil-smelling steam from his wet clothes. Noting his pale face, Mrs. Kavanaugh placed the back of her hand against his forehead, then clucked her tongue and busied herself with hot water and two small jars. From one she took bark of the chokeberry tree and from the other needles of Douglas fir. She boiled the concoction and forced Remme to drink it. Bitter to the taste, but savory to smell, Remme obediently swallowed the brew and was surprised when a few minutes later the chills that had been trembling his body disappeared.

Kavanaugh had been watching and smiling as his wife ministered to the pale, determined stranger who was chasing a horse thief. He chuckled to Remme and said, "Best cold remedy there is. Ma got it from an Indian woman over near Gold Hill. She swears by it. Sure makes me feel better when I get to ailing."

CHAPTER NINE

REMME COULD NOT HAVE KNOWN that a horse handler for the Mountain Express Company in Yreka, California had overheard the conversation between his boss, Tom Horsley, and the dirt-speckled rider with whom he had exchanged horses. Tom had listened to the man's story of chasing a horse thief and responded with the offer of the fastest mount in the company's corral, a tall mustang called Black Spot. He was fast alright. Del Hankerson had ridden him before the accident that broke his leg and reduced him to shoveling manure and grooming horses until his leg mended and he could throw away the cane he had to lean on.

Del, leg almost healed, had found it difficult to believe that the wiry, dark-haired stranger with a two-day beard was really trying to catch up with the rotten crook who would steal a horse. He didn't doubt for a minute that the rider had been in the saddle for hours. His coat and pants were stained with horse lather and mud. The horse he was riding certainly had shown every sign of hard wear. He ought to know. He was the one who had rubbed the animal down after walking her around in the corral to cool her off. He'd given her oats and water and put her in a fresh stall. Anyway, the man who said his name was Louis Remme didn't seem on the level to Del and the next words out of his mouth proved it, when he said to Tom, "I've been telling the horse thief lie since I left Sacramento because I'm in a big hurry. Adams Express went bankrupt last Monday and I've got to beat the steamer *Columbia* to Portland to save the money I've got in the bank. I've been in the saddle since noon Monday and I've got four days ahead of me. I can't take your horse on false pretenses!"

Del saw Tom Horsley step back, astonished, and stare at Remme. "Adams Express is broke and you've come more than two hundred miles in about sixty hours? My God, man, when have you slept?"

Quickly, he had called to Del to put Remme's saddle on Black Spot. While Del stripped Remme's gear from his tired horse, he overheard Tom warn the Frenchman about the Modocs who were stirred up and angry at the white prospectors. One of them searching for firewood had destroyed a sacred wooden platform in their graveyard on which a tribal elder lay gazing up with sightless eyes at the sky above him.

Del had never trusted banks and even if he'd had enough money to put in one, he would never have done it. Remme's story about beating the *Columbia* to Portland fascinated him because he was leaving for Crescent City to catch the steamer in just about an hour. He was going to visit his ailing mom in Portland who might not live. He wondered how far Black Spot would take his new rider north before he gave out? Whatever possessed the man to think he could beat a steamship that wouldn't be slowed or stopped by the hazards of snow, ice, muddy trails, crazy Indians, and freaky weather that could change from one hour to the next?

Del had decided that after he'd made sure his mom was all right, he'd see if he could wangle a grub stake from his brother Hal. He had a pretty good business going at Fort Vancouver selling hats just across the river from Portland. He felt lucky. With a little money from Hal he had a hunch he could make it pretty big if he could get to the diggings in British Columbia on the Frazer River. He'd heard nuggets as big as walnuts were being washed out of the water. He wasn't interested in the gold diggings near Shasta. They were showing thin, he'd been told.

As Dell saw the stranger off on Black Spot on his way to save his gold, he couldn't help feeling envious and jealous. What if the rider failed to get close enough to Portland, but the steamer arrived just ahead of time? What a heartbreak that would be. What if he had an accident or was killed by Indians on the warpath? Hell, it was common knowledge things were getting worse for both the valley and mountain Indians. Gossip had it that the mountain tribes were the most vicious. The Yreka paper got dispatches twice monthly from the *Columbia* which also brought mail by steamer. Every delivery seemed to bring worse news. It must have been about two weeks ago when a miner living in a lonely shanty on Indian Creek near the Klamath River was killed. The belief was that the Takelman of the Illinois Valley had committed the crime. Bent on justice, two volunteer companies crossed the Siskiyous and marched down the narrow canyon of Althouse Creek to the mining town of Kerbyville. Their bloody mission of vengeance left four Indian men and one woman killed. Only hours before, it was said, the new Indian agent for the district had anticipated troubles and had hurried several Indian families from the region to the safer reservation on the Rogue River.

A miner deliberately taking a murderous path of slaughter near his diggings on Humbug Creek, was beheaded by Indians. Still in a murderous mood, drunken Klamath Indians launched a two-day massacre of eleven other miners along the Klamath, Scott, and Shasta Rivers. While the volunteer companies formed an army, a lieutenant and some of the settlers near Fort Jones rounded up nearly one hundred peaceful "Shasties" and brought them to the military post for protection. Those Indians remaining in the mountains became prey for the white avengers.

Del was soon on his way to Crescent City, to catch the steamer *Columbia*. He'd been surprised when Tom Horsley had given him two gold beavers to help with his travel expenses to see his mom. He liked the feel of the solid gold $5 pieces in his pocket. Tom was a pretty good old boy when it came right down to it, but he paid Del $30 a month, which wasn't much to get by on. His short pay made him feel a little guilty about the fate of the Frenchman. What if he was killed and his money belt never found. What a waste that would be.

On board the *Columbia* when she thrashed out to sea, Del felt a little uneasy. He'd never been onboard a big boat and the deck wasn't too stable beneath his feet. His first night in steerage with ninety-four other people made him a bit panicky. Everything was so close. People sleeping in their clothes, breathing, grunting, wheezing, kids crying or complaining. And there was the creaking and groaning noise of the ship's timbers as the steamer plowed through waves, troughs, and swells that lifted and dipped the sluggish bottom. He got very little sleep. The thumping racket of the paddlewheels on each side of the hull kept up a nerve-wracking, repetitious monotony that Del couldn't shut out even when he stuffed cigarette paper in his ears.

He bought coffee in the morning from a steward serving it in the main salon for a dollar a cup and it was lukewarm and unfit to drink. The crush of passengers was so bad that he escaped to the windblown deck where twenty or thirty people had wrapped blankets around their shoulders and planted themselves in chairs they'd brought aboard, travel-wise enough to know there were no conveniences on the *Columbia*.

He encountered one man, an intelligent well-spoken individual, Sam Hardy, who looked as miserable as he felt. Short red hair decorated his scalp and a long canvas raincoat reached to his boots.

"This your first trip?" he asked Del. He nodded before Del could respond, and said, "Life aboard this cramped steamer is always like this. We are thick as flies in August. In the staterooms you can't turn around without bumping into somebody. We have to divide ourselves into eating battalions, and go twice for our meals. There is no privacy. Gamblers jostle preachers; women of the night share staterooms with fine ladies; honest miners in red flannels sit next to dandies from new York in French broadcloth. We breathe other people's air. It becomes so thick that we have to throw open the portholes to the deck even in bad weather and risk getting drenched in cold wind-blown sea water." Hardy saluted Del, wished him luck, took a deep breath, and headed back inside the ship.

Del found a space to crouch against a wall while he chewed on a day-old beef sandwich, and wondered what trade Hardy practiced. He was soon joined by a man dressed in a blue uniform with a single stripe on his cuff.

The man standing beside him was in his late thirties, Del surmised, and was, he assumed, one of the officers serving on the *Columbia*, but not an important one or he would be wearing more gold stripes on his sleeve. He was just under six feet, his light brown hair receding, his face open and friendly. There was a preciseness about him, with his carefully knotted tie, his sensible, black leather sea boots, and the sharp crease in his navy blue trousers.

Before the crewman had come to stand next to him, Del, with nothing to pass the time, had been thinking about Louis Remme. He was picturing the intense horseman in his mind, recasting his opinion of the man who had declared to Tom Horsley that he wasn't chasing a horse thief, but bent on winning a race with a steamboat so he could save his money. If Remme was desperate enough to try to outrace a boat with big engines and huge paddles that didn't have to stop to eat and rest, that plugged along night and day without interruption as long as it was fed coal and oil, then the amount of money the Frenchman stood to lose if he didn't win the gamble must be considerable. That was one thought—the other one was more confusing. What did a bank going broke in California have to do with when the steamboat arrived in Portland? That was a connection Del did not understand and it bothered him.

Not a shy man, Del decided to ask the officer standing beside him if he knew the reason for such a hairbrained idea. Taking in a deep breath of the brisk morning sea air, favoring his left leg which was still stiff, he stood and turned to the seaman. "Mister, my name is Del Hankerson, and I've got a puzzle I'd be grateful if you could help me solve."

Surprised, the officer accepted Del's extended hand and said, "My name is Ralph Meade. I'm the purser of the *Columbia*. I'll help you if I can."

Del thanked the man and described the circumstances on the day before when he overheard Remme's confession to Tom Horsley.

"What I can't figure out is why a feller would ride night and day, risk his neck, and maybe lose his life in a dozen ways to beat this boat to Portland. What does a bank in California that's closed its doors have to do with a paddleboat headed for Portland?"

The question struck Ralph Meade like a slap in the face. He fought not to let his expression reflect the sudden dismay he felt. How could it happen that this cowboy, horse handler, whatever he was—was a passenger on the same voyage taking Meade, himself, to financial ruin? It was beyond irony, unbelievable, the worst kind of luck, that he was being pushed by a stranger's innocent question to make the decision he was delaying which would affect his whole future!

Convincingly, he hoped, he frowned and said, "Mr. Hankerson, I'm not sure I know how to answer your question. It's intriguing. Right now I have to go on duty, but why don't I give it some thought and I'll find you later?"

"Sure," Del said, then quickly added, "I paid a dollar for coffee I couldn't drink. Can you do something about that?"

Relieved that Hankerson had changed the subject, Meade said, "Of course, tell one of the stewards I said to give you a fresh cup and refills. I'll see you later."

The gratitude on Del Hankerson's face was confirmation that Meade had a few hours before he would have to respond to the question that upset him. Hankerson, Meade thought, was not the sort to be diverted from an inquiry once it stuck in his mind. He wouldn't give up because he was the kind of person that clung to little mysteries like a dog worrying a bone. The last thing Meade wanted was to have Hankerson pestering one of the other ship's officers with his question.

As he reached his small office not far from the wheelhouse where the financial records, official papers, bills of lading, commercial shipping documents listing the ship's passengers and cargo and trip instructions were kept, Ralph Meade dropped into the chair at his desk and considered the reason for his panic when Hankerson had posed his question. Of course, he didn't know a man named Louis Remme, but he could certainly surmise why the clever horseman was desperate to reach Portland before the *Columbia* docked. He had to be one of the California depositors of Adams Express Company which had declared bankruptcy. He must have reasoned—and correctly—that the steamer was carrying the legal papers that would cut off Oregon depositors in the defunct bank from any hope of recovering their savings. If the rider could reach Portland before the steamer, nothing could bar him from collecting his money from Dr. Steinberger, the Adams agent in Oregon. Del Hankerson's question had raised Ralph Meade's fear for another reason. If any of the passengers learned that in the *Columbia* safe more than $1.8 million rested, waiting to be distributed to the preferential creditors by the bankruptcy court referee, he was certain passengers with money in Adams Express in Portland who did not know about the Writ of Attachment Meade had been ordered to serve on the agent in Portland would be furious. Not only would they demand their money, but might force the safe opened at gunpoint and count out what was owed to whom, if the secret cargo was somehow discovered.

Ralph's memory was fresh of the foggy night before the *Columbia* sailed, the approach up the gangplank of two bank delivery men, a third armed with a shotgun to protect the valuable cargo, carried in the heavy iron-bound chest. Once they were on board at 3 A.M., when not a soul was stirring on the dock, Ralph led the way to his office, opened the door, and pointed the way to the safe. The ship's Captain Dall was handed a cast iron key, and with it opened the chest. Resting on the bullion, sacks of gold dust, and gold slugs was an inventory signed by the Adams Express Bank manager, attesting to the total in the chest.

Dall studied the inventory for a moment and signed a receipt relieving him of the duty to confirm the accuracy of the amount of the treasure. He kept a copy for himself, handed the other copy to the men, and bid them good night.

Before he left Meade's room, Captain Dall remarked, "Strange cargo at a strange hour. It's your responsibility now. We'll sail with the morning tide."

What a brilliant, mad, foolhardy, remarkable, and dangerous idea! If Remme got through, it would be a miracle, Meade thought, and he'd deserve every dollar he saved from the law. In the same moment he admired the horseman, Meade cursed his own helplessness. For he too was a depositor in Adams Express and unless he could figure a way to cash in his own certificate representing $950 in Adams Express, he would lose every cent by virtue of the official action he must take the moment the *Columbia* tied up at the dock in Portland. This was the dilemma he'd been trying to outsmart.

He'd never forgotten the chain of circumstances that had put him in his intolerable position.

The previous Friday, February 23, a day off for him, he had been in San Francisco when he learned the steamer *Oregon* had arrived from Panama a few days earlier. It was the last long leg for the ship that had left New York with passengers, cargo, and mail about three weeks earlier. There were sealed pouches aboard the ship which were delivered to Page, Bacon, and Company Bank which had just moved into its new building on Battery Street in San Francisco. The news of the failure of the parent company in St. Louis was among the financial papers delivered in the bank's pouch from the Oregon.

The disastrous news spread like wildfire and the San Francisco branch remained open until Friday afternoon. By then, it had paid out more than $400,000 to panicked depositors and closed until Monday.

The run has resumed on Monday, February 26, and spread to other banks. Four of them collapsed by noon; four stayed open as did the venerable Page, Bacon, but later that day the old house closed its doors, never to open again.

At 2 A.M. Sunday morning, Delos Lake, judge of the 12th Judicial District was called out of his bed to appoint a receiver for the assets of Adams Express, Alfred Cohen.

One of Cohen's first duties was to prepare a document which was to be delivered by fast riders to every branch of Adams Express in California. It was William L. Dall, captain of the *Columbia* who, early Monday an hour before the boat was due to sail, received an envelope from Cohen, the bankruptcy receiver, with instructions for him to deliver the enclosed Writ of Attachment to the first duly authorized law officer to be found in Portland immediately upon docking the

Columbia in the Oregon city. Captain Dall ordered Ralph Meade to run down the gangplank before passengers were unloaded in Oregon and give the envelope to the sheriff or a deputy who'd been alerted by emergency blasts of the steam whistle. Dall did not know that Meade was a depositor in the defunct bank and that for him to carry out the task demanded a bitter personal sacrifice.

Even before the *Columbia* raised anchor in San Francisco on February 26, so intense and resentful was the public feeling against Judge Lake in San Francisco for his after-midnight ruling to approve the petition of Adams Express for bankruptcy, that he resigned on the same day the *Columbia* headed out to sea. And, though Meade did not know it, that was the same day Remme boarded a paddleboat that would take him to Knights Landing, the first leg on his remarkable journey to outrace a mechanical monster.

Aside from his personal frustration at not being able to figure a way to save the $950 he had on deposit in the defunct bank, Meade was concerned that if Hankerson told his story of the lone rider matching his courage and stamina against a floating steam boiler with wheels to the other passengers, their fascination might boil into an angry crowd reaction. Counting the contingent of U.S. army soldiers who would be disembarked near the mouth of the Umpqua River in Oregon, there were more than 270 people aboard. Many of the passengers, aside from himself, must have money to lose in Adams Express. They wouldn't know about their potential losses until they arrived in Oregon, unless Hankerson's story got out and passengers started asking questions. It didn't take much imagination to guess what might happen if they learned there was a chance to save their money. That could only happen if a few people desperate enough to turn to violence to save their gold decided to band together and overpower the officers and crew of the *Columbia* and take command of the sidewheeler before she docked in Portland. Then the mutineers would arrange to be the first off the ship after raiding the gold and destroying the Writ of Attachment Meade had instructions to turn over to the law.

Such a mutinous action at sea had happened on ships before, but certainly not on any ship owned by the Pacific Mail Steamship Company.

Far more likely when Hankerson's story started circulating among passengers, would be the main question of why it was so urgent for a lone rider to risk his life unless he stood to gain a fortune if he beat the steamboat overland. Risk his life to chase a horse thief seven hundred miles? What did the horseman value so highly? Certainly not a pony the thief was riding. And if not a horse, what was the real reason for the race? What motive did the Frenchman have? The only sensible answer was gold!

On the other hand, the more Meade thought about the conversation Hankerson had overheard, the more he thought there could be an advantage to himself if he quietly encouraged the tale of a solitary rider braving a hundred deadly risks and hazards to recover what he had worked so hard to obtain. A romantic at heart, Meade had understood instantly the reason Louis Remme had chosen to tell the lie that he was chasing a horse thief. It was simple to explain. And the declaration demanded immediate action so the pursuer of the horse thief was delayed for the minimum time required to change saddles from a tired horse to a fresh one. And it relied on a tradition of the frontier. The buyer of the fresh horse at an average cost of $60 to $80 had the privilege of reselling the animal to the original owner at a discount of ten percent if the horse was sound when it was returned.

The whole idea of one against the enemy, one against the wind, reflected the exciting spirit of the westering wave. And Louis Remme was an outstanding example of the individual's freedom to choose his own course and risk his life as the price of that choice.

Meade was suddenly excited. Louis Remme was a man to bet on. His ride and the hazards he had to overcome constituted the beginnings of a legend. Legends were bigger than life. Why not wager on the legend? Why not encourage Hankerson to tell other passengers about Louis Remme and the impossible task he had set out to do? Why not get talk going on Remme's chances of success, and risk some of his own money on the outcome? There were gamblers on board, fancy women, soldiers with army pay in their pockets, businessmen who liked to take a chance, and the officers of the *Columbia* who were not opposed to risking a few dollars on

Lady Luck. The excitement could divert questions about the *Columbia* cargo. Who would believe the steamship actually carried almost two million in gold? If it came to a showdown Meade could display the Writ of Attachment as proof of the bankruptcy action in San Francisco. It would provide the evidence to Oregonians of their misfortune. But it didn't answer his own disturbing question of why so much gold was suspiciously present in the heavy safe of the *Columbia*.

The lines of a poem Meade had not thought about in years, a poem he'd learned in school, popped into his head. It was so very suitable, as if written especially, to describe Louis Remme:

Such deeds ennoble a mortal,
Single him out of the herd,
Fling wide immorality's portal,
And make of his name a grand word.

Ralph Meade decided, win or lose, that he would bet on Louis Remme, and, without making it seem intentional, he would quietly encourage Hankerson to ask about Remme from new passengers who came onboard at the next stop at Gardiner, Oregon. If there was word of Remme, someone was bound to bring it onboard the *Columbia*. On the frontier gossip spread like chicken pox. It was always uncanny to Meade how news of events a hundred miles apart traveled overland without wheels. There was a small military post at Gardiner—expected to get much larger—where many frontiersmen, traders, army men and their wives, worked, lived, bartered, and traveled to and from the interior as far east as the Willamette Valley. By crow's flight the fertile region was only about sixty or seventy miles or so from the coast.

After Gardiner, the *Columbia's* last stop on the coast before heading upriver to Portland was Astoria. That too was a thriving town where gossip was a way of life.

CHAPTER TEN

DARKNESS WAS CLOSING IN when Remme left the Kavanaugh farm and faced the long, wet night ahead of him on a broad-backed horse that slowed into a bone-jarring trot whenever he thought Remme wasn't paying attention. But the animal's stubbornness was endurable because Whitey demonstrated remarkable strength. The horse would need it to get Remme over the muddied Indian trail they were following. There was no more than a trace of it in the darkness.

While Remme was certain that he had put the threat of Indians and mountain snow behind him, the obstacle facing him now until he reached Portland was drenching rain. In the wet months of early spring in western Oregon, the land became a giant sponge that soaked up water in every pore and cell. Time after time, immigrants had been stranded by thick, relentless rains that formed walls of descending water. Every blade of grass, crevice in the earth, curved leaf, nook, and hollow was filled to overflowing with the drainage from the skies. Men and women confined to frontier cabins learned to hate the insidious rain that filled every ditch, weighted every plant and tree, and invaded every human crevice that presented a dimple for water to find. Tables, chairs, door frames, and windows swelled with the insistent moisture. Tempers flared or people became cranky and morose. Settlers in wagons had been stranded for days at a time in driving rain that created shallow rivers and lakes on the ground and released the earth on hillsides to flow down in thick mud slides, like curdled molasses. A half a dozen rain-glutted rivers whose banks could be awash with overflow stood between Remme and his final objective, Portland.

Still, he forced the big horse to plod at a steady lope north, his hooves a sodden drumbeat on the flooded ground as he drove through the slanting wet. Soaked to his skin, Remme was grateful for small blessings. One was his durable hat that acted as a barrier to the descending drops. The wide brim of the sturdy felt had soaked up so much moisture that it flopped over Remme's forehead and the beat of the rain was like a constant roar in his ears. But the portion of the brim extending over his collar, also bent with moisture, protected his neck and carried the water pouring off the crown past his coat collar. If there was one thing Remme hated it was water trickling down the back of his neck.

About midnight in a gray curtain of persistent rain, Remme pulled Whitey to a halt, dismounted, and stamped his deadened legs to return the circulation. He was famished and removed a jar of peaches from his saddlebags. In the downpour, he screwed the lid open and drank the sweet juice in big gulps, then ate the peach halves and realized how hungry he was. He chewed on a piece of tough beef jerky as he climbed back into the saddle, heading into the dark side of dawn.

In the miles between midnight and daybreak the rain-blown rider thought again about his grandfather whose angry voice had raised him from the snow. He could picture the sharp face of the old man and wondered if, like his grandson, Paul Remme had ever had a moment of terrible weakness when he had survived the cold breath of death and lost faith in himself temporarily? His grandfather had believed that men and women who exercised self-discipline could accomplish virtually anything. Had he ever seriously doubted himself? Of course, he had, Remme realized, or he wouldn't have understood the weakness in another man. Somehow understanding that about his grandfather made him feel better, stronger.

Sunup found Remme on the banks of the South Umpqua River near the small settlement of Roseburg. The South Umpqua descended from the north, then made a U-turn and headed southwest, where it became the North Umpqua, until it flowed into the Pacific. It was his fourth day in the saddle. He knew what was ahead of him and he dreaded it. The rain had stopped and a golden radiance drew miniature rainbows and sparks of light from dozens of puddles in the grass. He smiled when he saw a new spider web hanging between two bushes. It was a reliable weather sign that clear skies had replaced the rain. So were the few clouds called mare's tails in the blue sky. His grandfather had taught Remme if the thin streaky clouds pointed downward the way a horse's tail drops naturally, the weather would be calm and dry. But if the mare's tail was held high, like ascending streaks that point upward, high winds and stormy weather were on the way. The configuration in the sky was a good omen.

Though the South Umpqua River was high and dangerous to cross—a torrent of brown water carrying uprooted trees, bushes, shrubs, and small dead animals—Remme's passage on Whitey was made much easier when he discovered a fir tree that lay across the river like a fallen giant. The big fir had toppled when its deep roots had been undermined by the swollen river digging away the bank where it stood. The barrier formed by the fallen tree created a lake on the upstream side of the fir. Between the small lake and the shore was a wet little island partially submerged. The question in Remme's mind as he held on to Whitey's tail as the big horse plunged into the river and churned the water, was whether or not the island was solid? It was an uneven platform of natural wreckage. The river had woven tangled grass, knotted twigs, leaves from bushes, splintered tree branches, and chunks of sod into a slow-moving mattress. It was dragging over the bottom of the river, collecting more trash torn loose by wind and rain. Probably a sizable chunk of earth had been gouged out of farm pasture by the thrashing current and carried downstream.

Remme found out soon enough about the nature of the island when the muddied horse pulled himself up on the grassy bar, and shook himself, spraying Remme with water, mud, and leaves. Even as Remme dragged himself erect, using Whitey's long tail to lift his body out of the water, he knew landing on the island was a mistake. For as he pulled himself up, Whitey screamed and his haunches suddenly dropped. He sank down to his rear knees.

His frantic squealing puzzled Remme only for the moment it took him to realize that Whitey's terror was not caused by the mushy floating island that was too waterlogged to support his heavy weight. Something far more frightening was threatening the sturdy horse.

On his hands and knees scrambling past Whitey, who was sinking deeper in the sucking mud and swampy morass, Remme pulled his rifle out of the leather scabbard tied to his saddle. For only an instant he had glimpsed the shaggy form that lifted his massive head from the swollen carcass of a small drowned calf he had snagged from the river. It was a grizzly, almost hidden behind a wild acacia bush where he was feeding on his prize.

Grizzlies were smart hunters, Remme knew and was certain the big furry animal had stationed himself on the bank of the river near the floating island and had waited patiently for a victim of the flooding water course to be carried to where he stood.

Remme had not seen the bear when he rode Whitey into the fast water, but when the big white horse boosted himself onto the swampy bar, he had smelled the bear, screamed, and backed away when he saw the giant raise his head, dripping with blood.

And now, as Remme feared, the grizzly abandoned the decaying carcass, and suddenly rushed toward the riverbank on all fours. A frightened horse, caught in a trap of weeds, sod, and grass was a fresh meal for a week or two at least. And Remme was certain the ravenous bear, probably just emerged a few days early from his winter hibernation, would be starved for warm flesh.

He knew his own life would be lost if he couldn't stop the bear before he splashed into the river and attacked Whitey. One swipe from one of his long arms, sharp claws, and thick paw pads would smash Whitey's head like a squash and Remme wouldn't escape the bear's rush.

He was shaking with fear. His hands and fingers felt numb, his body detached, as he raised his rifle. There was no doubt in is mind that he would be dead if his first shot did not stop the grizzly in his tracks.

As he aimed the rifle at the bear's right eye, he was the ten-year-old on his grandfather's farm in Quebec facing another grizzly with a secondhand gun and hot wetness in his pants from his fears dribbling down one leg.

When the grizzly splashed into the cold water, three things happened at once. Wild-eyed with fear, Whitey sprang from the island trap, like a scared rabbit leaping from danger, his powerful rear legs propelling him in a burst of strength out of water to the right of the grizzly's path. In the same moment—Remme, standing chest deep in the river centered in the flotsam of the island—pressed his finger on the trigger of his rifle. The rifle exploded—a fine spray of water spurting from the barrel. It made a trail of mist and the bullet struck the grizzly in his right eye. It gouged a terrible hole that blossomed with dark blood like a flower shredded by a high wind. The grizzly's momentum carried him forward past Whitey about four feet until he crashed across the island with his forepaws extended and his sharp claws sticking out. He landed with a huge splash only a foot from Remme. The grizzly's weight broke through the swampy mattress of the floating island, making a big hole where his body began to sink.

Holding his rifle high, Remme waded out of the river and climbed the bank. To his surprise Whitey was standing quietly, twenty feet away with his head down. Remme replaced his rifle in the leather scabbard. Then, talking softly to the big horse who, like him, was shivering from cold and the aftereffects of his fright, he readjusted the leather saddle which had slipped and loosened on the horse's back.

Exhausted, feeling stiff and frozen in every bone, Remme knew it was critical for him and his horse to dry out. He led the animal forward into the Umpqua Canyon, his teeth chattering and a dread weariness in his muscles, making walking an aching effort.

What cheered Remme was that Umpqua Canyon wasn't storming, unlike the October nine years earlier when he first passed through it.

Remme had originally traveled through the Umpqua Canyon about six months after he left his grandfather's farm in Quebec in 1845. Traveling by horse south and west doing odd jobs for about three years, he finally reached St. Louis, Missouri. He soon found a job with an outfitter who sold provisions to emigrants bound for Oregon or California. It was amazing to Remme how many families were completely ill-equipped for a covered wagon adventure of hundreds of miles. Practical items such as wheel hub grease, water-tight canisters to keep flour dry, salt, spare wheels, extra canvas to patch holes in the sturdy cloth when accidents occurred to the original covering, and medical supplies for people who became ill. At least three dozen indispensible items were stocked by the outfitter and he did a brisk business.

Remme caught the Oregon fever from the optimism of settlers headed for the last frontier and finally hired out for a train of nineteen wagons as a hunter. His job: keep the emigrants supplied with wild game. By the time the caravan arrived at Fort Hall, Idaho, Remme had become acquainted with most of the emigrants and was fond of the children who loved him to sing to them.

It was at Fort Hall that Remme met Jesse and Lindsay Applegate. There the two who had gathered a crew of volunteers to scout and build a southern Oregon route to the Willamette Valley convinced many settlers to take the Applegate Trail. It was to be the life-saving alternative to the Columbia River route. This wide untamed river had taken the lives of dozens of emigrants who built log rafts hastily lashed together, for a threatening ride to Fort Vancouver through rapids, whirlpools, and strong currents. Even those who constructed sturdy rafts upon which they tied down their wagon beds and canopies lost much of their belongings to the Columbia. There came so many thousands of emigrants in the mid-1840s that wood for both rafts and campfires was scarce. Most were obliged to endure the elements without protection. They shivered as the wet winds howled through the gorge and soaked them to the skin. Children and adults often disappeared when a sudden hole in the river swallowed them, then filled up again. Even with the losses and tragedies the people waiting for *bateaux* from the Hudson's Bay Company or renting Indian canoes were only slightly more safe.

Remme like the way the Applegates talked about their shortcut and he decided to head for the southern route on his own. Later he discovered that when the road builders had laid out the trail in the summer and early autumn of 1846, they had faced unbelievable difficulties. They admitted they had been confronted with the single most dangerous stretch through a part of the Calapoolia Mountains. It was a passage through the Umpqua Canyon where nature had created a boulder-strewn creek which was the solitary entrance to the country beyond.

The steep canyon was a formidable threat, for once a family entered the canyon creek, there was no turning back. The creek bed was the actual road over which oxen and wagons were drawn. The bottom of the creek was littered with boulders and large stones that had to be moved to allow the covered wagons to proceed through the low water. Still it was a backbreaking chore for men to guide their oxen over the slippery bottom. When the rains came pouring down in stinging waves of water, raising the level of the creek, many of the tired travelers all but gave up coping with the weather and the mudslides that came rumbling down from the high walls of the canyon.

Remme, unencumbered with a fragile and awkward wagon and its precious household contents each family had brought along, was as helpful as he could be. But many of the pioneers, either sick, disappointed, weak from travel and short rations, resented being hurried along. And they hated the rainstorms that chilled them to the bone.

One pioneer family named Smith was typical of those who delayed their canyon trek arguing about leaving their wagon and continuing on foot.

William Smith, their captain, would have nothing to do with abandoning the wagons. He built a large fire of logs and gathered everyone around. He insisted it was folly to give up their wagons, the rain would certainly stop and the creek would subside.

While he was deliberating, he sank to his knees in the middle of the trail and called out, "Lord, have mercy upon me." No sooner had he uttered the prayer, than he fell forward without another sound onto the trail and died. Smith left behind his wife, Ellen and nine children. The oldest was Rufus, fifteen.

From the little spring wagon his father had planned to use to carry his children through the canyon, Rufus went to work building a coffin box. They buried Smith in it beside the Umpqua Creek close to where he died, and built a crude fence around his grave.

There were other deaths and Remme helped with the burials. One was the son of J. D. Wood, Alonzo, who died in their wagon of a persistent illness. Shortly after Alonzo's death, the wagon turned over with his body in it, along with beehives which his father had brought all the way along the emigrant trail. The bees drowned in the creek.

The emigrant Remme admired the most was the sixty-eight-year-old woman named Tabitha Brown. On horseback, she had guided her husband, Captain Brown through the terrible stretch, with a resolve like iron. Fearing her husband, ten years older than she, would never survive their second night in the dark canyon, she spread a canvas sheet above their heads to protect them from the relentless, icy rain.

They sat miserable and wet under the tarpaulin with their backs to a tree and slept on and off with the drumming sound of the pelting rain beating against the canvas. Captain Brown did survive that awful night and the couple made it out of the canyon. A day later, as Tabitha led her horse with Captain Brown, weak, discouraged, and chilled to the bone, holding on desperately to the saddle horn, suddenly toppled to the ground. He had given up the ghost and Remme was one of the volunteers who helped to dig his grave.

As for Tabitha Brown, Remme later learned that her determination took her through to Salem where she started a school for orphans of the Oregon Trail.

Most of the pioneers made it through the wretched canyon and to an encampment at the end where there was grass for oxen to eat and sunshine that brightened the land. At least three other victims of the Umpqua Canyon never reached the end. They included a new mother and her firstborn who expired in the bitter rain a few hours after she delivered.

In the nine years since he last traveled through the canyon, Remme noted that in places the watery road was still a slippery, stumbling passage for animals, though improvements had been made.

Remme's hope was that the canyon this year was the site of recent gold mining activity. If what he'd heard was true, there were sure to be some deserted shacks where he could find shelter and build a fire after he washed himself in a cold stream and led Whitey to splash and roll the mud off his hide in clear water.

There was no doubt in Remme's mind that if he pressed on in his wet and mouldering clothes with his physical resistance low, he would be inviting a collapse that would end his race to beat the steamship to Portland.

As Remme led Whitey into the canyon where the water was high, he discovered a sudden plague of quicksand and shifting ground. So slippery was the bottom of the stream that it was difficult for Whitey to keep his balance on the mossy rocks which trapped his hooves in the spaces between the stones. With every step he took, pulling his feet out of the swift water there was a sound like a muffled gunshot—a gurgling pop!

Remme had given up riding the horse, and choosing the ground he stepped carefully to avoid the worst places. But his effort was futile. Whitey's half-ton of weight, even minus the burden of his rider, sank his big feet just as deeply into the rocky snags. Miserable, feeling feverish and fighting against the sinking feeling that he could not hang on much longer, Remme's spirits lifted when, just off to one side of the canyon, he spotted two deserted wooden shacks on the banks of a small tributary that flowed into the larger Umpqua stream.

Remme stopped his horse in front of the first cabin, walked slowly, and leaned against the wooden door. It was swollen shut with moisture. Impatient and peevish, he stepped back and kicked the door and it screeched open. At least the door was not a prisoner of ice like the cabin he had set on fire to warm the blood of the piebald and himself when they reached the bottom of the Siskiyous half frozen.

Inside, as Remme looked around, immense relief gave him a boost. There were a table and two wooden chairs, empty shelves for canned goods, and a cast-iron stove from which a rusty pipe ran up through the roof. The roof was made of rough planks covered with squares of dried mud held together with grass. Somebody had lived here for quite a while.

After Remme pulled his saddlebags off of Whitey's back, it took him only ten minutes when he returned to the cabin to pull down the wooden shelves, break them into small pieces over his knee, and stuff them into the cold stove. He adjusted the damper on the exhaust pipe so the stove would take in air to feed the fire when he lighted the wood. With a precious wooden match he took from a small bunch kept dry in his Prince Albert tobacco can, he ignited the tinder from a small pouch he carried. When the flames were burning brightly, Remme stepped outside, where he discovered a small lean-to at the back of the shack where he could put Whitey. Then, after leading the horse into the stream, he splashed water generously on Whitey and himself after removing the dirty saddle and blanket and all his clothes, which he washed free of mud in the running water. He scrubbed his hair, face, and body with a small bar of cold-water soap he always carried with him. Downstream he plunged into a deeper hole to rinse his body clean. When he emerged from the stream, his skin was puckered and wrinkled like a chicken whose feathers had wilted, and he was shaking and blue with the cold.

Smart horse that he was, Whitey, free of the saddle and bridle, rolled and kicked in the stream until his hide and mane drained clean. Then, standing on a grassy spot he shook himself, spraying water like a fountain. Still naked and shivering, Remme led the horse to the lean-to and gave him an apple from the small store of food he had packed in his saddlebags.

Inside the cabin again, he laid out his wet clothes and saddlebags on the bare floor in front of the hot iron stove, propped his head on his saddle, and dozed on and off for two hours. He rose to replenish the fire only when the roaring flames consumed the wood and required more fuel. The wooden table lasted until his clothes had almost dried.

It was not until almost three hours after he left the cabin that he pulled Whitey to a stop. They had left the canyon behind and he couldn't believe he'd been so stupid, so unaware of what he had done. After they had dried out and revived, they had trudged out of the terrible canyon, and he had pointed Whitey northwest instead of north. How could he have been so careless? Bitter and angry with himself, he realized his mind was so dull with fatigue that he had failed to notice how the prevailing wind, which always came from the ocean west over the coastal mountains, had grown stronger. Even now, it was striking him full in his face and body, instead of his left side as it had been while he rode north.

Sighing, Remme turned Whitey north, jabbing the big horse in his ribs to make him move faster. His was a foolish, time-stealing mistake, and he'd have to make up for it. Used to relying on himself, Remme did not resort to an appeal to the God that had made the world, and the sun and the stars. He knew there was a power immensely greater than his own. But he couldn't make an excuse for his mistake by asking God to help him overcome the consequences of his error. Instead, Remme had always put his faith in himself, for he was convinced that any man who acknowledged nature's immutable laws and exercised self-discipline could accomplish anything.

Later that same day, less than an hour before sundown, Remme entered the village of Winchester located on the north fork of the river. There he dismounted, almost falling to his knees, then recovering when his stiffness drained away. He introduced himself to Joseph Knott who owned a trading post and tavern. The early evening had turned suddenly bitterly cold and Remme was anxious to get Whitey into a warm stall with a bellyful of oats and a rubdown. The big animal was trembling with fatigue.

"You look done in yourself," Knott remarked as he led Remme, with Whitey trailing behind him, to the barn. Knott's observation was an invitation for Remme to tell the man why he was in such a hurry and Remme obliged by repeating the lie about chasing a horse thief he had told so often. Only once had he told the truth. That had been to Tom Horsley in Yreka. The older man's face had been a weathered map of wrinkles. Every line was a mark of toil and honesty. He had reminded Remme of his own father to whom he had never lied, for to do so would have dishonored the trust Robert Remme placed in his son.

"Horse thief or not," Knott said, "you look all in, son. If it was me, I'd take a snooze in some fresh hay for a couple of hours while I dry out your sheepskin next to the fire in the kitchen. Throw that horse blanket hanging in the stall around you and you should sleep warm. First, though," Knott said, pointing out two horses, "you'd better decide which one of those knotheads you want to trade for. So far, you've been lucky striking fair weather and hard roads, except for Umpqua Creek Canyon, but you won't carry it much further. It will be about all you can do to reach the coast fork of the Willamette on one horse. You can take your choice of those two. The roan is the faster by far, but the sorrel is much the strongest walker and my hunch is that it'll be pretty muddy from here to the Willamette. Rain's been heavy for most of a week. But the cold snap that's just hit us may mean light snow and icing coming up."

Acting on Knott's advice, Remme chose the sorrel, bought a thick beef sandwich and a cup of steaming black coffee from the trader who took his soggy sheepskin, and promised to wake Remme in two hours with his dry coat and the sorrel saddled and ready to go.

When Remme drew the horse blanket over his shoulder, he was asleep in moments and did not stir until about an hour later when his face reflected the anxiety of his sleeping mind. His body twitched nervously and his arms thrashed the air as if he were fighting off monsters. Suddenly, he sat straight up bewildered, frightened, and reaching for his gun. He looked wildly around him, then took a deep breath when he recognized the stable. Then he remembered the nightmare that had awakened him. The grizzly he had killed in the Umpqua River had revived an old memory of another grizzly he had faced when he was a ten-year-old boy. It flashed into his mind again, briefly, then, safe in the present he curled up under the horse blanket and was soon dead to the world.

Scarface would have killed Remme if it hadn't been for old Morey Whitetail. An Iroquois Indian, Morey had been a fur trapper and worked off and on at the farm of Remme's grandfather's in Quebec while Remme was growing up. As a boy he had always admired the copper-skinned, gray-haired man, thin as a rail who seemed to glide over the ground where other men walked. His dress never varied: he wore a deerskin shirt and pants and his narrow feet were encased in deerskin moccasins tied at the ankles. He carried all of his worldly goods in a thin blanket and he hunted with a long rifle that fired from the powder Morey kept in an old weatherproofed polished horn that dangled by his right side from a long leather thong that crossed his chest and back. A soft but sturdy leather belt around his waist supported a long, sharp knife in a buckskin holder. A large pocket was sewn on his shirt over his left hip and contained round lead bullets for his rifle, and his pipe was embedded in a small pouch of tobacco. Also in his pocket were some other odds and ends including a flint to strike sparks for fire making. His hair had once been black years earlier and though nobody knew exactly how old Morey was, Remme was certain from things he'd said that he was in his eighties and still lean and tough as whipcord. His father had fought and died in the French and Indian war which older folks still remembered vaguely when Remme was ten.

One night when Morey was a little drunk—he liked whiskey and was sleeping in the hayloft at the barn—he told Remme about how his father had died. Morey had learned about his father from his mother when he was a boy about Remme's age. She had told him that after the end of the French and Indian war the British finally caught up with Graylocks. That was the name his father was known by when he was a spy for the French during the long conflict for control of Canada and what became the Northeastern United States. Though the British won, their victory led to the American War of Independence. Morey's father got the name Graylocks because his hair was prematurely grey. His son had inherited the same trait.

Morey's mother was present when Graylocks stood before the British firing squad and she listened to words she didn't understand from an officer who described the reason for the death sentence imposed upon her husband. She was proud of the way Graylocks died and she knew he had acted crazy and dangerous at the end to spare the feelings of the young soldiers who were ordered to shoot him. He had done his best to look fierce and ready to spring at the men holding their rifles, as if he was going to tear out their throats. Before the roar of their guns, he spat out an Iroquois curse at them, which he knew his own people would interpret for themselves as his declaration of pride.

Of course, Graylocks' performance was a lie, but it was a great lie to convince his children and theirs that came after that he was a worthy example who could laugh at death. Actually, he had never killed a single person, or wanted to, and that was a reputation he left behind to be held close to the heart.

"Can I go with you to hunt the grizzly?" Remme had asked.

Morey had taken out his evil-smelling pipe, filled it with tobacco, and said, "Now, that's up to your grandpa."

"I'd be a big help," the boy said eagerly. "I could take a stand and help turn the griz, when the dogs run him, and I could rustle up firewood and make camp."

"I can't promise anything, boy. Not unless your gramps agrees."

"But, is it all right with you?"

"If it's okay with him."

Remme had known that his persistence would pay off. Now, all he had to do was to tell Grandpa Remme that Morey said he could go on the hunt if it was all right with him.

He thought about when he'd first seen the bear that he called Scarface. He was a medium-sized grizzly, not heavy, lean-looking and angry because his lower jaw was twisted so that his mouth was open in a snarl that revealed one of the long sharp upper fangs used for tearing. He was red-eyed and mean looking when Remme first saw him in the pasture where he had killed two goats and half eaten one. He came upon the grizzly when his path from a stream he fished passed by the fenced enclosure for goats and sheep. He had not seen the animal until he was less than 150 feet away and the bear suddenly reared up on its hind legs and pawed the air. One look at the huge creature and Remme dropped his fishing pole and the three small trout he'd caught and he ran. He looked over his shoulder once and the bear had dropped back on the ground to continue his feeding.

That was when the feeling of shame overcame Remme. He had run, so scared that he had wet his pants a little.

Even after he told his father and mother, and of course, his grandpa, Paul, what he'd seen, and was told that running from a mad bear was not cowardice, he could not square his behavior with his conscience.

When he learned a week later that the bear had been attacking small domestic animals on other farms and had alarmed folks with his huge scarred face, twisted jaw, and skewed left eye, he was not satisfied that he had acted properly. It was all right to run to avoid danger, to run if you are afraid for your life, but to run because you are too frightened to think clearly, that was wrong.

For the next two months Remme went out of his way to learn about the bear's habits. He asked questions of the boys at his school and listened in on the male gossip at the general store where the men gathered on Saturdays to smoke and drink a little corn liquor.

Little by little he put together the tidbits of information he overheard into an explanation for the bear's anger and his attacks on farm animals. Apparently, the bear had been in a fight with another grizzly and had suffered a crushing blow that broke his jaw and dislocated his left eye. Instead of being centered in the eye socket, it had healed so that the line of sight veered off at an angle. As for his jaw, it was a source of pain as it healed crookedly, but it kept the bear from clamping tightly on food. One of the big nerves was exposed, and any pressure on it brought excruciating pain. The bear suffered greatly but, like most wild creatures, learned to live with the discomfort.

It was necessary for the bear, which was a six-year-old male, to get by with his condition, and slowly he learned what actions caused the least pain. Naturally agile with his powerful forepaws, he soon learned to do all of his hunting and killing with them. No longer did he kill small animals quickly by sinking its teeth through the skull. Instead, he dealt a smashing blow.

Gathering his courage, Remme, who'd absorbed the ways of the forests by watching Morey carefully when he accompanied the Indian on hunting excursions, had begun to secretly follow the grizzly's trail. It wasn't hard to read. The grizzly survived on berries, insects, and fruit which required little grinding under his massive teeth. He varied his diet with an occasional small rodent, found alive or dead. Whenever possible the bear ate things that could be licked up on his raspy tongue and swallowed whole, like ants and grubs. As the spring wore on into hot summer, the bear preyed more and more on larvae and such things as frogs, minnows, and wild bees for their honey, rather than his preferred diet of grass, berries, and nuts. It was painful to chew on any object that was crushed between his teeth. Remme discovered that he had made a week of meals from the decaying carcass of an elk who'd broken its neck trying to free its rack of horns from the crotch of a tree where they were caught.

By adjusting to its new handicap, the bear managed to get by, but he lost about twenty percent of his weight in the first two months. Because of his handicap, the animal chose to sleep in remote thickets, small caverns, or holes in trees from which he could escape quickly if he was observed. He liked to wallow in shallow water, drank a lot to soothe his sore jaw, and traveled day and night to feed his appetite and find new prey over a twenty-mile area.

By fall, Remme felt certain he knew the habits the bear had adopted to suit his altered hunting ways and he was not surprised when he found one of the hounds who lived on the farm dead. With her eviscerated body were the remains of two pups who'd been nursing.

The bear was getting restless and Remme could almost think his thoughts. In another month the leaves would begin to fall and then would come the cold weather. Instinct told the grizzly that he must get fat before snow time or he would fail to live through the winter.

When the first cold mornings descended, Remme decided he had figured out what the grizzly would do next and explained his theory to Morey Whitetail. The Indian listened thoughtfully to Remme, then smiled at him and said, "You've grown pretty smart. I guess it's time we'd better go after Mr. Bear before he gets too close."

Remme's predictions came true before Morey got to talk to Paul Remme.

The grizzly attacked a small herd of shoats—pigs just weaned from their mother. They were about three months old, fat, and the perfect prey for the bear whose jaw had finally healed so that he didn't scream with pain when pressure was applied.

It was late afternoon when the grizzly, staying in the shadows of a fringe of trees a few hundred yards from the main farmhouse, spotted a solitary pig apart from the pack rooting for acorns at the edge of the forest.

With a quick swipe of his huge clawed paw, the grizzly smashed the piglet a deadly blow. It squealed once, a high scream that frightened the others in the pack and they ran back toward the farmhouse.

The grizzly feasted on the pig for two days. Then, encouraged by his success, moved on, close to the creek by the farm and the odor of the domestic pigs. The bear became very clever and wary. The first time he heard the dogs coming, he found a hole in a cliff and waited for the baying hounds from the farm to find him.

There was no way for the dogs to come at him, except by a ledge one at a time, and the grizzly killed two before climbing the steep bluff behind him and heading for the distant, deep forest.

Having found a food supply and defeated the dogs, he quickly adjusted to the domestic ways.

The night the grizzly broke into the pigpen, the squealing shoats and the terrified grunting and screaming of the hogs and the excited hounds who could smell the wild animal in the cold air, was alarm enough to wake the household including Morey, who was spending the night in the hayloft in the barn.

By the time Remme had pulled on his shirt and pants and stuck his feet into his lace-up shoes and tied them quickly, he could hear Morey, his father Robert, and his grandfather talking hurriedly on the front porch. Before he opened the front door, holding the second-hand rifle his father had given him for his birthday, it had already been decided that Morey would track the bear and Robert would take a roundabout reconnoiter with four dogs and head through the cow pastures on a wide semicircle that would take him to a rendezvous point with Morey near the river flats. They were at the bottom of a high stone ridge with caves in it some animals used to hibernate.

When Morey said, “I’ll take the boy with me; he’s got sharp eyes,” Remme held his breath. He saw his mother was about to object, then, as if she lost an argument with herself, she made the decision that ever after he was grateful for.

Feeling older because of his mother’s approval, Remme walked along, stretching his legs as far as they would reach to keep up with Morey’s effortless ground-eating pace. While they moved, Remme told Morey what he had learned about the grizzly and when he was finished with his description, Morey stopped, turned to Remme, placed a hand on his shoulder, and said, “You’ve got the makings of a woodsman. Where do you think the bear will head?”

Proud of the compliment more than he could say, Remme explained that it was his hunch the grizzly would head " . . . for the bluff just west of here. It's the only good crossing on the creek, a place where a bear could wade but dogs would have to swim. You know where I mean. Beyond is the swamp, where the frogs make a big racket at night and the canebrakes are thick as brush."

Morey nodded and led the way to the ledge where they would wait for the bear. He squatted and placed the unlighted lantern he'd been carrying at a wide place in the path where he could rest his back against a tree. He had matches for the lantern in his one big pocket. He motioned for Remme to sit crosslegged, put his rifle across his knees, and be quiet.

For Remme, it was an occasion he had dreamed of when he had hunted by himself, for deer and small game. Alone in the blue night that sang of life in every form was like participating in a mystery he knew was as old as the stars. Mosquitoes buzzed around them, but didn't light. Far away, the hounds' bellowing died as they crossed a hollow, grew loud as they topped a rise in the woods. Then their sounds faded altogether, and there was silence.

For a long hour the Indian squatted silently, Remme beside him almost not daring to breathe, listening to the night sounds and the distant dogs.

And then they heard it, the scuffing of the approaching bear, with the hounds tracking behind. It seemed to be only a minute but it was longer until the bear struck the creek with loud splashing that reached up to the bluff where Remme and Morey waited. Morey smiled to himself that the boy had guessed right. He'd calculated himself that the ridge was the best defensive spot for the bear. And Remme had come to the same conclusion by adding bits and pieces of observations together. A few more years and the boy would be acting on intuition, which was experience added to known facts.

As for Robert, he would not catch up in time to see the grizzly killed.

Though he couldn't pretend to know what Remme was thinking about at this moment, Morey knew the boy had pursued the bear because he was deathly afraid of it. Chasing something you feared was a sign of courage. The boy was learning that. Also, he bet the boy was admiring the grizzly for being a smart bear. A bear, who, if he lived, would father a generation that might outwit the white man farmers who would otherwise destroy him and his kind. That was the shame of it, but it was the truth of life. Life had to make way for other life.

Scarface had become an outlaw, an unpredictable savage that could outsmart anyone but the boy and Morey who understood him. Morey scratched a match and lighted the lantern, hid it in a rock crevice, and cocked his 45-70 with the octagonal barrel in his lap.

When the the sounds of the grizzly's scuffling out of the creek onto the north bank reached the Indian's and the boy's ears, Morey was certain the bear would climb to the narrow part of the path and turn on the dogs that were in the creek yelping behind him. Morey warned Remme to stay calm, cock his rifle, and listen for the bear climbing the rocks and his heavy woofing snort when he turned to face the hounds. Smart bear that he was, he had picked a stand midway on the ledge. It was narrow so only one dog at a time had room to attack him.

"When the first hound reaches the grizzly," Morey explained in a soft whisper, "the bear is going to stand on its hind legs and sweep the air in front of the dog with its long powerful forelegs and claws. They can tear the hide right off a hound."

Both Morey and Remme prepared themselves for what was to come.

Morey pulled the lantern from the crevice where he'd placed it and turned up the wick. The light flooded the area now, illuminating the grizzly who had reached the ledge and was still on his four feet. Remme could smell the animal—the wild, hot odor of him stabbed him with fear! He could hear his grunting breath. Not a minute later, a black hound, teeth bared, darted up the ledge and stopped just far enough from the bear's reach. The dog didn't pay any attention to the lantern, or Morey or Remme. His rigid focus and quivering eagerness was pointed at only one object—the big, grayish brown bear with the faint silver stripe down its back. Then, with sudden darting lunges, the black hound leaped into the range of the grizzly and out again, irritating the shaggy monster and calling to the hounds in the creek.

Morey knew he couldn't get a clean shot until Blackie dared the bear with a frontal assault that would force the grizzly to rise to his full height and sweep a murderous paw at the dog. If it connected, the hound would die instantly. Remme held his breath, his right hand grasping his rifle in an iron grip as he saw Blackie react to a sudden hiss from Morey. It was a signal for the hound to attack, relying on his faith in the man with a gun, as he had so often. Blackie acted on Morey's prompting. He darted at the grizzly, nipping his nose and raising blood with his sharp teeth. The bear stiffened, howled with rage, and rose to his full height, swinging his long right paw with the claws extended. Then above the bear's roar, Remme heard the distinct unnatural click. It was the sound of metal striking metal—and he knew, even as he swung his rifle to his shoulder, that Morey's gun had misfired. In that same terrible moment, he saw the grizzly swing his shaggy head away from the dog which lay quivering and bleeding at his feet and stare red-eyed and furious at Remme. And as Remme fixed fearfully on the monster—impelled by the wild bear's hot gaze on him—he heard the calm, firm words of Morey: "In his eye, Louis, in his eye. Shoot him!"

The rifle was already centered on the grizzly's head, on his skewed left eye. Then Remme pulled the trigger—unconscious of the pressure on his finger—of the sudden roar—the spouting flame, and the shock to his shoulder. The huge, bristly creature with the dark red hole in his head, who had started toward Remme, crashed to the ledge in a furry heap, then rolled slowly to the edge and flopped off, tumbling down the rocks, tearing up foliage, undergrowth, and tree sprouts in his descent to the creek where he came to a stop. The last thing Remme remembered clearly was the dogs shrieking and pawing at the limp carcass.

When Joseph Knott awakened Remme, the Frenchman thanked him and followed him to the house where Knott gave him his sheepskin. So vivid had been Remme's nightmare that for a moment he was lost in his recollection of that night twenty years ago.

He dwelled briefly, as he accepted a cup of steaming coffee from Knott, on the portent his killing of Scarface had meant to the ten-year-old boy. It was the single event in his life that had influenced his decision in the years that followed not to become like his father and grandfather, a farmer. The chilling close call with the grizzly in which his life and Morey's had depended on the courage of a frightened boy had been the turning point. From that time on, he had viewed life differently. Life was not a slow, lazy summer of lovely earth smells and green things growing to a slow dying, cold decaying and a spring of renewal. It was deeper than death and more inspiring than birth. It was a mysterious adventure full of complexities, joy, excitement, contradictions, wonder, anguish, and loss. For the first time, after Scarface's death, Remme understood old Morey whose eyes were always on the horizon. And that was where Remme decided he wanted to be, wherever indefinite promise took him. He had left home when he was nineteen and he believed his grandfather understood why.

CHAPTER ELEVEN

RALPH MEADE'S IDEA TO SUGGEST to Del Hankerson that new passengers coming aboard the *Columbia* at Fort Umpqua, Oregon may have heard fresh news about the progress north of Louis Remme received an enthusiastic welcome from the horse handler. A garrulous man who loved to chew the fat and palaver about controversial issues of any nature with anybody who'd give an opinion on a subject, Del was delighted with the purser's interest in the solitary horseman. His idea to question passengers already on board if they'd heard news of the fantastic race was bound to stir interest and it certainly did! The response Del got from the first man he spoke to about Louis Remme had been gratifying. A government surveyor, a stocky, bearded man with eyebrows and facial hair as thick and wild as blackberry tangles, whose name was Don Beecham, was fascinated by the idea of a man on horseback risking his skin in the wide path of the Rogue Indians raiding and killing whites in a swath of wilderness stretching east from the southern coast of Oregon.

"If what you say is true," Beecham sputtered, "the man's a fool or crazy. No amount of money would tempt me to risk my life like that. I wonder," he said, "how far he got after he left Yreka before he lost his scalp?"

While the prevailing view of the men and women aboard the *Columbia* was excitement and admiration over the image of a lone rider outsmarting a bank by his wits, endurance, and the running spirit of the horses he bought or borrowed, an equal number with money in Adams Express were clearly doubtful that Hankerson had got his facts right. Adams Express was as solid as Mt. Hood whose gleaming white mantle of snow reflected light on Portland sixty miles to the west.

"No sir," one doubter said, "the whole story is a lie, probably cooked up by the officials at Wells Fargo who're always trying to run down their competition."

When two sharp-eyed gamblers onboard heard about Remme's impossible ride, they seized on his adventure to start a wagering pool, a lottery. The pool would pay off the biggest amount in the pot to the better who wagered on Louis Remme winning the race with the *Columbia*. The second prize would go to the person who came closest to estimating Remme's arrival time in Portland after the *Columbia* docked. To add legitimacy to the wagering pool, Ralph Meade, the purser, was asked to hold the bets and disburse the money to the winners at the hotel where he was staying until the *Columbia* started her return trip to San Francisco. The price of each ticket was ten dollars. Obviously the more tickets a passenger bought wagering on different times of Remme's arrival in Portland, the greater his chances at winning the pot. The gamblers were to receive ten percent of the total pot for organizing the scheme.

Meade declined the responsibility of holding the pot. The gambler's second choice was Miss Elizabeth Teller, an old-maidish woman in her forties who taught school in Portland.

Dall, who like the other officers, had heard the gossip about Louis Remme, said it was wise for Meade to decline, but he could see no harm in the gambling pool as long as it didn't have the presumed approval of the ship's master by allowing one of her officers to hold the wagers.

As for Meade, he was undecided if he should risk some of his own money on a wager. If he won he would recover some of the losses he would suffer when the Writ of Attachment in his desk was served on the Adams agent in Portland. But if he guessed wrong, only the organizers of the betting pool would win a significant percentage of the pot. There was one strict condition imposed by Captain Dall on Meade. He was not to inform anyone aboard the *Columbia* that in the purser's possession were the legal papers that would close the bank to Oregon depositors. Earlier, Meade had decided that he'd be in a better position to make a wager if any fresh news of Remme could be gathered at Fort Umpqua. It would add to the betting fervor. Passengers were free to leave the ship after the *Columbia* dropped her anchor in the Umpqua River near the shore. The burden of secrecy weighed heavily on Meade's shoulders. He was deeply concerned that if the fact the *Columbia* was carrying almost two million in gold ever leaked, there could be a riot among the passengers, especially those who were depositors at the Adams branch in Portland. In a way, he was glad that Louis Remme was betting his life on beating the *Columbia* to Portland. It was an exciting diversion that increasingly dominated conversation among the passengers. It was fun for them to speculate on how far into Oregon the lone rider had reached. The betting pool encouraged curiosity and challenged the imagination. Meade had to admit to himself serious doubts about the truth of Hankerson's story. What man in his right mind—even a superb horseman—would dare to pit himself against steam paddles, the wilderness and all its dangers, on an impossible race? Still, Meade treasured his sense of wonder and excitement that persisted despite the illogic of such a mad purpose. But what if Louis Remme *was* real, a man who had thrown caution to the winds and embarked into the unknown with an inflexible backbone and the iron confidence to win over any obstacle?

Meade sighed. He had to walk a thin line or be caught in a violent uprising that could happen if anyone came aboard at the Umpqua landing who could confirm Hankerson's story. At the very least a witness would bring confusion and uncertainty to the *Columbia*.

Meade understood Captain Dall's reason for making the condition. The Pacific Mail Steamship Company might be held legally responsible for payments to passengers aboard the *Columbia* who managed to jump ship or reach the Portland office of Adams Express to recover their money before the Writ of Attachment could be served. It could be argued in court that without foreknowledge of the stop payment document a passenger would not have been motivated to reach the banking office before the writ was served. It was Meade's duty to be the first off the paddlewheeler to find an officer of the law to deliver at utmost speed the writ to Dr. Steinberger. But what was to stop a passenger from jumping ship based on the unsubstantiated rumor of Louis Remme's ride? Any passenger could leap overboard, risk the danger of being swept under the ship and drowned or swept into the thrashing side paddles and mashed to death. Still, if a man or woman was desperate enough, they might dive off the rear of the ship and swim to shore in the icy waters of the Willamette.

As he reconsidered how he had encouraged Hankerson to spread the story of Remme's ride and pump up enthusiasm for the betting pool, Ralph Meade felt guilty and ashamed. But now it was too late to change what he had started. He had to decide if he should make a bet in the pool, which he knew contained several hundred dollars.

Before he'd been overcome with dislike for himself, Meade had suggested to Del Hankerson that he stretch his legs on solid ground, and head for the sutler's store at the incomplete fort. He could discover if there was any word of the intrepid rider. As a matter of common sense, he warned Hankerson that the Indians of southern Oregon were still fiercely resisting the miners and settlers who were flooding into the forested lands of the natives. Among many of the whites mining for gold or settling on farms, there was a prevalent attitude that the Indians should be exterminated. Lives were being lost on both sides. It was inevitable, most Oregon frontiersmen believed, that with the Oregon Volunteers and army regulars fighting together the Indians would be defeated. One man in particular, Joel Palmer, Oregon Superintendent of Indian Affairs advocated a plan that would relocate Indians vanquished in the fighting to the central Oregon coast.

The Siletz Reservation would stretch for 125 miles along the Pacific shore surrounded on the east and the north by the Coast Range. The army had plans to establish four regional forts to enforce treaty rules that required the Indians to remain on reservations. One of those forts was located on the Umpqua River.

While there were some rudimentary buildings designated on the Umpqua as a U.S. Military Post in 1855, the whole lonely and isolated area between the river and the Pacific Ocean was home to about 2,400 native Indians and perhaps at the most two hundred white frontiersmen, settlers, and soldiers. The post was built principally to guard the Siletz Reservation. It occupied a large pine-covered flat about two miles from where the Umpqua emptied into the Pacific. At the mouth of the river the *Columbia* had crossed the bar and sailed upriver to unload soldiers, other passenger, cargo, and several thousand board feet of lumber for crews who would soon be at work to enlarge the fort.

Del was one of the passengers who went ashore from the *Columbia* to buy a meal at a reasonable price, order hard biscuits and cured meat to last him for the remaining days of his journey, and take a drink or two of whisky. The *Columbia* was going to be tied up unloading troops, supplies, boxes of ammunition and rifles for the army, and all the lumber for the new fort for several hours. Then, returning passengers would be summoned back to the paddleboat by signal blasts from its horn. They'd walk up the swaying gangplank along with new passengers who had bought tickets for the next stop, Astoria, or the final destination, Portland. It was late Friday afternoon and the *Columbia* was not expected to depart until after six o'clock, maybe later. Unloading the lumber was slow and her departure might be delayed longer as a result.

Hankerson used the delay to visit with the manager of the sutler's store. He was surprised to see five Indians squatting against the front of the log building to the left of the wooden stairs leading to the open door. In front of them were two ponies tied to a horizontal hitching pole supported at each end by an upright post. Just beyond was a wooden trough filled with water for horses to drink. Upon each of the ponies was a worn blanket. The Indians started sullenly at Del as he walked up the steps to the store. He had no idea if they were friendlies or what tribe they belonged to. As he stepped into the store, he saw it was well stocked. It carried provisions for the few soldiers at the makeshift fort, blankets, canned food, dried venison, gunpowder, handguns, rifles, clothing, some mining equipment, large sifting pans for gold, shovels, picks and other tools, candy, flour, nuts, wheat, and whatnots for ladies. The most popular corner in the low-beamed log house with its big stone fireplace was the planked wooden bar in front of which stood four handmade stools. Behind the bar were seven or eight unlabeled dark glass bottles of whisky.

The sutler was a big heavy man with a gray beard framing his broad face like a hairy halo. His face bore a discouraged, bored expression and it brightened a little when Del Hankerson sat on a stool and ordered whisky. When he was served and responded affirmatively to the sutler's question that yes, he was a passenger on the *Columbia*, the sutler said, "I wish I was."

The big man identified himself as Amos Holt and explained that Fort Umpqua ". . . is the loneliest place on God's green earth. Worse than that," he explained, "there's the rain. I swear to God, I'm not exaggeratin' an inch when I tell you, we get at least seventy-one inches a year here. I got it straight from a sergeant I know who told me that this hellhole is the wettest military post in the whole U. S. of A. I don't doubt it a bit."

Holt paused for a moment to take a deep breath and Hankerson did not interrupt his brief silence. It was obvious to Del that the man liked to talk, was lonely, and appreciated a stranger who listened to everything he'd saved up to let loose on somebody with a sympathetic ear.

Del was alone with Holt in the next hour except for several passengers from the *Columbia*. One was a man who wanted tobacco. Another was a woman looking for a souvenir. She bought a large seashell for twenty-five cents to listen to the ocean when she pressed it against her ear. The others fingered the merchandise, obviously killing time until the *Columbia* sailed. Two other men, soldiers in army blue were sitting at a table nursing their coffee. One of them was a black man with sergeant's chevrons on his blouse. Hankerson stared at the man; somehow his presence disturbed him.

Holt poured another shot of whisky for Del and confided his fears that the tiny garrison of soldiers was hardly up to keeping the peace with the Rogue and Siletz Indians. He pointed out that one of the Indian Agents, E. P. Drew, deliberately reported agitation between the Indians and whites that was exaggerated. "I heard from my friend a sergeant, that Drew lied about the Indians arming themselves and gettin' ready to leave the reservation. Hell, feeling between the officers and Drew are tetchy because once or twice Drew absolutely would not halt non-treaty Indians like Chief Jackson and his people from headin' down the coast. Drew says the band weren't covered by treaties and were free to return to their homes. He done what he did on purpose, I'll bet. It's no secret he's agitatin' for the army to send more troops up here. Hell, there ain't more than maybe thirty men here now."

"All the signs are here. No matter how many lies Drew tells, this post won't last. Oh, there'll be new bunches of army men sent here for a while, and the post will get bigger. But the writin' is on the wall. Hell, the ferry at Coquille River was shut down. And the mail coming to the post from Port Orford has stopped. Couple of years and this wet, lonely place'll be abandoned."

Vaguely disappointed, Del said, "I guess then that you don't get much news here from other parts of Oregon?"

"Well now that's not really so. We do get mail from Eugene freighted up here with flour, goods, and other necessities. Wagons show up to supply the fort and the store with what we need. People drift in here from all over. I do a fair business. Otherwise, seein' nobody but mostly Injuns, and no women to speak of, 'cept squaws, I'd go crazy."

"Have you by any chance heard about a man chasin' a horse thief west of here? I seen him in Yreka couple of days ago. He lied to my boss about chasing a horse thief, then said he was actually trying to get to Portland before the *Columbia*. Lookin' to save his money from a bank that went broke."

"Don't know about a broke bank, but I got a cousin lives near Eugene. He was here yesterday unloading supplies. He knows a lot of mule drivers. One from near Jacksonville told him he heard of a feller in a hurry. Bought a horse there. Said he was chasing a horse thief. Could be the same man."

Holt frowned, his forehead knotted when he said, "Now that I think of it, the idea of a man chasing another one on horseback just don't make sense. Where did you say he started from?"

"I think he told Horsley that he started out in Sacramento on Monday."

"Oh, I can hardly believe that! Why from Sacramento to Yreka, and then to Jacksonville, must be at least two hundred miles, probably more, nobody's going to chase a horse thief that far, not with the Indians raiding and killing."

"Well," Hankerson said, "that's what he told my boss, before he said it was a lie. He said he had to beat the *Columbia* to Portland to save his gold."

Holt rubbed his beard thoughtfully. "Must be seven kinds of a fool," he said, "to race with a steamboat." Then, as if he was talking to himself, he said, "I wonder what the steamboat's carrying that could be so important," he asked softly in a curious voice, "that a lone rider would risk his neck for?"

Hankerson shrugged, drank off his whiskey, slid off his stool, and said as he walked out, "Well we'll probably never know, but it's interesting to think about."

Del felt a thrill course through him. Louis Remme was telling the same lie! As he walked back to the steamboat in the rain he felt his lucky hunch about the horseman more strongly. After spending two hours with Amos Holt, his belly warm from the whisky he'd drunk, he was excited over the news of Remme's progress. Del didn't have much money on him, but made up his mind that he'd bet one of the gold beavers Tom Horsley had given him on the Frenchman. If he'd gotten as far as the mining town after passing through the Bobtail Mountains whose icy snows and killing winds had taken the lives of a lot of men in the winter months, and he had escaped Indians who must have seen him, then he was worth gambling on. Del decided he would spread the news on the *Columbia*. The more bets laid down on the Frenchman's race, the bigger the pot was going to be and the odds would improve. Also, he calculated that with his good fortune so far Remme would reach Portland by noon, Saturday. That was the time he'd select as the winning entry in the betting pool. When Del told Ralph Meade what he'd leaned about the progress of the wild Frenchman, the purser had a moment of doubt, then in a sudden surge of reckless clarity he decided he would bet that Louis Remme beat the steamship to Portland.

It was past eight o'clock and raining hard before the *Columbia* backed out of the Umpqua River landing and made a wide turn and headed north into the teeth of a lashing, streaming storm, which rocked the *Columbia* from stem to stern. The west wind raised white caps and billows of angry sea buffeted the *Columbia* from her windward side that drove the *Columbia* off course to sail into the force of the wind to avoid turning over.

During Hankerson's visit ashore, Meade, no longer willing to be kept in the dark about the gold the *Columbia* was carrying, decided to confront the captain with his single question: Was the treasure to be offloaded in Portland and turned over to Dr. Steinberger, the Adams agent? In all the trips he had made on the *Columbia*, hauling U. S. mail and gold in large amounts, there was always a destination to which it had been consigned.

But he had received no instructions from Captain Dall when the precious cargo was loaded in San Francisco long after midnight. The loading time alone had made him curious, but other than making certain the gold was stored properly, Captain Dall had not commented on where it was going. The whole business of the bankruptcy process of Adams Express was off color. And Meade had heard that I. C. Wood, the head of Adams, had secretly taken ship for Australia.

When Ralph Meade knocked on the door to Captain Dall's cabin, he resolved to be respectful, but insistent upon an explanation.

The captain opened the door dressed in nightclothes, slippers, and a dark green velour robe. He looked straight into Meade's eyes. "Come in," he said, "I've been expecting you."

He pointed to an empty chair and Meade sat down across from him in a comfortable overstuffed leather chair. Dall leaned forward with his elbows on his knees, and his forehead creased with deep wrinkles.

"It's the gold, isn't it, you want some answers to? All that wealth without a destination. Well, I'll tell you what I know. The man I report to at Pacific Steamship Company called me into his office about five in the morning, after all our cargo had been stored and told me, 'Captain sometimes in business we have to change some of out standard business practices to serve our customers. You're carrying an expensive cargo which has no specific destination. Your sailing directions will be to return it to San Francisco on your way back from Portland. At that time, we will have instructions for what to do with it.

"'Have a safe voyage, Captain.'

"Now Ralph, you know as much as I do!" Captain Dall said.

Leaning forward closer to Meade, Dall stressed in a heavy voice, "For God's sakes, man, discourage anybody from going to the cargo hold for any reason. Keep it locked and keep the key where no one will stumble on it."

Looking at Meade with misery in his eyes, Dall said, "Let's get to bed. I know I can trust you, and that makes me feel a lot better."

Amos Holt was discouraged with his job as sutler. He had been looking for something more satisfying. He was tired of the loneliness, the constant rain, the persistence of the shiftless Indians who stole whatever they could sneak away without being caught. Amos was bored, uninspired, and weary of the sameness of his life. Del Hankerson's story had set him to thinking, but he hadn't given away the idea he was scheming to the man who had related Remme's ride to him.

After Hankerson had finished his drink and walked away, Holt pulled out a writing pad and did some figuring. If the rider had left Sacramento on Monday morning and ridden day and night, counting time out for sleep, avoiding natural obstacles, like crossing streams and rivers, dodging around mountains, changing horses, and running from Indians, he probably couldn't have made more than five miles an hour to cover the distance he did. If Jacksonville was two hundred miles from Sacramento, that meant he'd been in the saddle forty hours. Nobody could ride that far in forty hours. Most likely, he averaged about two and one half miles an hour and that would put him in Jacksonville, with about four hundred miles to go. He couldn't be much farther north, if he was still alive, than Yoncalla or in Roseburg, maybe.

If Amos could ride east and intersect the man close to Eugene—ambush him—and take what he was carrying, it would be worth the risk. By a freighter's route he knew well, he could overtake the rider in a full day on a fast horse and wait for him a little east of Eugene.

Not for a minute had Amos Holt swallowed the idea that the rider had challenged the wilderness for anything less than his weight in gold. Nobody was that stupid. He didn't know in what form Louis Remme carried his treasure, but if he stopped the man, he'd find out soon enough.

It was not until the next morning after the *Columbia* sailed out of the storm and resumed her original course north to Astoria that Ralph Meade found Sergeant Moses Gunn, a black man, who had bought horses for the army at Fort Humboldt in northern California. His firm kindness, intuitive sense of how horses think, and his care and maintenance of them, had earned him the unofficial title of "horse master." His army career for eighteen years had been almost solely involved as a sort of unofficial horse doctor. He kept his charges well and content and was responsible for buying well-bred stock that could stand up to long days over rough country with army riders on their backs.

Ralph Meade had met Moses on several occasions when he traveled on the *Columbia* to Portland. Across the river was Fort Vancouver where he was detached occasionally to train horses for soldiers assigned to that military installation.

Meade had greeted Moses for only a moment to take an army voucher for passage late on the previous day. He was accompanied by a young soldier, Private Harold Privet, who had been transferred to Fort Vancouver.

Now, he located Moses in the dining room drinking coffee and was greeted by a smile from the black man that split his face in a wide grin, when he rose courteously.

"Mr. Meade," he said, "how good to see you."

Moses was dressed in fresh army blues, four hash marks on his left sleeve and three chevrons. Campaign ribbons and medals decorated his chest. One was for sharp shooting.

Meade returned the greeting and was about to ask the horse master an important question when two army officers—one a captain, the other a lieutenant—and a Miss Teller—the only female passenger on the *Columbia*, appeared for coffee. Even before they reached his table, Moses was on his feet standing at attention with Privet at his side stiff as starch. Both men saluted smartly, took salutes in return, and relaxed when Captain Robert Holmes, said, "Stand easy, soldier." He smiled at Moses and said, "Good to see you, Sergeant. I suppose you're heading to Fort Vancouver on temporary duty?"

"No sir," Moses answered, "I took my discharge at Fort Humboldt after eighteen years, on Monday. I'm traveling to the Fort courtesy of the U. S. Army as a fine going away thank-you. I have a sister who lives in the city and I'm going to visit her for a spell."

"Well, well," Holmes said, surprise on his face. "I don't think you're going to be easy to replace. But congratulations. You've earned your retirement."

Holmes held out his hand and Moses grasped it in a hearty clasp. As the captain turned to find a table where he and his guests could drink coffee, he stopped suddenly and turned around, "A question, Sergeant. Did you ever buy horses from a man named Louis Remme?"

Moses grinned, "Yes, sir, about forty or fifty in the last two years or so. He has a good eye for horse flesh. Probably the best man I ever saw on a horse."

"Well, that's interesting. There's talk on this boat about a man with his name who's trying to beat the *Columbia* to Portland. The rumor is that he started out in Sacramento on Monday and was last heard of in Jacksonville, on Wednesday, I believe. That doesn't sound possible."

Mosses shook his head. "My goodness," he marveled. "That man's a piece of work." He brushed a hand in a contemplative fashion over his curly hair, going gray at the temples. "Yes sir, he could do it, if he had a mighty good reason and a little luck. He's tougher than whipcord and when he makes up his mind to go after somethin' there's not much I know about that could stop him."

Captain Holmes studied Moses's honest face for a moment. "That's a pretty high compliment, coming from you."

"Yes sir, I reckon it is."

Captain Holmes nodded to Moses and guided his guests to a table.

CHAPTER TWELVE

OUTSIDE ON THE DECK with the sun shining and the wind soft for a moment or two, Meade protested to Moses, "What you told the captain was what I wanted to ask you about, Moses. You really believe this Remme could have traveled that far with the Rogues on the warpath, not counting the other hazards? Hell, man, from Sacramento to Portland overland has got to be close to seven hundred miles, not counting detours a horseman would have to take. How could anybody travel that far in six or seven days? Why, you'd have to go without sleep, fork a saddle day and night, and fight exhaustion every mile. The weather I heard has been the worst inland since '47. It multiplies hazards and would be against him all the way."

Meade was aware his voice held a strong note of disbelief and disparagement that any horseman could accomplish what Louis Remme was rumored to have done. "How could anybody do that?" Moses looked down at his feet, as if he could find confirmation in their shiny black polish. He shook his head and said, "You just don't know Louis Remme."

"You seem to have a high opinion of this man, Moses. A lot of people on the boat think the story of his whole ride is a lie, a fairy tale."

Moses smiled to himself, then said, "Let me tell you one story about Louis Remme that gives you an idea about how tough minded he is. I heard it before I ever met him.

"Seems Remme was convinced there were better opportunities in the California diggings than lookin' for gold. After his close call on the *New World*, he made up his mind to find something less dangerous than workin' on paddleboats that blew up all the time. Like a few others who were delivering mail from remote miners to ships sailing with mail from San Francisco, Remme decided to go into the express business on his own. First thing he did was to buy a thimble from a seamstress. He used it to measure a portion of gold dust as his fee to carry a miner's letter to a ship carrying mail to folks at home.

"As soon as he had collected a sackful of mail, he started on horseback to San Francisco. He always rode at night to avoid thieves and competitors who tried to trip him up. Most nights in the winter it rained and he carried his burden in a heavy canvas sack. Slugging through mud, brush, and water he always had the company of wolves and coyotes, waiting for his horse to stumble or show signs of weakness.

"When he reached the waterfront after forty or fifty miles with his heavy burden, he rented a boat and rowed out to the *California, Oregon, Panama,* or *John L. Stephens* where he turned over the letters. Then he canvassed the passengers for used copies of the *New York Herald* at one dollar a copy. Ashore, he resold them for $8.00 a piece and from a single ship he might dicker for several hundred copies.

"Remme quit doin' that work when other runners found out what he was doin' and lowered the resale price to $4.00. Remme closed down his business with a surplus of gold, I hear, and decided to head back to Oregon."

"What about sleep? If he called on miners all day and rode all night, when did he get to rest?"

"Far as I know he got along on three or four hours after he sold the papers." Meade shook his head. "Hard to believe anybody would willingly take on that kind of punishment. Sounds like an awful stubborn man?"

"Yes sir, you got that right," Moses agreed, smiling to himself over some personal memory of Louis Remme he treasured. One thing was for sure, the horseman was colorblind when it came to judging another man's character or complexion.

Shortly, Meade and the two soldiers parted company, but not five hours later as dawn broke through the fog that shrouded Astoria, Moses Gunn was awakened by a loud banging on his door. Harold Privet never budged an inch in his solitary bunk nor did the other passengers who shared the stateroom; they were dead to the world.

At the door, Moses opened it to find Ralph Meade in a wrinkled uniform, tie askew, and a face stricken with shock and dismay.

"Moses, I need help," Meade began. Apparently Tom Potts, one of the gamblers who organized the lottery convinced Miss Teller to open her door. He told her he thought there was a shortage in the lottery money and with her help, they needed to count it. She fell for his lie, told him to wait until she dressed, then opened her door. She had stored the gold coins and specie under her mattress and complained to him she had had a restless night. All the money, about $2,800 lay out on top of her bed. She started to object when Potts raked the betting slips and money into a leather bag he had brought with him. When she opened her mouth to scream, he clasped his hand over her mouth, wrestled her to the floor, and stuffed a handkerchief in her mouth. He tied her to a wooden leg of the bed with her arms secured behind her. It was an hour before she could work herself free from her bonds. She was furious that she'd let herself be tricked and told Meade that Potts was pleased how easy it was to fool an ugly old woman.

"I'm not ugly, and I'm not an old woman," she insisted, then she repeated some things Potts said.

"It comes down to the fact that Potts is armed," Meade said to Moses, "and believes he can overtake Remme before he reaches Portland. He's convinced Remme's carrying a lot of gold. He told Miss Teller he didn't care who she told about his plan. She wouldn't get free from the cords he'd used to tie her to the bed-leg for at least three or four hours and by then he would have enough of a head start to outrun anybody foolish enough to try to follow him."

Moses had listened carefully, then in a steely voice, much harder and sharper than his usual soft, velvety voice with its slight flavor of the south, he asked Meade, how soon would the *Columbia* start unloading passengers in Astoria.

"About forty-five minutes," Meade said. then, his eyes opened wide as he realized the importance of Moses's question.

"He took one of the life boats and headed for shore right after we crossed the bar. Wouldn't be much of a chore to row ashore when we're only about three miles out.."

"How many life boats do you carry?" Moses asked.

"Eight is our full complement."

"Let me get dressed and I'll join you. We'll let down another boat for me."

Meade stared at the determined black man. At that moment, he was suddenly impressed by the dread certainty the sergeant displayed. He was a much different man than the gentle soldier who had just retired from the army. There was an inner toughness that straightened his back, strengthened his hand, and imbued him with a quality that made him bristle with threat.

Moses pulled a blue coat and pants over his long, red underwear, fastened a loaded handgun and cartridge belt around his waist, dropped ten or twelve extra rounds in his pocket, and forced his feet into riding boots. He was almost ready. He rolled an army blanket and his overcoat tightly and wound the bundle with a strap around the middle.

Ralph Meade found his certificate of deposit in a drawer of his desk, which he unlocked. It was valued at $950 at the only open Adams Express Office in the Oregon Territory. On the back of the certificate, there were two lines, which with his signature, he could endorse the money the certificate represented over to another payee. He signed his name and wrote a short note to Dr. Steinberger in Portland. Steinberger knew Meade's signature well. Moses would have no problem collecting the money.

When Moses knocked on the purser's door, Meade welcomed him into his room and handed an envelope to the sergeant. He explained quickly what was in it and that he was carrying a writ of attachment that would close the Adams Express office in Portland.

"That's why your friend is riding like hell to beat the *Columbia* to Portland. His gold is at stake. You're the only passenger who knows that."

Before Moses could raise an objection, Meade said, "You're my only hope to salvage some money from my savings. You'll need money to rent a horse to catch Potts if you can and ride to Portland. There you can cash in the certificate and keep $300 for your trouble. If you find Potts and the money he stole, we can distribute it to the winners when the *Columbia* reaches Portland. Then, I'll buy you a drink and you can join your sister in Vancouver."

"Is that fair?" Meade asked, standing with his hand outstretched to Moses.

Moses gripped his hand. "More than fair, Mr. Meade."

"Good! After our stop here, unload and load whatever passengers are coming and leaving and shift cargo, then we'll be underway. But I doubt if we dock at Portland for at least thirty-six hours, probably a little longer."

"I'll check in the Adams office twice every day until you get in," Moses said. Now, we'd better get that lifeboat into the water."

As Meade watched Moses disappear into the slowly lifting fog, he thought about his scheme to collect some of his savings. His idea to utilize the black man to present his endorsed certificate to Dr. Steinberger in Portland depended on whether or not the $300 reward was inducement enough for the soldier to disembark in Astoria and cut across country on horseback to get to Portland before the *Columbia*. Given the time line, Meade believed any good horseman could get to Portland before the *Columbia* docked. It could not be more than seventy miles overland to the city on the Willamette, while the *Columbia* had to sail up the wild Columbia river, with its rampant currents, shifting sand hills, and racing tide that obstructed the progress of the steamer.

Meade hurried to Harriet Teller's room, knocked, and she opened the door immediately. "I was just coming to see you, Mr. Meade," she said. "We've got to inform all the other lottery ticket holders," she said with a stern sense of duty, "that their money has been stolen."

"Miss Teller, I suggest we wait for the outcome of a plan I've set in motion to recover the lottery money."

In a matter of minutes, he explained the mission Moses Gunn had taken on and concluded with the observation, "I believe Miss Teller that on a fast horse, Moses will overtake the thief. There's another factor in our favor. Potts boasted that you'd never loosen the cords Potts tied you with under three or four hours, but you got free much sooner. So Potts, who thinks he has a strong lead, is in for a surprise. And now with the weather getting colder by the minute it'll be snowing soon, making it easier for Moses to pick up his trail. I have a lot of confidence in Moses. He knows horses and was in calvary, I learned, as a young recruit during the Mexican War."

There was a sudden sparkle in Miss Teller's eyes. "You're betting Moses will recover the lottery money and get to Portland before Louis Remme. What makes you so sure?"

Meade confessed that he'd endorsed his Adams Express certificate in favor of Moses who would be rewarded for hard riding. He pointed out that barring unforeseen hazards, Moses would cash the certificate and wait in Portland for the *Columbia* to arrive.

"You're gambling on the honesty of a black man you hardly know," Miss Teller said in a dubious voice.

"Yes I am, ma'am, but I believe there's sterling character in Moses Gunn."

Smiling suddenly with a twinkle in her eyes, "I think I'll gamble with you, Mr. Meade," Harriet Teller said. "In the dining salon yesterday, I overheard Moses describe Louis Remme. If the black man you trust vouches so strongly for the Frenchman, then I'm going to make another bet in the lottery that he beats the *Columbia* to Portland. Won't it be fun if I win? We can always notify the other lottery players, Potts has run with our money and perhaps the *Columbia* will have to stand good for it if it values its reputation."

A little taken aback by Miss Teller's sharp reasoning Meade chuckled and said, "Miss Teller you are a shrewd woman and I'm happy to know you."

In the tiny village of Astoria, first a fur collection point for trappers, then a busy fishing village that pursued the thousands of salmon that crowded the waters of the Columbia as they headed upstream to spawn, Moses was directed to the hosteler in town who had horses to sell. Moses found the owner, a Swede named Peg Orville who'd never seen a black man. He was surprised by the army uniform and Moses's black complexion. "I don't have many horses, mister," he said. "You an African ain't 'cha. You ever ridden a horse? I never saw a ni—"

"Uh, uh," Moses interrupted. "If you value your teeth you'll swallow that word."

The Swede clamped his mouth shut and said, "Ninety dollars for Harmless. He's sound and the fastest horse I've got. You're the second man who wanted a horse in a hurry. Only he was whiter than a cod fish. It'll cost you ninety, in gold. If you ain't got that much you're wasting my time."

"Throw in a saddle and blanket and I'll give you a hundred."

"You must be in a might big hurry, but show me some gold and I'll get Harmless for you."

Moses unbuttoned his blouse, explored his money belt for gold coin, and extracted two fifty-dollar gold pieces, part of his mustering out pay.

"I'll be damned," Orville said, then bit down on one of the gold pieces and started to say, "How come a nigger is wearing a money belt and can pay in genuine gold coin?" He looked into Moses's eyes; what he saw changed his mind.

"Yes sir," he said. "Harmless is strong headed and pulls to the right a little, but she'll get you there."

When he was in the saddle, his heavy blue army overcoat buttoned to his neck, Moses asked about the man who earlier bought a horse.

"Well," Orville said, "He was in a powerful hurry too, and had a disposition like a polecat with his tail in a crack. He asked how to get to Portland the quickest way. I told him to ride down the river path about twenty miles, then turn right or south for about fifty miles or so. Keeps you out of the coastal range. You'll go through Birkenfeld and Mist; living there's just a few folks who hate crowds like Astoria. Stay on straight until you hit the wagon path to Forest Grove. There used to be signs tacked on a tree here and there but don't count on it. From Forest Grove into Portland is only about twenty miles, but with this weather making up"—Orville looked at the heaving gray sky—"you may have to hole up somewhere until it quits snowing."

Moses gave Orville a salute and pounded away on Harmless. About eight miles later when the horse insisted on drifting to the right, Moses leaned forward, grabbed a handful of the horse's shaggy main and bit down hard on her right ear. She whinnied, tried to throw Moses, but settled down after Moses gave her two sharp thumps from his heels on both sides of her stomach.

Twitching her bloody right ear for a few miles, Harmless nevertheless kept to the path Moses was following. Her ear stopped bleeding in the cold.

The snow came lightly at first after Moses turned Harmless south from the blustery river road.

Leaving a thin and lonesome cover of snow in the afternoon, the storm came down quietly at first, like an afterthought on this gray Friday night. An early moon almost broke through once, but toward daylight a little wind came up and started carving white mounds, making strange shapes on bushes. It was heavier now and at daylight it stuck to old drifts. Gradually, the snow thickened until the two ruts of the winding trail were covered and for the shaggy firs the wind favored, it tore away from the limbs what it left on the ground.

The storm which the *Columbia* had sailed into reached land in full force, and as the wind rose the snow whipped against the posts of a ranch fence across the trail, and caked against the broad trunks of cedar and fir trees.

Moses was concerned that the storm would soon erase the faint tracks Potts was leaving behind.

Moses decided to gamble on a hunch. By the way Tom Potts was riding his horse, unsure of the trail ahead, pushing the animal through deep, sunken spots covered by the snow and causing the horse to stumble, he was proving to be an awkward rider and would soon take shelter under a tree to avoid the worst of the storm. It was about then that Moses found the recent hoofprints he'd been searching for.

Moses dismounted and following the trail fast disappearing under a mantle of snow, noted that Potts, bewildered by the whirling disguise in white, had led his horse in circles, then turned suddenly into a copse of thick woods.

The snow cover silenced every normal sound, and Moses, smoothing his horse's nose with his glove, crept into the thick set of trees, tied Harmless's reins to a shrub, detached a coil of rope from the saddle horn, and shook the snow loose from the hemp. Reaching beneath his heavy coat for his handgun, he pulled it free and walked about a hundred feet where he saw Tom Potts kneeling in a bare place beneath a tall fir with a three-foot trunk trying to make a fire.

When he was less than twelve feet away, in soft snow, Moses said, "Any fool knows better than to start a fire under a tree heavy with snow. You'll be buried in a ton of it when the hot smoke melts it from the branches."

Potts, startled, turned around quickly, reaching for the handgun at his side. The metal click from the hammer on Moses's gun, stopped the gambler's hand in midair. "It's the lottery money you want, isn't it? I never thought I'd be cornered by a jigaboo."

"Well, this jigaboo's going to shoot your eyes out if you don't unbuckle that gun belt, drop it to the ground, and back against that tree." Potts was a medium-sized man with a slight stoop, a small potbelly, and a ragged beard. His eyes were flinty with hate as he debated with himself if he could draw his gun before Moses shot him.

Desperate, furious that an inferior black man had found him, Potts said, "Look, I was hasty. Let's divide it. You go your way and I'll go mine."

With his left hand, Moses made a loop in his saddle rope and tossed it over Potts's head.

"Hey, what're you doing? I ain't harmed a hair on your head. Take it all, the lottery money, just leave me with my horse."

Moses just grunted, jerked down on the rope, and forced Potts to sit on the ground hard. Then, soundlessly, he wound the rope around the tree six times, trapping Potts in a tight embrace with his hands bound beside him and his back against the trunk, with his legs stuck out awkwardly in front of him. He could breathe, but his arms and body position prevented him from twisting. Moses tied a stiff double knot in the rope out of his victim's reach. Eventually, he would be able to twist and stretch the rope enough to loosen it and get free, but that would take at least an hour of effort. Without his horse, which Moses intended to take, Potts was going to have a long walk to a town of any size.

It was the work of only moments to transfer the small leather bag from Potts's horse to Moses's own.

With his gun still held in one hand, he untied the reins of the roan and led the willing horse to where Potts was wretchedly trapped.

"You can't take my horse," he whined. "We're miles from anywhere. I'll freeze to death.

With a look of disgust, Moses said, "You should have thought about that when you stole the money and a boat and slipped away leaving Miss Teller tied up."

Moses mounted his horse and trailing the roan by her reins, he thundered off into the snow which had thinned and would soon stop. He ignored Potts's pleas and soon his hoarse cries were swallowed by the deep silence. About ten miles later, Moses released the reins of the roan horse who'd been trailing behind him. Sooner or later somebody would encounter the animal and take custody of her.

CHAPTER THIRTEEN

THE TWO-HOUR SLEEP, his dried sheepskin, and the meat sandwich he'd bought from Joseph Knott had given Remme a strong emotional boost. Instead of rain, a cold wind like a frozen breath from the north had stiffened the mud on the ground and Annie, the sorrel, flew over the hardened earth urged forward by the hurry in her rider's signals and to keep her blood moving and warm near the surface of her hide.

Alternating between long stretches of galloping and shorter ones of jogging along at a sprightly pace, Remme and Annie greeted early morning of his fifth day at the sturdy fir-shaded house of Jesse Applegate in the Yoncalla valley. Smoke curled out of a stone chimney into the brisk morning air. Remme had met Applegate once before, but wasn't sure the Oregon trailblazer would remember him. Annie, the sorrel, had been a good choice and he was grateful that Knott had recommended the mare. But as he dismounted Annie in Applegate's yard, part of Remme's saddle came with him. It simply fell apart. He looked at the tangled leather in a heap at his feet and was not surprised. It was an old saddle, thin, brittle with age, not well made to begin with. The rawhide stitching that attached the left stirrup to the saddle frame had frayed and torn. The $10 he had paid the farmer Kavanaugh for the saddle had been too much money. But he had not had a choice. He bent to pick up the fallen stirrup and leg guard when Jesse Applegate opened the door to his rambling house.

"Saddle trouble I see," he said with a smile. "Isn't that Joe Knott's sorrel?"

"I don't know if you remember me . . . ?"

"Remember you? Of course I do. You look like a man who's come a long way in a short time. Coffee's on the stove and I'm sure Cindy can find something to eat." He beckoned Remme to follow him and the cattle trader nodded, trying to brush some of the mud off his clothes before he stepped through the door.

Remme entered the house, removed his shapeless hat, and thanked Cindy Applegate for the cup of coffee she gave him with a smile.

"I remember you," she said, with sudden recognition. "You cut all that firewood that terrible winter of '47."

Remme acknowledged her recollection and sipped the steaming brew in his hands. He stationed himself before the cheery hearth, warming his stiff body from the leaping fire. He had nodded to the family daughters, Lucy, Rozelle and Suzie. They nodded politely and continued sewing, pulling their shawls more closely around their shoulders. Cindy left the room silently and returned bearing a basket of dried corn kernels she had taken from the provision room. She'd been about to start a conversation with their visitor and ask him to stay to lunch, but Jesse walked in, smiled, and said, "It's gonna take a few minutes for you to thaw out. By the time you've warmed up I'll have a saddled horse for you to ride." He stepped out through the kitchen.

Compared to the cabins of most frontier settlers, the Applegate house was a miracle to Remme. A warm, inviting smell of cinnamon and apples came from the kitchen as the cattle trader stood self-consciously in front of the fireplace. He was more aware of his coarse, dirty sheepskin, muddy boots, soiled shirt and pants, and bristly whiskers in the house where hooked rugs decorated the stained and polished fir-wood floors and pictures of Applegates hung from the cedar-faced walls.

When Applegate slipped back in the house and handed Remme another mug of coffee, the Frenchman tried to apologize for his appearance with a gesture, but Applegate put him at ease with the comment. "Cindy has some cinnamon bread baking and we'll have some when it's out of the oven."

Applegate eyed Remme with an expression of disbelief on his face. "I'm trying to believe," Applegate said, "that you have ridden almost four hundred forty miles in about four days."

Remme's head snapped up in astonishment.

"How did you know that?"

His face brightening, Applegate grinned. "A rider Joseph Knott sent on an errand to Eugene while you were asleep in his barn did not believe your story about chasing a horse thief. He thinks it's something far more urgent. From your appearance, you've had a hard ride."

Remme paused for a moment before he decided how to answer. Applegate was far different from the men who had exchanged horses with him so far. This was the scout, turned farmer, whose name was respected all over Oregon. Thousands of men and women entered Oregon Territory in ox-drawn covered wagons following the immigrant trail that Applegate and Levi Scott had discovered at a terrible price to themselves. Separated from their families for months at a time, unpaid for their labors, the two had fought freezing weather, the terrible white winds of the Siskiyous, Indian attacks, and brutal, punishing physical labor in the wilderness to map a trail emigrants could follow into the promised land.

As Jesse recalled, Remme had traveled over part of the trail—the Applegate Cutoff—when he rode into Oregon.

"You saved a lot of people a lot of misery back in '46 by helping emigrants through the Umpqua. Then in '47, you offered to cut wood for our families while my brother and I were off fighting the Cayuse Indians in Walla Walla during that awful winter."

Now, still puzzled why Knott would ask a man on an errand to go out of his way to warn the trailblazers, Remme decided to tell Applegate the truth about his mad race to Portland. Somehow, the idea of asking the man to believe the lie about chasing a horse thief was wrong. He wouldn't believe the horse thief story anyway. He had never before told the reason for his ride, except to Tom Horsley. Lying had always rubbed him the wrong way, and the horse thief story had not sat well with him. "It is like putting your pants on backwards," his dad had explained to him once when he was a boy. That idea had popped into his head years later whenever he was tempted to stretch the truth. When he explained to Applegate why he was in a hurry and how far he had come, Applegate was astounded.

"My God, man," he said, "what you've done is impossible. All the way from Sacramento in five days? And you came through the Bobtail Mountains this time of year? You're lucky to be alive."

Applegate paused, then said with a certain foreboding in his voice, "I guess you realize that your secret's out. An impossible effort like yours, no matter how closed mouth you are, spreads like the wind. It seems to pass by some power all its own. Like wind or fire, sweeping over the lonely farms on the prairie, and up onto the snowy ridges. Reaching into the most remote cabins where the trappers and their women have been holed up for months or years.

"Since I brought my family to Oregon, I've always been amazed at the speed of frontier gossip. The story of a lone rider chasing a mythical horse thief for seven hundred miles is hard to swallow. But one who carries a secret message of great import to the passengers of a steamship is bound to tickle the imagination.

"Well, we've got to get you moving," Jesse said. "You've got a long way to go." Then he added, "A lot of people in Portland are going to be hurt when Adams Express closes after the *Columbia* docks." He looked Remme squarely in the eyes and said, "I hope you make it. I can help by giving you the names of men who know me in the Willamette Valley. They will trade horses with you—no questions asked. Just tell 'em Jesse sent you."

Applegate insisted that Remme drink a third cup of coffee and eat a big piece of Cynthia Applegate's fresh-baked bread while he brought the horse he had selected for Remme up to the house. Outside, he told Remme he could pay for the saddle and horse when he came back. Remme asked Applegate one question before he mounted: "How far to Portland?"

"About one hundred and forty miles," Applegate answered.

While Remme had stood soaking up the heat from the burning logs in the fireplace, he had cast his thoughts back nine years to 1846 when he had first heard of Jesse Applegate. He and Levi Scott were determined to find a southern passageway for immigrants to Oregon that would avoid some of the treacherous pitfalls of the northern Columbia River trek and the Barlow Road, east of Portland.

As Applegate walked Remme out of the house to a saddled horse, a worried frown wrinkled his forehead. He looked up at Remme who had swung into the saddle. "If I were you," he warned, "I'd watch my back. Joe Knott's messenger said Knott had heard rumors that somebody may try to stop you, convinced you're carrying something of great value worth your life."

Remme had no choice but to accept the truth about the frontier tongue wagging that spanned great distances without logical explanation. Remme remembered 1847 when all of Oregon, it seemed—united by news of a massacre that had traveled more than two hundred miles by frontier telegraph gathered together to hunt down the killers of Marcus Whitman. Remme was new to Oregon and his lasting affection for Morey Whitehead, the old Iroquois trapper who had shaped his views about Indians when he was a boy, stood in his way to join the armed volunteers. He had paid his first visit to Jesse Applegate and said he was good at chopping wood and protecting the women the men were leaving behind.

Jesse, with his strong memory of the Umpqua Canyon passage the year before and the happy-go-lucky Frenchman who saved lives with his unstinting labors to help exhausted emigrants, accepted Remme's offer without a thought.

Remme had stayed on for five weeks until Jesse returned and discovered enough wood had been cut to fireplace size to last the harsh winter.

From Jesse, Remme heard the story of the killing of Reverend Whitman and the capture of about forty women by the Cayuse Indians who were holding them as hostages after the bloody murdering was finished.

Reverend Whitman who had been a stalwart source of inspiration, prayers, and encouragement on the Oregon trail, was found in Walla Walla near his mission with a Cayuse "tommyhawk" embedded between his shoulders. His male helpers had lain all around him in bloody disarray, and for long minutes their screams for help were unheard and they expired with unanswered prayers on their lips before they were found.

Applegate was a thoughtful writer and sent reports to Cindy almost weekly and she always invited Remme along with her older children to listen to Applegate's bloodcurdling details. In Cindy's mind, as her husband's words formed images for her and her daughters, she saw Narcissa Whitman's coiled hair twisted between the bloody fingers of the Indian who had killed her with whip and knife. To think this was the same gracious woman in whose home the Applegates had been welcomed to rest and dine on their way to the Willamette Valley, brought tears to Cindy's eyes. Her mind pictured Narcissa with her proud face and mud-smeared skirts drenched with her blood when she died asking her God to forgive the heathens for their violence. There in the slimy mud and darkness of the irrigation ditch that in happier times had carried water to her flowers and fields, she died.

Remme was new to Oregon then, but had learned that Applegate and Scott had defied the governor. Furious and vengeful, Abernathy so detested the "damnable southern road" that he had deliberately sent printed notices to Fort Hall, Idaho in 1847. The message on the bills warned immigrants who had stopped there that they risked their lives if they followed the Applegate cutoff. He enhanced the quality of venom in his warning by stating that " . . . any individual connected with the road or having the gall to offer his services as a guide is reprehensible, untrustworthy, and then some."

As Remme clattered out of Jesse's spacious yard, he knew it would be foolish for him to ignore Applegate's words of caution.

The trail Remme took north seated on Blackie, in a saddle that was strong and firmly made, was a boggy path that sucked at the hooves of the horse. The weather had changed from clear to soggy again and Blackie was going through the same kind of clinging mud that had trapped Whitey. It was a foot deep in some stretches, forming thick mud pies around the mare's hooves. She skidded and slithered and threw clods of dirt that peppered Remme's pants and his saddle with mudballs. Soon, the front of his clothes, from the toes of his boots to his belt, was studded with mud that hardened into a thick layer. It wasn't until late afternoon that the laboring mare finally escaped the quagmires and mud traps and broke into the clear. That same night as Remme descended out of the hills into the main Willamette Valley the stars came out to speckle the sky with diamonds. Under the spangled sky, he pressed his horse with urgent prodding and breathed deeply the sweet odors of balsam and the curiously bittersweet tang of spring oak and madrona borne to him on the wind.

Though dead tired, his eyes drooping with fatigue, Remme forced himself to stay awake, sometimes by pinching the skin on his arms with his fingers. He also thought about Joseph Knott's intuition and the gossip he'd heard that concerned him enough to send a messenger to Applegate. Despite his best intentions, twice before dawn Remme fell asleep and woke with a start, sliding precariously sideways in he saddle—the falling sensation warning him at the last moment.

It was near daybreak of the fifth day of his race when Remme galloped through the muddy streets of the little settlement of Eugene City. He barely paused, staying in the saddle a dozen miles more to the farm of John Milliron. when he gave Applegate's name to the man as the trail-breaker had suggested, Milliron appraised the Frenchman approvingly with his eyes and said, "The wife's got breakfast on the table. Eat while I put your saddle on a fresh horse." Twenty minutes later, still munching on a biscuit, Remme waved to Milliron and clattered out of the farmer's yard.

About eighteen miles later near Junction City, not alert as he should have been, Remme saw too late a tall, heavyset, gray-bearded man dressed in a heavy black coat with a hood that partially concealed his face, step from behind a thick oak tree about one hundred feet away with a shotgun pointed straight at Remme's chest.

"Pull your horse to a stop," he shouted, "or I'll shoot him out from under you."

Remme heard the distinctive click of the hammer drawn back, as he pulled back on the reins, bringing Blackie to a halt. Remme cursed himself for not heeding more carefully the parting words of warning from Jesse Applegate.

"What do you want from me?" Remme asked.

"Want from you? Why just about the same thing everybody seems to know you're carrying. Gold man, gold. Your name's Remme isn't it? You're the man who's ridden more than six hundred miles to cash in what you've got in those saddlebags.

"Now, no more talk. Climb down from your horse, after you drop your gun belt. Careful, now, I've got an itchy finger. One wrong move and you're a dead man."

Remme tasted bitterness in his mouth. To have come so far, only to be stopped by a thief with a gun who knew how to use it. What would he do when he discovered there was no gold in his saddlebags? If he forced Remme to take off his clothes and found his treasured certificate, would he be smart enough to leave Remme behind dead and pretend to Dr. Steinberger to be the real Louis Remme? After all, few men carried documents that identified them.

As Remme unbuckled his gun belt carefully and it slipped to the ground with a solid thump, he believed the man was not smart enough to try to fool the Adams agent. He was nervous, the shotgun in his hand unsteady as he watched Remme pull out his rifle from its place in the saddle and toss it a few feet to land in the grass.

"Now," said Amos Holt who was gaining confidence that his ambush was going just as exactly as he had planned it, after he rode fourteen hours from Fort Umpqua, exchanging horses twice, "get down from your horse. Next, remove your saddlebags. Move slowly as if they were babes asleep and you don't want to wake them.

"Okay, now spread them out on the ground, unbuckle the flaps, and take out each item, one at a time. My shotgun is aimed at the back of your neck. Just one false move and you'll be deader 'n a doornail."

Slowly as directed, Remme removed his canteen, the remnants of the torn shirt he had used to cover Becky's eyes during the Mt. Shasta storm, a sack of coffee beans, one empty jar of peaches, and a pouch containing tinder.

"What else you got in there?" Amos thundered. "Quit stallin', get the gold out."

"I'm just going slow like you told me. I don't want a bullet in my back."

"Well, move it along! I ain't got all day."

Remme nodded his head, reached deeper in the left leather pocket and placed his hand around the coiled pig-skin whip he always carried and had used to pop above the ears of poky cows or lazy mules. He found the handle quickly, glanced at Holt's shadow stretching on the ground, made a grunting sound as if he was pulling out a heavy weight, then like a viper striking, Remme rolled over and his right arm shot out, the cracking whip whizzing through the air like an extension of his hand. The slender end of the whip lashed Holt's hand holding the shotgun, winding snakelike around his wrist and rasping skin from the flesh. Howling with pain and horrified to see blood welling to the surface where the whip had struck, Holt screamed louder, as if burned, dropping the shotgun.

Before he could regain from his shock, he was staring at his own weapon held with rocklike firmness not three feet from his belly. Amos Holt seemed to fall apart at once. he slumped to the ground, tears running down his cheeks into his whiskers.

"I should have known better," he mumbled sorrowfully to himself. "What'll I do? What'll I do?"

"You have any other weapons?" Remme asked in a voice cold with rage.

"Only a hip gun. It ain't accurate."

"You're a pitiful example of a man. Toss the gun, I'm not going to kill you. Get to your feet and replace the stuff I pulled out of my saddlebags and tie them on my horse. I'm going to take yours and let him go in about five miles. I'll empty your guns."

Disbelief and tears in his eyes, Holt scrambled on his hands and knees and soon returned the items Remme had dumped on the ground. He placed the saddlebags where they belonged and tied them in place.

Remme had rebuckled his gun belt around his waist, returned his rifle to its sling, and led Holt's horse next to Blackie. He mounted quickly, then ejected the shells from Holt's shotgun and pistol into his free hand and dropped them in his coat pocket. "Now," Remme said, "I think you'd better take up another line of business. As a holdup man you're a failure. Now step back thirty paces. You'll have to hike for your horse. You'll find him up ahead. The grass is good around here."

As Remme touched his heels to Blackie's sides and wheeled away, his voice sailed back to Holt: "I'm not carrying any gold."

CHAPTER FOURTEEN

THE FOLLOWING MORNING, Saturday, dawn of his sixth day in the saddle, Remme exchanged a tired horse for a fresh one at French Prairie. Earlier, forty miles south when he crossed the Willamette at Peoria, he had thrown the cartridges from Holt's guns in the river. Established by retired French-Canadian trappers of the Hudson's Bay Company, the settlement of French Prairie was populated by men and women who knew the cattle trader by sight. He answered greetings from several men while he wolfed down a quick breakfast and by noon, he was in Milwaukie, Oregon, leaving Willamette Falls in Oregon City behind.

There on the banks of the Willamette River Remme could see the river was high, swollen, and angry with spring flood waters. Anchored next to a wooden landing was the log ferry that transported men, cattle, and supplies across the river. It was a floating contraption constructed of big, heavy fir logs, fully five feet thick, locked together by iron spikes four feet long. The spikes were driven through the wooden planking deep into the logs which were reinforced with thick rope bindings. Side rails six feet high formed barriers on both sides of the raft to keep barnyard animals and horses from falling into the water. Power to move the ferry back and forth across the river came from a system of ropes and pulleys that reached from one side of the Willamette to the other. By pulling on the ropes in one direction, the ferryman launched the raft from the east side of the river to the west bank. When he embarked from Portland to cross back to Milwaukie, he hauled in the opposite direction. The thick ropes also served another purpose: they prevented the raft from drifting too far off its course.

A man who Remme assumed was the operator of the ferry stepped out of a small shack that was built on the wooden landing. A spare, long-legged individual with a dour expression, he looked up at Remme and said, "If you're thinking about getting across, forget it. Ain't no amount of money could make me try the river high as it is." Remme was stunned. So close and yet so far! He eased his horse closer to the ferry landing and said earnestly, "Mister, I've ridden more than seven hundred miles to cross this river to get to Portland. I can't wait for the river to go down. I've got to get to Portland now."

The ferryman frowned. "What's so important that it can't wait a day or so?"

"Everything I own depends on it," Remme said desperately. "If you won't take me across I'll have to swim it with my horse." The quality of conviction in Remme's voice made the ferryman look up into his eyes. Startled, he peered more closely at Remme, taking in the cattle trader's mud-smeared clothes, the horse lather stains spreading from his belt buckle to his knees, and the anxiety in his frank black eyes. The ferryman turned to look at the strong, swift, muddy water rushing by. The current carried limbs of trees, splintered logs, and tufts of grass. The partially submerged body of a drowned sheep swept by and behind it was the smashed frame of a small wagon with one wooden wheel still attached. Small leaves bobbed and fluttered like green flags on the choppy surface.

The ferryman heaved a sigh and said to Remme, "Get your horse on board. You'll have to help with the ropes. If we get hit by a big log or the strain's too much for the ropes and she tears loose, you'll have to pay for the damage, that is—if we don't drown."

Remme nodded; he couldn't speak. The last hurdle had fallen. He dismounted and led his horse, clattering nervously, onto the ferry and tied the reins to a bar on one of the side rails. He stood behind the ferryman, and like him, took a firm grasp on the ropes and pulled. He was surprised at how easy it was to get the barge moving. He felt the power of the river a minute later when the two of them had hauled the ferry out of its calm shelter by the landing. The barge shuddered and creaked loudly when the river grabbed it. The strength of both men was necessary to keep the ropes moving; Remme could see them smacking the water in front of the ferry and soon his arms and shirt were dripping with water that ran off the wet ropes as they passed through his hands after being pulled by the ferryman.

It was when they were in midstream, navigating through a tricky and dangerous section of fast water that Remme heard a sound that brought a cry of despair from his lips.

Boom! Boom!

"Is that the *Columbia*?" he yelled, beseeching the ferryman for an answer.

"Don't stop pulling!" the man shouted. "Keep a steady strain. It could be the *Columbia*. Sometimes they fire the cannon when she's just been sighted. Other times when she's docked. Can't tell till you get there."

Bending his back over the whip-cracking ropes and peering anxiously through the wet wind spray off the river, Remme could not see the shape of the steamer. Where was it? He could see a few buildings, but the docks where the big boats tied up were upstream from the place the ferry landed.

A few minutes later the ponderous barge entered calmer water and the ferryman said, "I'll take her in by myself."

Remme dropped his arms amazed at the ache in his muscles. Work he was not used to seemed a lark for the ferryman. When the ferryman asked Remme for the crossing fee of two dollars, one for Remme's horse and one for Remme, the Frenchman placed two $5 gold pieces in the man's outstretched hand.

The ferryman looked at the coin and then at Remme who was climbing aboard his horse. "I didn't do it for the money," he said.

"I know that and I'm grateful." Remme answered. Then he waved his hand in a salute and kneed his pony into a run. An hour after leaving the ferry behind, and guiding his horse through a sticky mire of mud that concealed the trail, Remme handed the reins of his horse to the hosteler at Stewart's Stable. He was almost afraid to ask the question he had put to the ferryman. "The *Columbia*—has she arrived?"

"She's hasn't been sighted yet," the man said casually, "But if she's running late, sometimes they fire a cannon when she turns into the Willamette. She moves slow. Could be a couple of hours before she docks."

Remme left his horse to be rubbed down, fed, and watered, and hastily asked for directions to the Adams Express office. He started running before the stablehand's last words were out of his mouth.

He stopped to calm himself and collect his wits as he saw the sign above the door with the painted letters: Adams Express Company. Squaring his shoulders and taking a deep breath, he reached for the doorknob.

Oh God, he shuddered as the knob refused to turn in his hand. Locked! The door was locked! Cold fear, utter despair gripped him. Was it possible that the news of the failure of Adams Express had reached Portland by some other means than the *Columbia*? It seemed impossible, and yet? What other explanation could there be for the disaster that confronted him? He swallowed hard and actually felt chilled, faint. For a moment he couldn't catch his breath. To lose at the very last moment was unfair. It was wrong. It was almost more than he could bear. Suddenly angry, he reached for the knob to rattle the door when he heard a distant voice behind him. Remme whirled and saw a man wearing glasses and dressed in a dark brown suit and a small-brimmed gray hat.

"Hello, may I help you?" he asked. "I'm Dr. Steinberger. I've been to lunch."

By sheer will power, Remme forced his voice to sound casual. How many hours had he dreamed of this moment while he swayed in the saddle listening to the creak of leather beneath him?

"I'd like to get a draft cashed. I've bought a herd of cattle and the longer I wait to pay for them the worse off I am."

"Come in."

Remme followed numbly thinking of the minutes ticking by as the *Columbia* edged up the river to dock. She couldn't be alongside yet, not according to the stable-hand. She had to navigate the traffic on the river. But what if he was wrong? What if deck hands were now lowering the gangplank for the passengers to disembark?

His throat was dry as he extracted his certificate of deposit from its hiding place in the oilskin packet next to his chest. The agent took Remme's draft and examined it leisurely from behind his money counter. He cocked an eye at Remme who certainly looked authentic, mud spattered, smelling strongly of horse lather, and tough-looking for his medium wiry height. Then Steinberger held the draft up to the light and peered at it intently. Finally turning it face up, he noted the signature of W. B. Rochester, the Adams agent in Sacramento.

"Looks authentic," he said. "Let's see," he added, figuring on a pad with a pencil. "That's $12,500 less my agent's commission of one half percent. That comes to $62.50. That'll be $12,437.50 net to you." The agent pushed the pad across the counter. "See if you agree with those figures," he said.

Remme stared at the pad numbly and merely nodded. Surely by now the *Columbia* had docked. The purser was probably on a dead run from the boat right this minute with the news of the bankruptcy.

"Hurry, man, hurry!" he screamed at the agent in his mind.

From his safe Dr. Steinberger unhurriedly transferred several stacks of gold to the counter top, then trimmed them evenly with his fingers so that each pile of $50 gold pieces stood in a small, neat twinkling column. He stepped back slightly, pleased with the commission he had earned.

Remme could not control the violent trembling of his hands as he scooped up the piles of gold slugs. For even as they fell into his saddlebags, he could not quite believe he had won an impossible race of almost seven hundred miles in six days. Still dazed, exhausted from lack of sleep, body fatigue beyond any challenge of physical endurance he'd ever pitted himself against, he staggered as he walked, headed for a clean, comfortable hotel with a big iron safe not far from the waterfront.

As he stumbled into the lobby of the Frontier, he weaved his way to the front desk and heaved his heavy burden onto the counter.

The hotel clerk who was proud of his strong memory for faces was not certain the strong-smelling, mud-stained, bearded, drenched, and weary cattle trader who dropped his heavy rain-soaked saddlebags leaking water on the counter was the Louis Remme he knew. This man's loose-fitting clothes, torn and ripped sheepskin, his misshapen hat with three small suspicious holes in the dirt-streaked crown, his drawn features, bore no resemblance to the Frenchman who had stayed at the Frontier before.

When the bedraggled figure leaned forward, placed a gold beaver on the counter, and said in unmistakable French mixed with English, "*Mon Dieu*, Clark, I'm all in from a long ride. Put my bags in your safe, and get me a room and bath and somebody to wash my clothes."

"It is you, I apologize," the clerk said, thrusting a key across the counter, and, surprised at the weight of the saddlebags as he dragged them across the counter, muttered, "What have you got in here? Gold?"

An hour later, Louis Remme stepped out of the bathtub in his room, wound a bath towel around his hips, and pointed to his discarded clothes in a heap on the floor when he opened the door for the hotel housekeeper after she knocked.

When she'd gone with her burden, and after shaving, Remme stretched on the bed and slept two hours until a knock on his door woke him. He opened it for the housekeeper in whose arms were washed and pressed clothes. He opened her hand and pressed a gold beaver on her palm. Astonished and grateful she bowed her way out of his room.

After dressing in his clean clothes, Remme stopped at the front desk and asked Clark if the steamer from San Francisco had arrived yet.

"No, sir. We always know because they shoot off a canon when she's sighted. When she docks she gives two blasts on her horn, three if there's an emergency."

Remme thanked Clark, walked into the restaurant, and ordered a steak, eggs, biscuits, and coffee. He was still too excited to give in to sleep. Besides, he had a chore to perform. As he ate his late breakfast, he reflected on the ride he'd made and when he weighed all the hazards he had faced and overcome, he felt a sense of awe. He realized deeply and fully that he had been blessed by some greater kindness, some beneficial expression of unlimited power that had guarded him and inspired him with courage and endurance. When he thought back it was amazing. From Knights Landing, in daylight and darkness on horses he traded, borrowed, or bought, over Indian trails, chased by savages, he had ridden through snow storms, rain, swollen rivers, and had reached Eugene City in just 148 hours. From that number he'd slept thirteen hours. Twenty-one hours more had taken him to the ferry at Milwaukie. In the Grave Creek hills he'd lost a brave horse, shot a bear on the wild Umpqua, and in Umpqua Canyon he did not make two miles an hour, hindered by the deep mud and slippery bottom. And his horses had struggled valiantly against the deep snows in the Trinity and Scott mountains. His average time he calculated was just five miles for every hour that passed over a distance of more than 650 miles. At least forty of these miles were deep snow and eighty miles were of hoof-sucking mud. Five times his horses gave out and he had to lead them. Once he'd lost his way and had to retrace his footsteps. And yet he would have lost if he had not outwitted the bushwhacker who menaced him with a gun.

He rose from his table, left money for his meal, and decided to return to the Adams Express office and warn the agent that his bank had failed and to save himself before the *Columbia* arrived. A block away from the building where Steinberger was located, Remme changed his mind. He was certain the banker would demand to know what facts Remme possessed to authenticate his claim. He could see disbelief change to suspicion on the man's face after he'd heard the preposterous tale of Remme's ride to save his gold. He could guess what Steinberger's accusation would be: "I don't know what your game is, mister, but I'm not playing along with it. You'd better get out of here before I call the sheriff and have him confiscate the gold I paid you until I can get confirmation by mail that your certificate is genuine . . ."

That was the moment when Remme was startled by three long blasts from the horn on the *Columbia*. It was the emergency signal summoning a lawman to the dock where the steamship was being piloted to her berth. As he glanced down at the river, he couldn't believe his eyes. Sitting on a tightly coiled pile of heavy rope was Moses Gunn. He was unmistakable; smart in his blues, his chevrons, and his black face. With a shout, Remme headed down to the horse master who stood up as he grew close and cracked his face with a grin from ear to ear. Moses clasped Remme's hand and said, "You won your race. Congratulations. Your gold is safe?"

"Yes, but how did you know?"

Moses shook his head as if bewildered. "That's a long story."

Two hours after the *Columbia* docked, Ralph Meade, with a deputy sheriff who had answered the three emergency blasts of the ships cannon, served the Letter of Attachment on Dr. Steinberger. Then, he joined Louis Remme, Moses Gunn, and Harriet Teller for dinner at the Frontier Hotel. Meade was bright eyed and in awe of the Frenchman who had made a place for himself in western history. Moses's story of recapturing the lottery money was like adding spice to a sweet drink. Dr. Steinberger had refused to honor the certificate Moses presented because he claimed he wasn't positive Meade's signature was genuine. Harriet and George Meade each contributed $150 to Moses, to compensate him for the amount Meade had promised him. Harriet was pleased that she was the big winner in the lottery along with Meade and when the four were talked out, Moses Gunn asked Remme a final question. "What will you do now with your gold safe?"

For a long moment Remme didn't answer, the image in his mind so eloquent and deep feeling that he could not express it. He was remembering a night in July when Iron Bird, silent as a ghost, came to his side and slipped her hand in his. It felt as natural as breathing. Both of them stood together as the wind came rushing from the sea into the timber, rousing at the stillness, making a rumbling voice to the night, blowing clouds across the moon. They thickened above the trees and a harsh invisible rain came striking in the wind cutting at their faces. There were no answers except one: Remme and Iron Bird came together and in each other's arms found peace and excitement and knew a longing that would unify them for as long as each of them lived.

He said to the three at the table. "I have to find a woman who's waiting for me. I've kept her waiting too long and she's too important for me to sit here any longer."

He turned to Moses, "I'll need another horse and will buy yours for the same amount you paid if you're willing."

It was mid-afternoon in his hotel room on Saturday, March 3, 1855 when Remme loaded the golden eagles Dr. Steinberger had counted out for him into the leather pockets of the saddlebags he had placed in his hotel's safe. He would tie them in place against the cantle on the saddle of his two horses. Remme had wrapped his gold into two equal portions in laundry bags he bought from the Frontier Hotel's housekeeper. Gold was heavy and by distributing the weight between Harmless and the gray horse he was going to ride, neither animal would be overburdened.

His plan was to head southwest the next day until he reached the prairies of Josephine Valley, avoiding the swamps and reaching the Illinois River which wandered among the Siskiyous until it entered the Rogue about forty miles from the coast. He'd follow along the Rogue, then swing north to the village of the Takelman Rogues.

His breath caught as he pictured Iron Bird as he had last seen her. Tall, with long lustrous black hair she tied at the back of her neck with a single bow, it covered her ears, fanned over her shoulders, and emphasized her high cheekbones, oval face, and firm chin. A wide forehead, pride and a lofty bearing set her apart giving her features a hawk-like appearance that was softened by her large, expressive eyes that looked on the ironies of the world with a certain humor. In her eyes also was her love for Remme—a trust and a knowing that was beyond explanation.

Remme had been on the trail several hours, his cleaned sheepskin buttoned under his chin against the cold of the late day, the legs of his animals wet with rain-soaked grass, when the sun sinking in the west blazed brightly as it dropped over the forest of trees in front of him, leaving an afterglow that painted the green-pointed tops of the firs with gold.

Remme looked through the boughs down at the sloping tumble of the low mountains opening out westward under the pale pink of the sky. As the sky darkened, he admired the early silver frost stiffening the grass along the trace.

Now, free of the long pressure of his seven-hundred-mile ride, Remme felt strong and good, his doubts about himself which had plagued him, vanished. As he looked back at what he'd done, he did not feel any deep sense of satisfaction or pride. He regarded his trial as a chore that had to be done. And now that it was accomplished, he could get on with his life.

By early morning the next day, Remme and his two horses came down a gentle slope to a long plateau rimmed with mountaintops. They rode out upon the level, in grass faintly gold from first frost. The stalks were stirrup high and they rustled with the tread of the hooves in the sunny quiet.

That night, he built a fire, removed the saddles and bags from both animals. Then from another leather bag filled with corn he had bought from the hosteler in Portland, he hung it behind the ears of one horse and listened to the munching until it was time to refill it and transfer it to the second animal. While they were eating, Remme fried bacon in a pan and when it was done, poured off the fat and added canned beans. Later, after his stomach was full, he boiled coffee over the coals, leaned back against his saddle, and spoke quietly to the gray horse as he looked up the slope at the bright stars of the Pleiades.

"See that cluster of stars, gray horse? If you look closely there are seven that shine the brightest. In Greek mythology, they are the seven daughters of the Titan Atlas and the Oceanid Pleione. They all fell in love with the gods, except for Merope who loved a mortal. She, like her sisters, was pursued by the giant hunter, Orion, who loved Merope the best. Across the sky he chased them and to prevent their capture, Zeus turned them into stars. Merope is the faintest of the seven sisters because she is hiding her light from Orion. Old horse, I believe Merope was the fairest of the Pleiades and had pledged her heart to the mortal. She makes me think of Iron Bird who is the star in my life.

"Isn't that a foolish story, horse? But when I was a boy on my grandfather's farm, I loved to see the Pleiades appear above the trees when the sky darkened. I love the myth my grandfather told me. It was a fascinating mystery and I believed the sisters smiled down at me, especially, Merope, and they made me feel important."

"Sleep now good horse," Remme sighed and fell silent, his voice fading like a small wind soothing the dark night.

The dying coals glowed red, dimming in the silence beyond the sound of the wind and the water from the nearby creek. Remme lay down to the comfort of the earth, wrapped in his blanket, with his gun by his hand. An owl's hooting awoke him in the dark, and the wind blew harder before he rose in the blackness and rebuilt the fire, with the morning star above the rim. He warmed his leftover bacon and beans in the growing light, hearing wolves cry from beyond the dim ravines.

Excited when he mounted the gray horse, he rode west. After a few hours he felt the sharp, spring slant of the weak sun at noon as he came over the edge of the mesa and rode under trees again. By a high myrtle on a stream bank he unsaddled, and dozed for an hour or so while his horses grazed in the shade. Squirrels, bluejays, and red-headed woodpeckers chattered at him. Cloud shadows moved, patches of rich blue, along the slopes. He washed in the cold water of the stream and drank, before he saddled again and rode on. Antelope tracks were thick along the trace he rode, but he saw none of the tawny animals in the bushy shade.

As the tangle of tracks climbed from the rocky stream, up the shoulder of a hill, a familiar sound reached his ears and he stopped to listen. It was the distant whispering of the sea and he kicked the gray in the ribs. "Hurry horse," he said. "I've kept her waiting long enough."

An hour later he struck the beach, turned north, and galloped the horses along the edge of the ocean where the sand was firm.

He saw the empty grass huts first, windblown and vacant and his heart skipped a beat. He rushed past the deserted village, leading Harmless on the gray and penetrated the forest where the stream he had found moved fast with the tidal current. Still solemn and quiet were the big aromatic trees, the myrtles, the big-leaf maples, the aspens, and the tangles of cucumber vines he remembered, but the stream was dirty, cloudy and filled with debris. Where he had watched the villagers fish for salmon, the banks of the stream were caved, wooden planks were half submerged in the clogged stream, and a broken rocker discarded by some vagrant miner sat abandoned in a small pool.

Remme was frightened, a sense of deep irretrievable loss overcame him and for a long moment he couldn't catch his breath; he couldn't believe that the woman who had become the substance of his dreams was gone. Anger and bewilderment replaced his confusion and he was unable to control the sudden shaking of his body. He was lost in the sorrow and numbness that took away his strength and his purpose. He wanted to lash out, to punish those who had taken her away. He slumped on the gray, helpless, tears streaming down his face, salty and bitter on his lips. He had failed the one person whose life was more important than his own. He felt abandoned, utterly alone, robbed of his reason, of who he was. He glimpsed a future of emptiness and it was gray and hopeless.

He stirred finally; the gray moving under him to munch on grass, but he lacked direction. What should he do? A question without a meaning or answer.

Remme allowed the gray to drift slowly toward the sea without guidance, Harmless following behind. On the beach, he slid off his horse and walked toward the water. It was the one constant that promised a certainty, a rhythmic endurance that was beyond pain or feeling.

As he gazed out at the even rollers moving in and out again, the cry he heard was his own scream of desperation. When it sound louder, insistent, he was confused and he turned. His world was transformed in an instant and when he saw Iron Bird running toward him, flying, the tears in his eyes washed away his sorrow and emptiness. In his arms, vibrant, alive, grateful, and excited, Iron Bird said, "The army moved us to the reservation a month ago. I've been camping out a few miles up the beach, waiting for you. I knew you'd come."

She flattened her body against his and held him fiercely with all her strength and he came alive again.

EPILOGUE

AS IT TURNED OUT the depositors of Adams Express Company in Oregon never received any money after the single payment to Remme on March 3, 1855. As for him, he went on to prosper as a cattle trader and his remarkable ride became one of the most exciting legends of the American West.

It was the kind of legend that was especially appealing to lonely settlers on the Long Tom, the Calapoolia, or the Umpqua. These men had no love for banks, especially after 1855. Here was the story of a man much like themselves who, with great effort, had outsmarted the wicked bankers. They chuckled and slapped their thighs as they retold the story.

When men in remote cabins awoke at night to the clatter of hoofbeats in the distance they rolled over in bed and said to themselves or to their families: "There's that crazy Frenchman going to Portland after some more money. Wonder if he'll beat the steamer this time?"

Two days after the *Columbia* made port in Oregon, she slipped her ropes and headed up the Willamette to the Columbia which would take her to sea and to San Francisco with the treasure she was carrying.

Fraud was openly charged by irate California depositors who claimed the bankruptcy of Adams Express was illegal, but some persons profited from her failure and California courts were the scene for several years of bitter dispute.

Ralph Meade never learned in whose hands the gold in the safe of the *Columbia* landed.

SOURCES AND ACKNOWLEDGMENTS

The bankruptcy of Adams Express in San Francisco in February 1855 is a recorded fact, as is the remarkable overland race of Louis Remme, a depositor in Adams Express, with a steamboat. His purpose was to beat the *Pacific Mail Steamboat Columbia* to Portland before the purser could serve a bankruptcy Letter of Attachment on Dr. Steinberger, the Adams agent in Portland. If Louis Remme could present his certificate of deposit before the *Columbia* arrived, he could save his $12,500 at jeopardy.

Newspapers and Periodicals:

The story of Remme's race first appeared in the *Oregonian* of April 12, 1882. Approximately the same version was published in the *Oregon Business Review* of January 1962.

A brief history of Adams Express Company was published by Richard Frajola on July 12, 2004.

Books:

The Applegate Trail of 1846, William Emerson

A Century of Paddlewheelers in the Pacific Northwest, The Yukon and Alaska, Edward L. Affleck

Long Day's Journey, The Steamboats and Stagecoach Era in the Northern West, Carlos Arnoldo Schwantes

Over the Applegate Trail to Oregon in 1846, Bert Weber

Requiem for a People, The Rogue Indians and the Frontier Man, Stephen Dow Beckham

The Rogue River Indian War and Its Aftermath, 1850–1980, E. A. Schwartz

Seeing the Elephant, Voices from the Oregon Trail, Joyce Badgleiss Hunsaker

Skookum, An Oregon Pioneer Family's History, Shannon Applegate

Treasure Express, Neill C. Wilson

ABOUT THE AUTHOR

A journalist for twenty years with major daily newspapers, including the *Chicago Daily News* and Associated Press, THORN BACON became a prolific assignment writer for such national magazines as *True*, *Argosy*, *Popular Science*, and *National Wildlife*. He published several books before he wrote *Race for the Gold*. Bacon makes his home in Oregon.